Ciao Don Camillo

Volume Two

Giovannino Guareschi, known as Giovanni to his millions of English-speaking readers, was born at Fontanelle di Roccabianca in la Bassa parmense, the lowland plain on the banks of the Po River in northern Italy, on the 1st of May, 1908. He found his vocation after a package containing cartoons, jokes, prose and proposals was sent to the Milan-based publisher Angelo Rizzoli, who was planning a new satirical magazine, to be called *Bertoldo*.

For two years during the war, Guareschi was incarcerated in one prison-of-war camp after another in Poland and Germany, where he was reduced to a state of despair. Out of it he brought himself to the polemic that would underwrite all his work post-war.

Shortly after he was liberated by the English and returned home in September 1945, he was commissioned by Rizzoli to found *Candido*, the satirical magazine in which Don Camillo, Peppone and the speaking Christ first appeared in December 1946.

So effective was *Candido* in its satirical swipe at life in post-war Italy, where the communist party formed the most effective opposition to Christian Democracy, that the hugely popular *Life* magazine, published by Time Inc., reported that the 1948 elections had effectively been won by Alcide de Gasperi, leader of the Christian Democrats, and Guareschi together.

In 1952 the first of six films was made, based on the Don Camillo stories, helping eventually to take book sales to more than twenty-three million copies worldwide. In the same year, Guareschi moved back to la Bassa, bought some land at Roncole Verdi, where the composer Giuseppe Verdi had been born in 1813, and built the house he had been dreaming on for years.

Since 2013 Pilot Productions has, in collaboration with the Estate of Guareschi, published twelve collections of the Don Camillo stories, bringing the translations more faithfully in line with the author's original manuscripts and a great many of them to the English reader for the first time.

Titles in the Series

The Little World of Don Camillo
Book 1: E-book ISBN: 9781900064132;
ASIN: B00HAMIVUC. Paperback ISBN: 9781900064071.
Audiobook: ASIN: B07CZPFQDT.

Don Camillo and His Flock
Book 2: E-book ISBN: 9781900064194;
ASIN: B013TFT1YS. Paperback ISBN: 9781900064187.

Don Camillo and Peppone
Book 3: E-book ISBN: 9781900064279;
ASIN: B01CIWE1T8. Paperback ISBN: 9781900064262.

Comrade Don Camillo
In Book 4: E-book ISBN: 9781900064354;
ASIN: B0722G6GY4. Paperback ISBN: 9781900064330.

Don Camillo and Company
Book 5: E-book ISBN: 9781900064460;
ASIN: B07DKBHFJH. Paperback ISBN: 9781900064408.

Don Camillo's Dilemma
Book 6: E-book ISBN: 9781900064484;
ASIN: B08KJ6GT7W. Paperback ISBN: 9781900064477.

Don Camillo Takes the Devil by the Tail
Book 7: E-book ISBN: 9781900064521;
ASIN: B089KLX8KK. Paperback ISBN: 9781900064514.

Don Camillo and Don Chichi
Book 8: E-book ISBN: 9781900064552;
ASIN: B096SMTL48. Paperback ISBN: 9781900064569.

Merry Christmas Don Camillo
Book 9: E-book ISBN: 9781900064644;
ASIN: B0BGM2S6R7. Paperback ISBN: 9781900064590.

Don Camillo of la Bassa
Book 10: E-book ISBN: 9781900064668;
ASIN: B0CHMNK8FC. Paperback ISBN: 9781900064651.

Ciao Don Camillo (Volume One)
Book 11: E-book ISBN: 9781900064682;
ASIN: B0DJ3GJZM7. Paperback ISBN: 9781900064675.

Ciao Don Camillo (Volume Two)
Book 12: E-book ISBN: 9781900064705.
Paperback ISBN: 9781900064699.

CIAO DON CAMILLO

Volume Two

GIOVANNI GUARESCHI

EDITED BY
Piers Dudgeon

PILOT PRODUCTIONS

Published by Pilot Productions in 2025
Grove Farm Sawdon, North Yorkshire YO13 9DY

A catalogue record for this book is available
from the British Library

Paperback ISBN 978-1-900064-69-9
Ebook ISBN 978-1-900064-70-5

Cover design by BerniStevensdesign.com
Typesetting and e-book production by
epubknowhow.co.uk
Printed and bound in Great Britain by
Clays Ltd, Elcograf S. p. A.

Contents

Editor's Preface

THESE STORIES SPAN the years 1952 to 1960. Immediately, in the first story, we are back in the violent aftermath of the Second World War.

The war had passed, but with its passing 'hatred and land mines' were scattered through the towns and cities, particularly in la Bassa, as Guareschi recorded in 1947. Anyone who had sided with Mussolini's government since its inception in 1922 was fair game. Monarchists were targeted because Italy's King, Vittorio Emanuele III, had rubber-stamped Mussolini's appointment as Prime Minister. Priests were in the frame because in the 1920s and '30s, the Vatican and Mussolini had used each other to preserve and protect their respective institutions.

So this is the setting for 'The Flood' and explains the prevalence of war-time weaponry concealed by both sides in the conflict between the communist Peppone and the village priest Don Camillo, formerly comrades in arms in the Resistance.

Then, in 1956, Soviet troops and tanks kill and execute thousands when the people of Hungary rise against their communist masters, local support for Mayor Peppone is on the wane. 'Smilzo's Intervention', written in that year, turns on this and on Soviet chief Nikita Khrushchev's apparently paradoxical policy of 'peaceful coexistence'.

In Don Camillo's little world conflicted politics is what life is all about: 'This newfangled business of *détente* seems designed specifically to confuse us,' says Brusco to Smilzo, who has immediate plans to knock it on the head. Khrushchev's *volte face* must have seemed as baffling to Peppone's gang as President Trump's sudden backing of Putin's invasion of Ukraine must have been today. Even Don Camillo finds the new policy a hard one to swallow: in 'Music', he fears an alignment between the Soviets and Heaven, before the steadying voice from above the High Altar in the village church puts him gently, but firmly, in his place.

Next, Russia launches a notable propaganda victory by rocketing Sputnik into space, the first man-made object ever to leave the Earth's atmosphere, an event that swings Peppone and his gang back into the ascendancy and colours quite a few stories here.

Elsewhere, Guareschi discards all political ideology and finds his anchors in the Land and in the Risorgimento, which brought unity to the land he loves and Italy's first king.

'Giovannino was of peasant stock,' writes his son, Alberto: 'his heritage comes from his paternal grandparents. He loves the land.' His characters, based on people he knew, emerge out of the land and throughout this collection, land defies ownership, inheritance and exploitation, and is an important issue in the class war between Landowner and Sharecropper, not finally resolved in Guareschi's lifetime.

Even the funniest moments have their inspiration in real episodes, as the photograph, taken in 1956, of the massive bell of the church of Santa Maria degli Angeli (Perugia), which appears in 'Peppone Has a Problem', shows: 'My father,' writes Alberto, 'is between two people in front of the church wearing a beret on his head.'

'People crowded around the massive bell,
stunned as if petrified into a fossilised form.'

However, it is not events or episodes in the real world but the values that underlie the playing out of them which are his purpose to explore. The stories are parables for all times and all places.

It was a great personal disappointment to him that the films based on the stories, for all their commercial success, failed to grasp his purpose. They are, nevertheless, wonderful period pieces and generally available in DVD form today, as I discovered through the generosity of a Don Camillo reader.

Between 1952 and 1972, six films were made. *The Little World of Don Camillo* (1952); *The Return of Don Camillo* (1953); *Don Camillo's Last Round* (1955); *Don Camillo, Monsignor ... but not too much* (1961); *Don Camillo in Moscow* (1965). A sixth film, *Don Camillo e I Giovanni d'Oggi – Don Camillo and the Youth of Today* began shooting in July 1970, but was left unfinished after the death of Fernandel, who played Don Camillo. A film of the same name, starring Lionel Stander as Peppone and Gastone Moschin as Don Camillo, was then shot in 1972.

As an eyeglass into the making of the third film, *Don Camillo's Last Round*, the story 'Letter to the Reader' takes some beating. Its background is that in January 1954 Guareschi was arrested after he published two wartime letters in his satirical magazine, *Candido*, apparently signed by former Prime Minister Alcide De Gasperi, requesting the Allies to bomb the outskirts of Rome in 1942 in order to demoralise German collaborators. The Court refused a demand by Guareschi's lawyers to let handwriting experts express their opinion on the letters' authenticity. Subsequently, he was found guilty of libel and sentenced to a year in jail. Damages were limited to one lire, but being under a suspended sentence for making fun of President Luigi Einaudi three years earlier, he faced the prospect of an even lengthier stay in Parma's San Francesco jail.

Conditions were atrocious. He lost weight; his cell was one of the coldest; in winter the temperature reached minus twenty degrees. Besides being banned from publishing any stories in Italy, he was allowed neither a newspaper nor, at first, materials with which to write. After months he was permitted a typewriter and paper, to be stamped and handed in before eight o'clock each evening. But then came a worse problem: Don Camillo and Peppone declined to join him in jail.

It is a terrible moment in the story, yet magical because, with real writers, there comes a point when their characters take on a life of their own, and Don Camillo and Peppone 'did not show the slightest intention of coming to keep me company in cell No. 38.' His imagination had run dry.

Reading this I thought immediately of one of my favourite Don Camillo stories, 'The Village of Don Camillo' (see page 211 etc. in *Merry Christmas Don Camillo*), where Guareschi runs Don Camillo and Peppone to ground in their village, leading his real wife and children into his imagination to find them. Suddenly I realised the significance of the year in which it was written, 1954, the year of the author's incarceration. It must have been one of those stories handed in before eight o'clock each evening, which coaxed all his friends from Don Camillo's village back into life.

By 1956, on account of his prison experience, Guareschi's health deteriorated and he began to spend time in Switzerland, in 1959 making a second home at Cademario, a village in the district of Lugano in the Swiss canton of Ticino. By now he had retired from the post of Editor of *Candido*, although he remained a contributor until the magazine closed in 1961.

Piers Dudgeon, August 2025

Part One

The Flood (1952)

AROUND THREE O'CLOCK Lightning growled. Lightning was a hunting dog who had never done anything but hunting in his life, and, as a result, had always been uninterested in things not related to hunting, not because he put on airs but because he possessed a certain professional dignity.

However, finding himself in exceptional circumstances, namely that flood of 1951[1], he had felt morally mobilised and carried out his function as a guard dog with commendable diligence. It is on occasions such as this that you see if a dog is a true gentleman.

Lightning growled dully, and Don Camillo woke up and looked around.

But throughout the house everything was perfectly as expected. On the ground floor the water had reached half a metre from the ceiling, the rooms on the first floor were unusable because they were full of junk, and the pig and the chickens regularly dwelt in the attic. But Lightning continued to growl and so Don Camillo, who had the utmost respect for

---

[1] One of the worst natural disasters in Italy was the flooding of the Po River in 1951. At its height, hundreds of hectares of agricultural land were submerged, killing over eighty people and leaving 180,000 homeless.

the dog's integrity, thought it his duty to inspect the roof too, and he slipped into the attic.

Even the roof seemed to be in order, but the dog persisted in his growling and so Don Camillo widened his field of observation and looked around and about. It was a dark night, though with no fog. Hearing a splashing sound to the west that made him suspicious, he espied a small light, quickly extinguished, and was sure that he had seen a boat moving among the deserted houses.

Lightning made it clear that he would have preferred to remain on guard at the house, but with his shotgun seeming to promise a hunt, Don Camillo convinced him to climb on board the now famous craft with him.[2]

'We're going hunting for jackals,' Don Camillo explained in a low voice, carefully starting to manoeuvre the long pole.

The small boat slid silently across the water, and after a while Lightning, who was on the lookout, leaned toward the port side and instinctively pointed his muzzle at something, as if it were game.

Don Camillo put down the pole and took up the double-barrelled shotgun: 'Who goes there?' he shouted in a thunderous voice that made the waters ripple.

Immediately, a clatter of oars was heard and a dark mass broke away from an isolated house and headed out to sea.

'Stop there!' the priest shouted. But the mysterious boat increased its speed and then Don Camillo let loose two barrels simultaneously, which sounded like a cannonade, and again shouted: 'Stop there, or I'll shoot!'

Lightning, who had reprised his role as a hunting dog, had leapt forward into the water. Not until he was up to his neck did he regret how foolish he had been. So, Don Camillo had to ignore the jackal and think instead about fishing him out, a particularly difficult manoeuvre, given the craft was clad with

---

[2] Don Camillo had himself built the craft with four empty gasoline cans and a wine press, upon which he could punt on his knees into the church, floating above the High Altar and coming to rest at the foot of the crucified Christ.

empty gasoline drums for buoyancy, hampering the dog's attempts to get back on board.

Meanwhile, the mysterious 'pirate' boat had disappeared and Don Camillo pointed his craft toward the isolated house from which he was sure the boat had broken away:

'I want to go see if that scoundrel managed to pull off a heist or if we got here in time to prevent one,' Don Camillo explained to Lightning, who was dripping and shivering with cold.

The front door of the house was set higher than most above steps, five of which were visible. Crouching down, Don Camillo managed to manoeuvre his craft through the front door and into the hallway.

Turning on his flashlight he was immediately startled by two eyes glaring at him from the far end of the hall. But he soon recovered: a large portrait, nailed to the wall, was up to its eyes in water.

'All but drowned!' he muttered.

Having reached the stairs he soon found himself on the first floor.

Still pondering whether 'that damned pig' had managed to pull off a robbery, he found that the doors on both sides of the upper corridor were locked. But they were not forced and it could still be that the jackal had opened and then closed them again, even that an accomplice, unable to get back into the boat in time to escape, was still in there.

Don Camillo had a large bunch of keys of his own in his pocket and one by one the doors on the first floor yielded to them and were carefully closed after the priest's conscientious inspection. Nothing seemed to be amiss, but it would be foolish to leave the house without visiting the attic. If some scoundrel remained, he could have slipped into the attic. And, having climbed two flights, Don Camillo, holding the shotgun at the ready in his left hand, worked with his right inside the lock of the attic door. And the lock clicked. But the door wouldn't open. Someone had bolted it from the inside or had propped something heavy against it. And now, with his muscles tense, Lightning was pointing at something that must surely be behind the door.

It was a case of holding the shotgun with both hands and ramming the door with both feet. Now, as Don Camillo had shoes like the treads of a large Panzer and, inside the shoes, feet to match, the door flew open at the second blow.

Lightning darted in and, after a moment's hesitation, Don Camillo leapt to the attack like a battalion of Alpine troops.

The dog was standing in front of a pile of rags in a corner, growling, and Don Camillo said in a hollow voice:

'I'll count to three and then I'll shoot. If there's anyone there, come out! "One..."'

At "Two" the rags shook feverishly and an ugly face emerged.

'Put your paws up!' Don Camillo ordered.

From the pile of rags two trembling hands framed the face.

Don Camillo grabbed the man by the scruff of his neck and pulled him up. Then, in the light of his flashlight, he studied him carefully, then let him go.

'Oh, what do we have here?' he said. 'What did you come to do?'

The man looked at the priest in amazement.

'Answer, big guy! Who was the other one or others who escaped in the boat?'

'I - I - I don't know,' stammered the man. 'I was here. I have nothing to do with anyone on a boat. I haven't done anything... I've been here for months.'

Don Camillo looked at the pale face and unkempt beard. He looked at how the unfortunate man was dressed and was convinced that he was telling the truth. Then the penny dropped.

'So, the police have been looking for Moretto for two months and they can't find him, and everyone says they know where Moretto has run off to: and, instead, Moretto has been here all the time, hiding in this attic!'

Moretto threw up his arms.

'I didn't do anything' he exclaimed. 'I don't want to go to jail.'

'I understand: no one would want to go to jail. But if justice is out looking for you, it means you must have done *something*! If justice is looking for you because you beat Tonino Brezzi to death with a stick and if you're hiding, it means you have a guilty conscience…'

Moretto lowered his head.

'I did what they ordered me to do,' he said. 'I've never had anything against Brezzi. I beat him because they ordered me to beat him, but I felt bad about it.'

Don Camillo turned to his dog:

'Do you understand, Lightning? He had nothing against that good man, but they ordered him to beat him and he beat him even though he felt bad about it! You tell me, Lightning: can a man be more of a beast than that?'

Lightning didn't elaborate, but he made it clear that, in his opinion, a man could not be more of a beast than Moretto.

Don Camillo sat down on a box and lit a half-Tuscan.

'I am a wretch!' exclaimed Moretto. 'I have been living here for two months like a mouse… I am dying of cold, of fear, of hunger… I have not eaten for three days… They have forgotten about me!'

Don Camillo shook his head. 'They have not forgotten,' he said. 'Probably those from the boat came to bring you food and take you away. They couldn't take you away when there are still a few people in the village.'

Moretto's teeth were chattering from the cold.

'Taking me away, no,' he explained. 'It's not worth the risk. And then I have to guard the stuff.'

Don Camillo stood up:

'Don't worry, I won't report you. You're worse off here than if you were in jail. Here you'll really pay for your sins! Best wishes, Moretto. Be happy.'

Don Camillo started towards the door, but Moretto wouldn't let him go: 'Reverend, enough! I can't stand this filthy life anymore! Take me away, hand me over to the police, do whatever you want, but don't abandon me here, or I'll end up shooting myself!'

'God's will be done,' Don Camillo replied. 'I'll take you, but if you're planning on doing something stupid, think twice.'

'I've done enough already,' muttered Moretto.

They punted on in silence to the churchyard and, landing under Don Camillo's bedroom window, pulled themselves up.

Moretto was as hungry as a lioness and ate everything that Don Camillo put before him.

'Now, let's go,' Don Camillo ordered when he'd finished, heading towards the window.

Moretto followed him and embarked with him again on the small boat – a short crossing. When they reached the bell tower, Don Camillo indicated a little window:

'Go in, and on up. On the landing there's a straw bed, some blankets and water. If you need it, give a light bang on the small bell. Stay there quietly, calmly: I will bring you something to eat and drink and then, when you have thought carefully about your business, you will tell me what you decide to do.'

Moretto disappeared into the bell tower and Don Camillo changed course. But, when he reached the window, something he'd said came to mind: Moretto had also said he'd stayed up there in the attic to 'guard the stuff'. Don Camillo thought it would only be polite to find 'the stuff' and take it up to the bell tower, so that Moretto could be more at peace. So he set off again, returned to the house and climbed up the stairs to the attic.

Now Don Camillo was a conscientious man and if he decided to do something he did it with the utmost commitment. So he inspected the attic with all possible care and found nothing anywhere. Only finally, throwing out the rags that had served as a bed for Moretto, did he come across a box. And inside the box there was some paper of no particular value and some iron junk.

He stayed there for a while because he was uncertain whether or not to take the box to Moretto. Then he decided not to take it to him and went to sleep.

A few more days passed and Moretto remained where he was, safe and sound in the bell tower. Then the water began to subside and, one evening, Don Camillo heard the small bell sound.

He went up the bell tower and Moretto, who by then had straightened up and shaved, told Don Camillo that he was ready.

'Ready for what?'

'Reverend, the water is subsiding,' explained Moretto. 'People will start coming back soon and we must settle the matter. I will never go back to the attic again. I want to live with my soul in peace. I want to go to jail peacefully. Let them keep me inside as long as they want. Then one day they will put me on trial and, if I have to pay, I will pay. But I will tell you how things are. I will say that they ordered me to do that dirty thing. I know, I have thought about it again, Reverend: I was a beast. But if they will not have compassion for the man, they will, I believe, have compassion for the beast. Take me to the city and hand me over to the police there. Not here.'

'God's will be done,' replied Don Camillo. 'I'll take you to the city tomorrow evening.'

*

People were returning to the village because the floodwater had subsided and now there was a lot of mud to clear out of the houses.

Don Camillo, with his sleeves rolled up, was yawning in church when he heard the voice of Christ.

'Don Camillo, for some time now I have not seen your usual serene self. Is there something wrong?'

'No, Lord: everything is fine.'

Christ sighed:

'As you wish, Don Camillo. I have no difficulty believing what you say. But do *you* believe it?'

Don Camillo began another yawn, even with his head bowed. Then, at the appointed moment, he threw down his shovel and approached the altar.

'Lord,' Don Camillo said through gritted teeth, 'among all the good people that you regularly see here before you, devoted and composed, there are six scoundrels who belong to the Reds and (though only the big bosses know it), in a secret register, they are marked as "on a special mission".'

Christ smiled: 'Don Camillo, your head is full of novels.'

'I have no novels in my head, Jesus. And if you want me to tell you, in this secret register there is also a complete list of all those cowardly landowners who have given and continue to give money secretly to the Reds. The payments are marked there, down to the last cent.'

'Don Camillo,' said Christ. 'All this is of no importance. Because, among those whom I always see kneeling devoutly before me, there are many others who, although not listed in the secret register, are certainly no better than the six on a special mission and the others who secretly give money to the people you mention.'

Don Camillo was full of anger and suffered particularly because he could not shout:

'Jesus,' he said, 'do you think it is insignificant that, together with the secret register, there were four machine guns in perfect working order?'

'Yes, Don Camillo,' Christ replied, smiling. 'Even this is of no importance because those weapons are now in the attic of the presbytery and, in half an hour, they will be reduced to shapeless scrap.'

'Jesus,' protested Don Camillo, 'I don't...'

'God gave you two strong hands that you may use them for the good, Don Camillo. Divine Providence will provide you with a large hammer and something to serve as an anvil and then everything will fall into place.'

Don Camillo went to look for the big hammer and something that would work as an anvil and, shortly afterwards, there were blows enough to shatter a Breda 30 piece.

*

Don Camillo then came across Peppone and asked him how he was doing.

'Like someone who is alive by a miracle,' replied Peppone. 'The other night, while I was inspecting the flooded township, some damned coward of a jackal sent a shotgun after me!'

'No miracles, I'm afraid,' Don Camillo pointed out. 'I fired the shotgun and I shot high. I took *you* for a jackal. But you might have said it was you!'

'Sure,' muttered Peppone. 'Then you would have shot low.'

As they chatted, they arrived in front of the People's Palace, where Smilzo and the team were cleaning up.

'My, look how much mud there is in here!' Don Camillo observed with lightly veiled solicitude.

The door was wide open and you could see, at the end of the hallway, the large portrait of Stalin stuck to the wall. The water level had reached his eyes and left its mark.

'Too bad it was only water,' he sighed.

Peppone advised him to keep going because he didn't like the idea of getting into trouble for strangling a provocative priest.

The Lockout (1952)

DOWN THERE, TOWARDS the Great River, the land is good not only for wheat, corn, tomatoes, beets, etc, but also for making bricks. Hard, compact soil: and the bricks are heavy, but ring like bells. Yet people build little.

People are almost ashamed of having a nice house, and they are right because nice houses are usually unbecoming of the landscape, which, down there, is seriously tranquil.

The kilns supply mostly for building elsewhere and then their problem is cost of transportation. There are long periods when someone who has a kiln must scratch his head for work.

Two or three kilometres from the village, Dino Caratti had a kiln, an old furnace that gave work to about fifty people, among them men, women and children. It was the only big industry in the area, and it was the one that gave the most worries because the Reds, if you take them one by one, are already a damned problem in themselves: but, if you take fifty all at once, they become a sort of antechamber to the October Revolution. Men, women and children of the Caratti furnace were all Reds and having to handle *that* merchandise you were sure to get burned.

Dino Caratti was forty-five years old and, for five or six years already, everyone in town had been wondering how he had reached such a respectable age despite having always lived at the furnace in direct and daily contact with these people who worked it.

Whenever some new strike was called by those at the furnace, everyone declared: 'This time Caratti will lose his skin.'

Now it cannot be said that furnace workers come from another world and wear rings in their noses. They were Red, but then ninety percent of people were Red in those parts, in those days, and among the Reds there were good and bad, just as among the greens, blacks, yellows and so on. But, apart from the fact that the Reds of the furnace – unlike the others – worked in groups, one has to keep in mind that Caratti was one of those men who seem to have been brought into the world with the precise task of transforming even the most innocent discussion into an argument.

He had principles that were in open conflict with progress. So, for example, he was forever shouting that, since he paid the workers lire of 100 cents each, they should give him working hours of sixty minutes each. And that, since he paid with complete and functioning banknotes, the workers had to repay him with complete and functioning production.

Dino Caratti was, in addition, one of those guys who 'keeps his cards close to his chest': he dressed like a dude, drove his Millecento with his left elbow out of the window, lived in a nice house with a bathroom, radiator, telephone, electric icebox and all the rubbish people in the city have. He kept away from the people of the village and, the few times he went to church with his wife, it seemed like he did it as an extraordinary concession to the Eternal Father.

In the village he made everyone feel uncomfortable, because, to be respected in a small community, it is not enough never to ask anything of anyone, you also have to *give* something:

and Caratti had never given anything. If they greeted him he returned the greeting, but if they didn't he carried on as if he were a stranger passing through.

The workers at the kiln hated him not only during working hours, but also off duty, and if, when democracy arrived, they didn't immediately give him what he deserved, it wasn't out of respect for the diligence with which Caratti – immutable under any and all regimes – had worked to make himself detestable to all, but rather, because they knew that somehow or other Caratti would drag them into disgrace, given half a chance.

But then, one fine day, on account of his claims on them and lack of social justice, they presented him with their first strike. And Caratti simply retorted that if they didn't like it, they could find another boss.

'There are *no* bosses anymore!' replied Giobassi, the cell leader. 'These days there are workers and employers, and workers have rights, while employers have duties. Now, the people are in charge!'

'Fine,' exclaimed Caratti. 'If the people are now boss, go get your wages from the people.'

Caratti was at the works gate, and, having said this, he locked the gate and made to go back into his house.

'Exploiter of the people!' Giobassi shouted at him angrily. But Caratti didn't blink.

Representatives from the Chamber of Labour came, but Caratti didn't even let them speak: 'The people are master? Go, discuss things with the people.'

The workers stopped work and, every morning, they arrived punctually at the usual time, punched their time cards and went to sit in front of the works gate and discussed things amongst themselves. Their conclusion was always the same: either kill him or give up. And since it was a little early in the proceedings to kill him, they gave up.

'Then we'll do the maths,' Giobassi said threateningly.

Naturally, when the law on wage increases came in, Caratti had to adapt like everyone else, but this poisoned him the more and so the relationship between him and the workers became even more tense. But hate always binds more than love, because, as hate increases, the value of the hate-object increases in parallel. In short, to hate is to overvalue. And so unrest continued for a long time.

Then, one day, the bomb really did explode. Caratti managed to get back into his house only because he had a gun in his pocket and was quick on the draw. The building was like a small fortress, with a very high wall all around and a formidable gate. Everyone knew that if someone were seen climbing over the wall, Caratti would certainly not welcome him with sprays of cologne.

Peppone intervened and ordered calm and then went himself to present Caratti with a list of demands. Caratti let him in and when he had looked through the list he handed it back to him.

'I don't feel like joking,' he explained.

'Do you have anything else to say?' Peppone replied grimly. Caratti spread his arms.

Peppone returned shortly thereafter. 'Either you accept our terms of employment or the workers will strike,' he said.

Caratti shook his head: 'We're just beginning a period of full-scale production,' he explained calmly. 'Every day that's lost is an order that goes to hell. Either the workers go back to work immediately or I cancel the orders and close up shop.'

'A lockout is not permitted by law!' Peppone shouted.

'Blackmail is not permitted by law either,' Caratti replied.

'Let them go back to work: then, once the urgent orders have been processed, we'll talk again. Now, we cannot waste even an hour.'

The workers, hearing this, marched straight to the house, but fortunately stopped a little before getting there because they thought they saw something unpleasant peeking out from a crack in the shutters of a window on the first floor.

So, they discussed things the more and came to a conclusion that seemed logical to everyone: if we strike, he declares a lockout. If he declares a lockout, we occupy the furnace.

They occupied the furnace, appointed a management board and resumed work.

'From this moment on, work begins under the new conditions that are exactly those that we have imposed,'

Giobassi explained solemnly. 'Then, that damned pig, when he gets tired of staying at home, will come out and have to pay. And the arrears. He has exploited us shamefully for too many years: now is the time to settle accounts. And if he calls the police, we will resist to the last and defend our victory tooth and nail!'

A sentry service was set up and, to be even more certain that Caratti would not call the police, the telephone wires that connected the building to the town switchboard were cut.

They didn't for a minute let the building out of their sight and so, the very next morning, when Caratti's maid slipped out of the wrought-iron door at the side of the house, someone raised the alarm.

The girl was immediately stopped: 'Where are you going?'.

'Home.'

'What for?'

The girl shrugged: 'The boss says he doesn't need me anymore and doesn't want me to run any risks. So he let me go.'

The girl had a suitcase with all her stuff inside.

'You're talking nonsense!' Giobassi shouted threateningly. 'I believe you were going out to call the police.'

'The police? Why? Yesterday he spoke on the phone with the Marshal and told him not to show up because it would only complicate things. He explained that everything would be fine without any problems. If he needed help, he would raise the alarm by sounding the building's siren.'

Rosso, who was the deputy foreman, slapped his forehead: 'We should have cut his electricity wires right away.'

'It doesn't matter,' muttered Magro, the other deputy foreman: 'he has a generator in the cellar. I installed it for him when the electricity restrictions came in. If he wants to ring, he'll ring for a whole month. His tank is full of diesel.'

Then someone from the vanguard arrived to warn that the *carabinieri* were wandering up and down the embankment. Another two days and two nights passed: the situation was becoming difficult because production was ongoing, yes, but people were starting to think about how the goods would be disposed of since the contracts on the orders were inside the house, along with all the accounting. The coal supply was good, but what would they do for the naphtha that was needed for the excavator and the little train that carried the earth from the quarry to the furnace? And to pay for electricity…?

On the morning of the fifth day, Don Camillo arrived at the furnace and immediately Giobassi, Rosso and Magro strode up to him: 'If you've come here to try to weaken worker resistance, you can go back whenever you want,' they told him. 'It is better that the clergy do not interfere in the affairs of the people.'

'All right,' Don Camillo replied calmly. 'Then I'll go back and tell the Mayor that I couldn't do what he asked me to do because the people didn't allow me to.'

They grumbled a bit and then left him free to go wherever he wanted.

Don Camillo went up to the house and rang the bell for some time before a voice told him to enter through the little wrought iron door.

'So?' Caratti asked, when Don Camillo appeared before him. 'If you come with Holy Oil for the last rites, it's still too early.'

'I come to try to enlighten your mind,' Don Camillo replied. 'This isn't about giving in: it's simply about showing a little good will. Give something and everything will be back in order. I have good reason to assure you of this.'

'I won't give a thousandth of a millimetre,' Caratti affirmed. 'I can't.'

'If you want to, you can,' Don Camillo insisted.

'I know my business. Nor do you have the right to question my actions. Have I ever come to meddle in your "*dominus tecum*"? Everyone does his job. I'm an industrialist and you're a priest. If you want to be a demagogue, tell Giobassi to give you a place in the commie cell.'

Don Camillo had promised himself he would remain calm at all costs: 'I come as a priest,' he said, 'because it is precisely the function of a priest to bring back to reason two factions that have lined up as enemies against one another. Before coming to you, I spoke at length with Peppone and made him concede on several counts. You should concede on at least a couple too.'

'Caratti has only one word,' the other man stated dryly, 'and he never backs down.'

Don Camillo sighed: 'I thought you didn't want to complicate things.'

'If I had wanted to complicate them, I would have asked for the intervention of the police,' Caratti replied categorically. 'I am someone who knows how to do his own thing without needing anyone's help. Tell your friends that this time they'll be hit by the biggest blow of all.'

'May God enlighten your brain, if you still have any of it left,' Don Camillo muttered, heading toward the door.

Outside the walls of the Giobassi building, Rosso and Magro were waiting:

'Well?'

'I will report to the man himself,' Don Camillo explained.

*

A few days and more nights passed and, one morning, the word suddenly spread that Caratti's house was empty. He who raised the alarm had been the first to discover, stuck to a pillar of the gate, a piece of paper:

NOTICE

Due to cessation of activity, all the employees of the Caratti Furnace are fired and will receive their legal dues within one week. Go to hell, one and all.
DINO CARATTI

He really had left and no one knew how or where he had gone. By the following Saturday, each of the workers had received their due severance pay along with a formal letter of dismissal.

'You can send all the letters you want, we won't abandon the kiln, even if the Panzers arrive!' shouted Giobassi. 'No one will send us away from here!'

This was met with a ferocious shout in support and everyone went on the defensive as if they were in a besieged fort instead of a furnace.

Days passed and no one came to disperse them. They continued to make bricks with anger: 'We'll show him who's going to hell!' they shouted. 'Now all the money that damned man earned will go into our pockets!'

Journalists came from the city to study the experiment, and people also came to make speeches: 'The deserter who abandoned his ill-earned command post to starve the workers deserves the contempt of all honest people and he will have it! Let him stay in his remote hideout and revel in the millions stolen from the people! The people will be able to teach him and all exploiters how much genius, how much intelligence and how much tenacity the workers have at their disposal.'

But, day-by-day, the situation became more and more difficult: production was okay but little was being sold. And those who bought had no intention of paying immediately. The coal and fuel supplies were dwindling. And so, day by day, the hatred for Caratti grew:

'He's abroad drinking away our money!' the workers said. 'If we had the capital he has, things would be different today. Nobody lends us money... That coward should come around here for a moment!'

In the fifth month, when supplies were almost gone and shopkeepers refused to give credit to the workers at the furnace, when everyone was horribly enraged and cursed Caratti, who probably knew everything even though he was abroad devouring chickens as big as calves – who knows how he was enjoying himself at their expense – an extraordinary piece of news arrived: Caratti was not abroad but in Milan. Someone had seen him in a shiny Buick together with a splendid girl, all bejewelled, and they had also seen the gates through which the car had been driven.

A hair-raising scene occurred in the furnace, so enraged and furious were everyone. Peppone had come to bring the news and, at one point, intervened:

'Everyone keep it zipped and leave it to us. Woe betide anyone who lets it be known that we know his secret. Giobassi, Rosso, and Magro are leaving for Milan tonight and we'll go and fish him out afresh. And we'll talk...'

'He has to pay! We want our money! Bring him here, we'll have his guts for garters!'

*

Peppone and the other three, dressed as if they were going to their Confirmation, arrived in Milan at eight one morning.

Rosso checked in the phone book at the station but couldn't find any Caratti. Peppone snickered – 'Imagine if he's such a fool as not to go ex-directory! No matter, we have his address anyway.'

At nine o'clock they arrived in front of the fabled gates. 'He doesn't waste our money in any small way!' exclaimed Rosso. 'Look at this building!'

'Damned pig!' muttered Magro.

'You wait here,' ordered Peppone. 'Giobassi and I will go in.'

They ambled into a courtyard glittering with marble, and knocked on the glass of the concierge's lodge.

The concierge came to the door and opened it.

'Please, does Cavalier Dino Caratti live here?' Peppone asked politely.

'Yes, why?'

Peppone and Giobassi looked at each other.

'Come on in,' said the concierge, 'and bring in the other two as well.'

The four of them entered the concierge's lodge and on into a small adjoining bedsit. A large painting framing a panoramic view of the kiln works hung on one wall.

'So you've come all the way here to give us more bother!' said a woman, her voice full of hatred. 'What do you want!'

Peppone couldn't find the words to answer.

'What do you want?' the woman pressed. 'Haven't you had your money down to the last cent?'

'Signora Caratti...' Peppone stammered.

'Yes, you may well say that,' the woman shouted. 'Signora Caratti. Finally I feel a *signora* since being shot of your ugly faces!'

At that moment a man in a chauffeur's uniform entered the room, and it was Dino Caratti.

'Well?' he exclaimed, seeing an unexpected gallery of cod faces before him.

'Look at that: they came all the way here looking for me. And what more are you after? Double time vacation? Back pay? Oh, you also want the furnace and the quarry? Take them: come to an agreement with the mortgage people. I used up all my capital to keep the whole thing afloat: I still had my name as a gentleman, my competence and my will, and perhaps, by smashing my head against the wall to find money, I would have kept the whole thing afloat. But thank God it's over. Now, finally, we've stopped eating our hearts out and risking our skin. Now we're rich. We both have a good job, a little house with a radiator, and I drive the nicest Buick in Milan! No worries: every end of the month an envelope. And the tips! Is that not true, Maria? So many tips!'

'Yes, so many tips!' repeated the woman.

The phone rang and she ran into the other room.

'It's the *Commendatore*,' she explained, returning shortly thereafter. 'He wants to know if you're ready … you have to take him to Varese.'

'All good,' replied Caratti. 'Get me a drop of coffee, I'll be there on time.'

The woman went into the kitchenette and brought back the steaming coffee pot and a cup.

'Offer these gentlemen a coffee too,' said Caratti. 'Even a shot. Just yesterday the lady gave us a magnificent bottle of grappa that she doesn't like because it's too strong and it's bad for the *Commendatore*.'

The four were still standing there, like dried cod.

'It's a disgrace!' Peppone suddenly said.

'What's a disgrace?' Caratti asked aggressively, who in the meantime had sat down and was sipping his coffee.

'A disgrace to the country,' Peppone explained gloomily. Giobassi, Rosso and Magro nodded. At that moment an angry voice was heard coming from the other room: 'Well? Where is he?'

'The *Commendatore*,' the woman hissed in dismay. 'Dino, hurry up!'

Caratti wanted to get up, but Peppone pressed a hand on his shoulder and held him down. Then he went into the other room and, seeing his elephantine figure approaching, the *Commendatore*'s eyes widened.

'Sorry, but the driver can't come,' explained Peppone.

'I am Mayor of his township and I came to tell him that he has inherited a large brick kiln. And, poor thing, the news was such a shock that he's taken a turn.'

Peppone took out his ID card and the *Commendatore*, somewhat reassured but not entirely, attempted a smile.

'The trouble is that I have to be in Varese right away... I have an important appointment,' he stammered.

'No big deal,' exclaimed Peppone. 'I'll lend you my driver.' He went into the other room, tore the chauffeur's jacket off Caratti, made Magro put it on, and stuck the cap on his head.

'Here,' said Peppone, reappearing, 'take the *Commendatore* to Varese and remain at his disposal until further orders.'

'Yes, sir!' replied Magro.

The man left, completely stunned.

'Get yourself properly dressed and come with us,' Peppone said to Caratti. 'Your place is not here. Come at once: in a couple of days your lady can come back too.'

Caratti tried to wriggle free, but Peppone's hands were of steel and those of Giobassi and Rosso were no joke either.

'Go, Dino! Go!' the woman shouted at him, bursting into tears.

Caratti looked at the woman, then looked at the picture of the furnace. 'Now who's going to get that thing back on its feet?' he cried, waving his hands.

'Get on with it,' Giobassi muttered. 'You're the boss, the master, not us.'

Caratti started off. 'I'll make you spit blood!' he said.

'That remains to be seen,' Giobassi replied with great pride.

His lady returned to HQ three days later.

But Magro did not return. He remained as driver for the *Commendatore*, awaiting further orders.

Cinema (1952)

O N THE WALLS around the piazza appeared posters of a film that was showing in the nearby city.

There were only a couple of posters in all, but there was a lot of talk in the village because the film had been the scandal of the previous summer. In fact, the exterior scenes had been shot in the surrounding area, and the Reds had immediately taken advantage of this to start a damned cancan around the forces of reaction wanting to defame the workers of la Bassa, and so on.[3]

A film, in short, in which the main characters were a parish priest and a communist mayor who were always fighting each other; a rather laughable story, if you think about it: but the Reds never laugh and, if they see someone laughing, they label him an enemy of the people.

Peppone was immediately informed of the fact. He was working in his office in the Town Hall and the team arrived to give him a full report: how many posters there were, where,

---

[3] Note by the author: 'He refers to the making of the film, *Don Camillo*.' (French title: *Le Petit Monde de don Camillo*).

how and by whom they had been put up and what effect they had on the people.

'I would say eliminate them without further ado,' said Smilzo, who did not like half measures.

'First, we need to see if the posters contain provocative content and if direct action is advisable, or not,' replied Peppone gravely.

So, followed by the team, he went down to the piazza.

In truth, there was nothing provocative about the posters: in fact, given the funny face of the actor who played the part of the parish priest, there was, if anything, something to be enjoyed.

But Peppone was vigilant:

'They are the usual underhand expressions of bourgeois propaganda,' he explained. 'The people see a funny priest on the posters, believe in good faith that it is an honest film, go to the cinema and are fooled because, underneath, there is denigration of the proletariat. They are not mistaken: where there is a priest there is a scam. *"Chi disse Vaticano disse danno."*'

The reference was stretched, but the concept clear.[4]

'We must warn our comrades,' warned Peppone. 'Explain that this film is the rubbish of last summer. That the author of the book from which they took the story is that reactionary journalist[5] who draws the communists with three holes in their noses,[6] and that the film is a piece of disgusting bullshit from beginning to end, as explained by *Unità* and *Corriere della*

---

[4] Literally, 'Whoever says Vatican says Damage'. Peppone's reference is to a public warning to Pope Innocent X (1574-1655), to let him know that the Italian people hated his sister-in-law: 'Whoever says woman, says damage / whoever says female, says misfortune / whoever says Olimpia Maidalchina, says damage, misfortune and ruin.'

[5] Note from the author: 'He is referring to the Director of *Candido*, an independent Milanese weekly.'

[6] Famously, 'in a happy moment of satiric inspiration', Guareschi drew a cartoon of a Communist as a man who needed an extra nostril to exhale the copious amounts of hot air created by a ceaseless diet of communist propaganda. It so caught the public imagination that it is remembered in Italy to this day.

Sera. We need to gather our comrades, read them the two articles and say, loud and clear, that if someone goes to the city to see this film, he is committing a serious act of indiscipline.'

A lot of people were gathered in front of one of the posters. Peppone walked resolutely toward the group and said aloud: 'Of course it's convenient to go and laugh at the people's expense in a cinema! We should be able to do that here. It's easy to make fun of communist mayors in movies. I'd really like to see a bully capable of making fun of me.'

No one said a word and Peppone was about to walk away when Don Camillo arrived.

'The Reverend certainly won't forbid his sheep from going to see this film!' Peppone exclaimed. 'When you make fun of communists, nothing you draw or write is immoral.'

Don Camillo turned slowly: 'Excuse me, which Reverend are you talking about?' he asked calmly.

'About a certain reverend who, for once, will not be saying that this is a film that leads young people into perdition.'

Don Camillo lit his half-Tuscan:

'Excuse me, Mr Mayor: why are you so angry with this film? How can you judge it, if you haven't seen it?'

'And you, excuse me, Reverend: have you ever seen the Devil? Answer, if you have the courage!'

'No, I have never seen the Devil,' Don Camillo admitted.

'And if then you, to believe something, don't need to see it but it's enough that it's written in your books, so I, to believe that the film is rubbish, don't need to see it. It's enough for me that it's written in my newspaper.'

'Bravo!' Smilzo said aloud. 'That's the clergy sorted!'

Don Camillo didn't lose his cool.

'You see, Mr Mayor,' he explained, 'I don't wish to argue. I simply want to ask you: if tomorrow, in your newspaper, it were written that there is a flying ox at Pioppetta, would you believe it?'

'My newspaper never prints stupid things and cannot print them!' replied Peppone categorically.

'Admit, for a moment, that in your newspaper there is a damned traitor who, taking advantage of a moment of inattention by the director, puts in the provincial news that there is a flying ox at Pioppetta…'

Peppone shrugged his shoulders. 'That has nothing to do with it!' he muttered. 'If there is a traitor in the newspaper, that's another matter.'

'The matters are one and the same, Mr Mayor,' replied Don Camillo. 'The traitor has accomplished his feat and you open your newspaper and read that at Pioppetta, that is to say three kilometres from here, there is an ox that has grown wings and is now flying. You, who have blind faith in your newspaper and ignorant of the fact that a traitor of the people is hiding within it, what do you do? You take the news as good and believe it? Is your faith that great?'

'It's not a question of faith, it's a question of common sense,' protested Peppone. 'Because it's easy to go to Pioppetta to check.'

'Here's the difference,' exclaimed Don Camillo. 'What is written in the sacred books cannot be checked because it is beyond the powers of the human mind, and then dogma, faith, comes into play. What is written in your newspaper is all checkable and so truth is no longer a question of faith, but of not giving up on personally evaluating the facts. When I, without ever having seen the Devil, believe in his existence because that's what's written in the sacred books, I give proof of faith. When you, without ever having seen the film and even though you could see it with extreme ease, believe that this film is rubbish, you do not demonstrate your faith in *L'Unità*, otherwise you would also believe in the flying ox: you simply demonstrate that, out of party discipline, you give up evaluating the facts with your own brain. So your comparison does not add up. *L'Unità* is one thing, the Holy Scripture is another.'

Peppone shook his head.

'So, in your opinion, what is this film like?'

'I have no idea: to be able to tell you what I think of it, I would have to have seen it. To my knowledge there is no film criticism in the Holy Scripture.'

'But,' Peppone shouted triumphantly 'on the door of the church there is a menu of films that can or cannot be seen. So, when my newspaper says that a film is rubbish and I believe it without going to see it, that means that I give up reasoning with my own head. If your list says that a film is rubbish and you believe it without seeing it, with what brain do you reason?'

Don Camillo shrugged his shoulders. 'You see, Mr Mayor, we were wrong from the beginning, when we did not better specify the difference that exists between the Holy Scripture and *L'Unità*. Up to this point we have discussed matters as if we belong to two opposing organisations of the same nature. In reality, they are two substantially different organisations, because mine is headed by Christ, yours by Stalin. I work for the Kingdom of Heaven, while you work for the Soviet Republic. I am the custodian of the House of God, while you are the custodian of the People's Palace. How can we come to a conclusion if we do not first establish which is the true Eternal Father – the one in Heaven or the one in Russia – and which of us therefore belongs to the right administration? And what *is* the right criterion for evaluating human manifestations?'

Smilzo intervened: 'The usual story; when they see a bad situation, they bring God into it and throw everything into politics: "God is always right!" So if God is right, the priests are right. But God is nothing more than a geographical expression to establish the boundaries of clerical power into infinity!'

The team walked away satisfied with the visible dismay that Smilzo's statement had aroused in Don Camillo. Arriving at the headquarters, Peppone turned to Smilzo: 'Where did you read that stuff about "a geographical expression"?'

'I thought of it,' explained Smilzo. 'I study a lot, these days.'

'*Bene*,' Peppone approved gravely, 'see if you can explain that we must respond to the manoeuvres of reactionary forces by not taking up their provocations and not going to see the films that the opposing propaganda puts out to vilify the cause of the people.'

*

'Jesus,' Don Camillo said to Christ above the High Altar, 'it would be as well if you don't take into account the "geographical

expression" and the other stuff by Smilzo. He probably didn't
even know what it meant. I am sorry for having discussed
that film. It might seem that I, in a certain sense, have incited
people to go and see it. Thinking back on it with a clear mind,
I fear I have committed a foolish act. Not seeing that film, I
was obliged not to talk about it. Because, if by chance it were
really rubbish, the very fact of having spoken about it in public
without disapproving of it would be enough to create a tragic
misunderstanding in the minds of the faithful.

'One of the two main characters is a priest, and the idea of
dressing up a movie actor as a priest is already frowned upon
from the start. But what kind of priest would come out of it?
Tomorrow is Sunday and I, during the sermon, should be able
to dispel the misunderstanding, clarify the faithful's ideas, and
warn them against the subtle danger that may be lurking in
that film. The criticisms: yes. There are the newspaper reviews:
but how does a film critic observe a film? Does he perhaps
worry about highlighting the distortions or discrepancies of a
religious nature?'

Don Camillo paced a bit up and down, then stopped:

'The reviews in the Catholic newspapers? All right: but
who has seen them? And, even having seen them, can they
be considered valid in all respects always and everywhere? Or
shouldn't we instead take into account the different situations
in each of the various countries where the film is being shown?
What is good in Rome or Milan is one thing, can it be good
here too? Or maybe, in the film, there is a detail that in Milan
means nothing, while here it can be interpreted as an allusion
to a particular fact and possibly be counterproductive?

'And not knowing what to say, tomorrow! Not being able to
trust anyone because, apart from the fact that no one is going
to the city tonight, unfortunately there is no person so calm
and collected as to be *able* to provide a truly reliable opinion.
And so, tomorrow afternoon, a lot of people will leave this
church to go and see a film that my imprudent words have led
people to believe is worth seeing, while instead it is stupid, if
not downright sacrilegious! It's a big mess!'

'Big mess?' sighed Christ. 'I don't think so, Don Camillo. Considering the fact that you, by some lucky chance, have Perlini's motorcycle in front of the garage and that, under your cassock, you have a complete civilian suit, I don't see any mess.'

'Jesus,' replied Don Camillo, shaking his head sadly. 'Would you want a priest to disguise himself, jump on a motorcycle and go to the city to mingle with the crowd at a movie theatre?'

'I do not want anything, Don Camillo,' Christ replied softly. 'It is you who wants. Otherwise, why would you have borrowed the motorcycle and why would you have disguised yourself?'

'When the mind is troubled by serious worries,' sighed Don Camillo, 'one commits acts of which one is not materially aware. I realise now what I have done in a moment of recklessness, and I regret it.'

Don Camillo went out with his head bowed and with the firm intention of going to bed. But an unpleasant accident happened to him. While he was fiddling around with the motorcycle in the dark to take it to the garage, his foot fell on the starter crank, the gear engaged somehow and the machine would have slipped out of his hands, had Don Camillo not jumped on it.

So he soon found himself beyond the Molinetto bridge and, since it was cold, Don Camillo stopped the motorbike, took off his cassock, put on an overcoat that was in the top box tied to the back, put on a cap and then continued on his way home. Evidently, because of the darkness, he took the wrong road, for after a mad dash he found himself at the gates of the city, at the entrance to an old stable where, in those days, an aged cobbler looked after the motorcycles and bicycles of people coming into town from the countryside.

Don Camillo knocked and the old man came to the door shortly afterwards:

'There is not much movement tonight,' he informed Don Camillo. 'You are the first and I think you will be the last.'

This pleased Don Camillo no end and, putting on a pair of rather foggy glasses, he set off at once towards the city.

And here was his first problem: the film was being shown simultaneously in two cinemas; which would be the safest?

Don Camillo tossed a coin. Heads: cinema A, tails: cinema B. It came up tails and Don Camillo headed towards cinema B and, once there, he entered and stood near a door so that he could make a fast exit if he saw any familiar faces.

All this was done so speedily that when Don Camillo was entering the cinema, the old man at the stables was still busy closing the old stable door. But he didn't have time to lock it before another motorcyclist arrived and asked to leave his bike.

The rider went to park his motorcycle next to the only other one and started to take off his overalls, when he almost had a heart attack: in front of him was a vehicle he knew only too well! Perlini's old Norton.

While the caretaker-cobbler was minding his own business, the motorcyclist looked around and immediately found what he knew he would find around any old cobbler's workshop. There in the corner was the man's bench: the motorcyclist reached out and fished from a bowl of tacks, fished out a good one.

Then, delicately, he stuck it on the tread of the rear tyre of Perlini's motorcycle.

'Damn reactionary, you'll know about it once you've passed the Fontanaccio!' he muttered to himself. And there was really no doubt that the whole thing would work as planned, because even if the tack failed to pierce the inner tube along the smooth road up to the Fontanaccio, there the road was awful, grid-like, with bumps one after the other. For sure, there the tip of the tack would pierce the inner tube and the rider would be left stranded, with no alternative but to push the motorbike for about ten kilometres. Perfect!

Taking off his overalls, the man ran towards the city: evidently he had very urgent things to do.

*

Don Camillo drank in the film undisturbed and, as soon as the credits came up, he darted out and in three seconds was on the road. The idea of positioning himself near the door had been a good one. He found a taxi waiting outside the cinema, which took him to the old stable. He shoved a hundred-lire note into the cobbler-keeper's hand and ran to get his motorbike. But his eye fell on the other bike next to his and he almost lost his breath.

'Damn! Talchetti's Guzzi!' Don Camillo muttered. 'He'll catch up with me whenever he wants! I can't run the risk. It's too bad it's him: as soon as he gets home, he'll phone Stalin!'

It is extraordinary how the same ideas are destined to pop into everyone's head in certain situations: even the head of Don Camillo, who fished around in the cobbler's bowl for a tack and delicately stuck it into the rear tyre of the motorbike that had so riled him, and thought: 'If I can get past Fontanaccio, Talchetti will never catch up with me!'

He took off like a 105-mm cannon shot with one thing in mind – getting past Fontanaccio, and went past it at full speed, bouncing. But 500 metres further on, Don Camillo was on foot.

He felt like crying, finding himself after midnight on a road where not even ghosts passed, with a flat tyre and a ten-kilometre foot-slog to the village.

'Jesus,' he whispered, 'it is right to punish me because I did a dirty deed dressing up and running away to the city: but...'

Then he remembered that he had also done the really dirty deed of sticking the tack in Talchetti's tire. He cut it, walking slowly, pushing the heavy motorcycle.

Immediately he felt damnably hot and decided to take off his overcoat and put on his cassock. If someone passed by and discovered him in disguise, things would only get worse. He walked on for a long while and then stopped to rest on the parapet of a bridge.

As he was about to continue on his way, he heard the thud of footsteps approaching, someone coming from the direction of the city. A man pushing a motorcycle. So much the worse if it were Talchetti: although at two in the morning, even Talchetti's company would be bearable.

But while the motorcycle was Talchetti's, the motorcyclist on foot was Peppone.

'An expert mechanic like the Mayor, on foot?' probed Don Camillo.

'As if the misfortune of having a flat tyre wasn't enough!' exclaimed Peppone grimly, 'now I have a priest in my way! What are you doing here at this hour?'

'I'm teaching Perlini's motorcycle to walk,' Don Camillo explained, jumping down from the low wall and starting to push the motorbike again.

They walked in silence side by side for a while, then Don Camillo said:

'Shouldn't we try to fix the problem?'

'Yes, in the dark. And what can I use to fill the hole in the tyre, spit? I don't have anything.'

The Norton's box was also empty. They continued walking, panting...

'It would be convenient, wouldn't it, if real communists were like those in the film!' Peppone suddenly exclaimed.

'What film?' Don Camillo replied in surprise.

'Well, what did you come to do in the city? Count the bricks of the Ponte di Mezzo? It would be convenient if the communists were like that! Big words, big chatter, big red handkerchiefs around their necks, and then everyone else good and listening to the priest!'

'It's not that, in the film the Mayor listens to the priest: it's all about conscience. In fact, the film shows that communists also have a personal conscience and, finding themselves in situations where conscience is involved, they act like normal men and women.'

Peppone bellowed: 'They act like normal idiots! That mayor is not a communist, he's an imbecile! He's a puppet! *L'Unità* was right: the reactionaries would like the communists to be the idiots the film portrays. But, thank God, they are very different. You will see!'

Don Camillo intervened:

'Comrade, why are you so angry? Save your breath for the motorbike: I agree with you completely. The wretches who put the film together don't understand a thing. They give us communists who act like gentlemen, who even make gestures of generosity, who even, at certain moments, become poets.

Communists who have a personal conscience stronger than the conscience of the Party!

'Wretches, they will see! The strength of the communists consists precisely in having renounced their own freedom of ideas, in having accepted a discipline without discussion. Rather than kissing the ring of the Bishop and saying goodbye to the priest who is leaving – all of it just sentimental bourgeois nonsense. The communists have *no* sentimentality and go straight to the goal. Whoever is an enemy of their ideology is an enemy of the communist. If the wife is against the party, away with the wife. If your son is dangerous to the party, kill your son.'

'You will kill your son!' replied Peppone.

'What utter nonsense?' exclaimed Don Camillo. 'We can't have children.'

'Luckily: we'd be in trouble if the priesthood were hereditary!'

Don Camillo didn't get angry: 'Don't misunderstand me, Peppone: I don't mean to say that communists normally kill their children and wives. I mean to say that if, tomorrow, your son were to become a powerful political opponent and the life or death of your party depended on him, you, having to choose between the death of your son or the death of the party, would, as a good communist, choose the death of your son!'

Peppone mumbled something: 'My son will always think the way I think and he certainly won't start acting like an enemy of the people, otherwise I'll beat him to death.'

'Precisely what I maintain: if the son is an enemy of the party, the son is eliminated.'

'What I said is just a figure of speech! Let's not take everything literally!' shouted Peppone. 'Let's leave the children alone, they have nothing to do with it.'

'Let's leave the children alone; but, getting back to our discussion, only someone who doesn't know the communists could put on the stage a communist like the one in the film: imagine if a communist could get along with a priest! Priests are public enemy Number One! I mean, where do these film-makers live? Don't they even read the newspapers? Haven't they noticed all the priests you communists have killed here in Emilia? And another nice one: a communist mayor who plays the scab and goes to milk the animals together with the priest so as not to ruin our common heritage![7] Where are these people's heads! Don't they know about the thousands of vines cut off at the root? About the bombs placed inside the threshing machines? About the iron stakes planted in the grass to break the mowers? About the scabs trampled underfoot and killed? About the barns set on fire? About the dams destroyed? And the roadblocks? And the farmers killed, like the famous one over there in Ferrara who was one against 400? Poor deluded bourgeois: one day you will hear what time it is! You will understand whether communists are like those in the film or if they are something else altogether.'

Peppone stopped him, snorting. 'Listen! In your opinion, are all communists bloodthirsty, arsonists, saboteurs, destroyers?'

'Of course.'

'No, sir: there are many ways to be a communist!'

'No, Comrade Peppone, there is only one way. And the only feeling that can dwell in the soul of a communist is hatred!'

'You have the gall...!' shouted Peppone. 'You, who excommunicated us! Excommunication is the greatest act of hatred there can be!'[8]

'No,' replied Don Camillo calmly. 'Not hatred. If someone has cholera, a contagious disease, I, as a doctor, have the duty to isolate him. I do not isolate him because I hate him. I isolate him because, by doing so, I warn people: be careful, Peppone has cholera. And, if people know, Peppone knows too. I do not hate Peppone nor do I want to kill him. I want him not to infect others and to recover. I treat him, but I isolate him. I isolate him, but I treat him.'

---

[7] 'Men and Beasts', *The Little World of Don Camillo* (Pilot, 2013).

[8] In 1948 *L'Osservatore Romano* (the Vatican City newspaper) published a decree which excommunicated those who propagated 'the materialistic and anti-Christian teachings of communism'. This was followed a year later by Pope Pius XII issuing the famous 'Decree against Communism' which excommunicated all Catholics collaborating in communist organisations.

'Moral arrogance is what you have!' protested Peppone.

'It would be if, by excommunicating you, the Church prevented you from believing in God. No one can prevent you from believing in God. And, if you believe in God, you will soon realise that you have cholera. And, as soon as you realise it, you will be cured.'

Peppone shouted that he was not there to listen to a sermon and Don Camillo changed his tone.

'You are right: here we were talking about the cinema. In conclusion, we are at least in complete agreement in recognising that the film is a piece of junk, that presenting communists as banal gentlemen denigrates communists and underestimates the danger of communism in the eyes of its opponents. The communist is a man who shuns all sentimentality and, since conscience is deemed sentimentality, if a good communist sees a poor priest dying of desire to smoke at three thirty in the morning, instead of giving him half a Tuscan he pretends not to notice, because the Party orders him to be a scoundrel.'

Peppone took a half-Tuscan from his pocket and handed it to Don Camillo.

They were by now in sight of the village, so they sat on the parapet of a small bridge to smoke and stayed there for a long time watching the smoke.

'Now that we've arrived,' muttered Peppone, 'I can tell you that I put the nail in the tyre at the depot. I thought you were that damned Perlini.'

'Then I'll tell you that I put the nail in your tyre, at the depot,' Don Camillo admitted. 'I thought you were that road-jumper Talchetti. If I had imagined it was you, I would have put one in the front tyre too.'

'Imagine what I would have done if I had known it was you!' Peppone shouted.

They both remained silent for about ten minutes. 'A nice coincidence, though,' Peppone suddenly said. 'It seems like a story from the movie.'

'A nice coincidence, yes,' Don Camillo added. 'You fool me, I fool you and so we both end up stranded. It seems like the eternal story of the life of the poor in that wretched movie.'

Dawn was slowly rising behind the river and the sleeping village looked to them gloomy and depressing. Don Camillo asked Peppone: 'If you could get everything you wanted right now, what would you ask for?'

'To die!' replied Peppone. And his voice was soft, calm and sincere. Don Camillo looked at his worn and dusty shoes and sighed, and they continued on their way. And when they reached the fork in the road, one took the right and the other the left without saying goodbye, each pushing a motorbike which wasn't his.

And, as one moved further and further away from the other, the same useless effort united them.

The Brigade (1952)

THAT AUTUMN, SIGNORA Cristina had an attack of her usual illness and called Don Camillo as a matter of urgency:

'Reverend,' she explained with a great effort, 'if Santa Rita gets me out of this mess, I'll redo your little chapel.'[9]

Signora Cristina was eighty years old and lived alone in the Palazzone. She owned a thousand *biolche* of land[10] with 300 and more head of cattle, but she remembered she had a heart only when she was short of breath.

---

[9] Rita of Cascia, an Augustinian nun, came to be known as patron of women troubled by all sorts of things, including bodily ills.

[10] A biolca (plural, biolche) is a unit of land measurement traditionally corresponding to a field estimated to be ploughable on a working day with a plough drawn by two oxen.

Don Camillo looked at the old woman, who was panting as she lay in her armchair, then replied:

'I will report back. If the deal suits Santa Rita, I will return.'

He made to leave but the old woman called him back:

'Reverend, you should have more respect for a poor, sick, lonely old woman!'

'And you, madam, should have more respect for the Eternal Father!' replied Don Camillo. 'God is not a merchant in grace, nor am I his agent. No one asked you to redo the chapel of Santa Rita: if you are devoted to Santa Rita, pay homage to her, but do not try to arrange a contract with her. For my part, I will pray to God that he will heal you, even if you do not commit to embellishing my church.'

'If I have blasphemed, God will forgive me because he knows how confused my illness is making me... Go to an architect, Reverend, and have him make you a plan for the chapel of Santa Rita... Something grandiose. No expense spared... Go immediately, and pray for me.'

When Don Camillo returned to the Palazzone with the plan, the old woman was better and looked carefully at the drawing. She was okay with it and asked how much it would cost.

'You wanted something grandiose,' Don Camillo explained. 'The estimate comes to a million and a half.'

'For such a luxurious chapel, it really is not much,' Signora Cristina observed. 'Leave me the plan so I can study it and see if anything is not agreeable to me.'

Don Camillo received the plan back that same evening and, along with the plan, a letter and a cheque.

'I am sure that you can do something beautiful even if less grandiose. Please leave a note of receipt to the bearer of this.'

The cheque was for 350,000 lire and Don Camillo acknowledged receipt of it under the title 'restorations to the chapel of Santa Rita.'

Signora Cristina improved further in the following days but, both because of her mania of going around checking if anyone was stealing her stuff, and, perhaps, because of the torment of having thrown away 350,000 lire when she would have got better anyway, without turning to Santa Rita, two weeks later her heart became engorged and she became as thin as a rake. And when she died she did so without leaving a will, because she was the sort of person who could never submit to leaving her stuff to anyone.

Everything went to distant relatives and so, for the people of the village, the old woman was even more dead than dead: it was as if she had never been born.

In the meantime, winter had arrived and everything was at a standstill, except the hunger of the unemployed people, and Don Camillo decided it was a good time to take out the old woman's money and give the unemployed a little work to do. He looked into making a few tweaks to the little chapel of Santa Rita project document, made a fair copy of it, put the original in a drawer and went to see the Bishop.

*

'Your Excellency,' Don Camillo began very agitatedly, 'I have had an idea.'

'I realise what a serious situation that puts us in,' replied the old Bishop. 'But you mustn't let it get the better of you, Don Camillo. Just think of something else … venture in the opposite direction … and you will restore your balance again.'

'Your Excellency,' protested Don Camillo, not a little humiliated, 'are my ideas ever so bad?'

'Certainly not,' explained the Bishop. 'Don Camillo thinks up many good ideas: but then he never comes to tell them to the Bishop. When Don Camillo comes to the Bishop, it means that he has thought up some crazy idea and, since he does not feel like taking on the responsibility of putting his plan into action on his own, he tries to involve the old Bishop in the enterprise.'

Don Camillo spread his arms wide: 'Your Excellency,' he exclaimed. 'I never...'

'You *always*!' the Bishop interrupted him. 'You are a trouble factory! I have always had nothing but trouble from you. You are my main supplier of trouble! And you always take advantage of the fact that I like trouble, to load new instances of it onto these poor shoulders. Shame on you, Don Camillo, and tell me what new diabolical plan you have come up with! Speak!'

Don Camillo began to speak and the old Bishop stood there admiring the spectacle of his doing so. For Don Camillo, as a speaker, was not a man, he was the speech. He spoke with his whole body, and where he could not express what he wanted to say in words, he did so by waving his hands, shrugging his shoulders, rolling his eyes. Only the ears remained impassive, and that was only an apparent impassivity because, at a certain point, the ears did actually change colour and became red as a ripe cherry.

The Bishop let Don Camillo empty the bag completely and when he had finished and was drying his sweaty face with a handkerchief, the old Bishop observed:

'Sometimes I ask myself: is Don Camillo a poet or is he reckless? Then I think that it is often difficult to establish a precise boundary between poetry and recklessness and I leave that decision to the good Lord. But, in this, I have no doubts: only a reckless person can think of undertaking such as you suggest without having any means at all to pay for it!'

Don Camillo smiled: 'I do have the means, Your Excellency: 350,000 lire in cash. An old lady, before dying, entrusted me with this money to renovate the chapel of Santa Rita...'

The Bishop interrupted him and stated categorically: 'Don Camillo! The will of a dead woman is *sacred*!'

'Your Excellency, when she gave me the money she was still very much alive and had no intention of dying. Furthermore, I am not taking anything away from Santa Rita: I am postponing the work to a more suitable season. Santa Rita can wait: those who are hungry, No!'

The Bishop shook his head for a long time, then pointed his stick at Don Camillo's chest:

'Your project does not interest me,' he exclaimed. 'In fact, I don't even understand how you plan to undertake it. You ask me for twenty days leave. I will grant you a month. You will answer to God and man for what you do in that time.'

Don Camillo was a little perplexed: 'Your Excellency,' he stammered 'if you do not approve of my idea...'

'A Bishop can never approve the crazy ideas of crazy priests!'

In the meantime he had made his way over to a cabinet and taken a book out of a drawer. From the book he now took an envelope and handed it to Don Camillo:

'I hear that you are actively involved with Santa Rita,' he said. 'These 150,000 lire were given to me a little while ago by a very faithful follower of the good saint: put them together with the rest.'

Don Camillo puffed out his chest: 'Your Excellency, with half a million in cash, not even the Devil can stop me!' he shouted.

The old Bishop sighed and wanted to say something, but said nothing because disappointing a poet is like cutting off the wings of a little angel.

*

Don Camillo worked well on the project and in silence, so when the bomb exploded, it did so unexpectedly and the whole town gathered in the piazza, with Peppone and his staff on the balcony of the Town Hall.

No one knew what the hell would happen: the poster that Don Camillo had put up ignited interest but was very vague, and everyone was waiting anxiously. And then the bells began to ring in celebration and a team of young men wedged themselves into the crowd and opened a wide corridor among the people, starting in the churchyard, crossing the piazza and exiting into the main road.

'If this is one of his damned dirty political tricks,' Peppone said grimly, 'this time it's going to end badly for real.'

As he spoke, something was happening in the churchyard, but it didn't give the impression of having a hidden political purpose.

A small procession began to pass through the corridor without any sort of aggressive intent: first a small group of cyclists, then a cart pulled by two horses and, towed by the cart, two 'cassoni' as they call them down there: two of those carts with very high wheels that can be tipped over and are used to load gravel and sand into the river.

Having arrived in front of the town hall, the small procession came to a halt. Don Camillo jumped out from somewhere and climbed onto the cart.

'Brothers! Citizens!' he thundered.

Peppone gritted his teeth and waited for the storm.

The people fell silent.

'Brothers! Citizens!' repeated Don Camillo. 'Listen to me, listen calmly. Forget for a moment the Party card you have in your pocket. This is not a deployment that should worry you. Twenty-five men, a cart, two crates, two horses and a priest: it is not an army that should frighten you. And if you hear the clanking of metal under this sheet, do not think of hidden weapons. Twelve shovels, twelve pickaxes, twelve wheelbarrows, twenty-six mess tins, a kettle and a frying pan are not dangerous weapons.'

The people still didn't understand and Peppone was still full of suspicion.

'Twenty-five men, two horses and a priest!' continued Don Camillo. 'I present to you the first *Brigade of honest seekers of honest bread.*'

'Where there is no work for the people, we will go and look for it. We will wander the muddy streets of this sad winter, we will stop in front of every farmyard. We will offer our labour in exchange for bread. We are up for anything: to repair or build roads and cart tracks, to restore irrigation canals, dig drainage ditches. And we are equipped to undertake all the work that someone who wants to make improvements to a farm may need.'

'There are people here capable of handling a trowel, but who are ready to work with shovel and pickaxe. The two crates will be used to transport gravel, sand, lime, earth, whatever is needed.'

'We will not ask for money: give us flour, eggs, lard, butter, wine, milk. The workers and their families will eat. We will sleep in haylofts and straw stacks.'

'Can work become an adventure? Let us set out proudly to be adventurers in work. Citizens: the men of this Brigade are free from all political agenda and, if any of them are members of some party, they recognise a single great motivator that permits no fantasies or indiscipline: the hunger of children!'

'I am merely the chaplain of this work department. If I go with these people, or if, dissatisfied with having created this Brigade, I dissolve it, it is not so much to remind these men that there *is* a God who helps and comforts, but above all to remind others, who can *give* work and bread, that there is a just God, who punishes the selfish!'

'So now, brothers, before we set off on our adventure, let us raise our battle flag on the flagship!'

An old man planted a Tricolour flag as big as a handkerchief on the wagon.

No-one applauded. No-one said a word.

Don Camillo and the others got back on their bicycles.

The Brigade moved forward and the people watched it pass by with eyes full of anguish.

Peppone retreated with the gang. 'It's a damned farce!' he shouted when he managed to re-establish internal connections. 'This is how you denigrate the concept of work and workers!'

Mental confusion abounded. 'What about the emigrants, those who go abroad?' Brusco objected.

'Emigrating abroad is one thing, emigrating at home is another!' Peppone shouted. The concept was not very clear, but Peppone sought to clarify it:

'If a poor man is hungry and asks for alms from a stranger, it is one thing, but if he asks for alms from his son, then both are pigs: the father because he does not kick his son, the son because he does not feel obliged to feed his father!'

Then he thought about it again and concluded:

'If it is not like that, it must be something like it!'

*

First stop was in front of Bersini's farmyard. The Brigade remained outside, waiting on the road, Don Camillo went in. Bersini let him speak then replied that the idea was excellent.

'They should do stuff like this everywhere!' he approved. 'Because, as you rightly say, Reverend, you feed the hungry, and you take people away from those that sow hatred. Too bad I have no work to offer. But I'll gladly give a kilo of flour per person.'

'We're looking for *work*, not charity,' explained Don Camillo.

The Brigade continued on its way. But before long it was midday and the men put the pot on the fire and sat down happily to eat.

In the afternoon they marched off again. Don Camillo knocked on two more doors of big farmers. Unfortunately, the first had had a lot of trouble with his grapes, the second with his milk. They offered 1,000 and 500 lire respectively, which Don Camillo refused.

Evening fell and, while the men were preparing a fire and the pot on a dirt road, Don Camillo made for the nearest farmyard to ask for lodging.

They had by this time progressed far beyond the village and the people here knew Don Camillo only by name. They had no room for the Brigade, they said, and directed him to an abandoned shack, about half a kilometre away. Here, that night, the Brigade took up residence and before throwing themselves onto the straw with the others, Don Camillo comforted his companions thus:

'Let us not allow ourselves to be discouraged: God will help us.'

*

The next morning they set off again and the day started well. When Don Camillo knocked on the first door, he found himself in front of someone he knew. He was offered a drink in a warm and welcoming room, Don Camillo was listened to with great sympathy. But then came the man's reply:

'Reverend, I know very well who you are and you know very well who I am. You know my ideas and you know that I agree with you on everything. So you must believe me if I tell you that what you are doing is not working. Leave these initiatives to others. To the lefties and the pro-lefties. Forgive me, but you are in the realm of demagogy with this – yours is an emotive appeal rather than a rational one. You are playing the game of our adversaries. Think again and take the whole Brigade home.'

Don Camillo had made a solemn promise to Christ: he had sworn that he would never let his hands or his feet speak for him again, and that, whenever occasion arose, he would limit himself to saying only words that were strictly necessary. He thought calmly about the situation now, pondered what had been said to him and considered that, in reply, one word would be enough. And, in fact, he said only one word. And, in turn, the other man, very agitated, replied that if Don Camillo and his band of gypsies did not leave immediately he would call the police.

*

The March of the Brigade lasted as long as the money of Santa Rita lasted. Then, one sad morning, it found itself on the embankment. And there, no more than a kilometre away, lay the village.

Seeing his bell tower again, Don Camillo's heart sank. Then he looked at the men of the Brigade: gloomy, sad, with their long beards and muddy clothes and straw in their hair. Not even a dog had given work to these wretches! Not even one!

The crackling of a motorcycle startled him out of his thoughts and he found himself confronted by Peppone.

'Let's say welcome to the returning Brigade,' said the Mayor. 'Be of good cheer, I have some work for you. The connection between Strada Quarta and Strada Lunga is under construction. There's work for all of you... For everyone except, of course, the Reverend... Unless...'

'Thank you, I have my own work,' replied Don Camillo.

The men of the Brigade were suddenly rejuvenated and, getting back on their bicycles, raced towards the village, the horses trailing behind.

Left alone with Don Camillo, Peppone, who knew everything, from A to Z, about the Brigade's misadventure asked, 'Did the experiment go well?'

'Very well,' replied Don Camillo.

Peppone lit a half-Tuscan.

'Reverend, may I offer you membership of the Communist Party?' he inquired between one snort and another.

Don Camillo felt like shouting something, but he looked at the bell tower and did not shout.

'Thank you,' he replied, 'too kind. But I have decided to remain a Christian.'

'At any rate, I am grateful to you for the service which you have rendered to my Party at your expense.'

'I did not render it to you,' Don Camillo explained calmly. 'Thank all those who closed the door in my face. Send them the honorary membership cards.'

*

Don Camillo made his report to Christ and Christ sighed: 'It is easier for a camel to pass through the eye of a needle...'

'Jesus!' Don Camillo interrupted him. 'Be careful, or they will accuse you of playing the communist game.'

The Good Earth (1952)

EVERY TIME THEY talked to him about Magnaschi, Peppone made a disgusted face and spat upon the ground. For many reasons he had never liked the man and in the final reckoning, Magnaschi was the first to be called before the people's tribunal.

'You are guilty of carrying out political activities contrary to the interests of the people and of liberty, activities aimed at strengthening the tyrannical fascist regime,' Peppone told him.

'I have never been involved in politics,' Magnaschi replied calmly. 'Everyone knows that I have barely even left my farm.'

'You never left, but everyone knows that on your farm there was a constant stream, of comings and goings of bigwigs in heavy boots with pigeons on their caps[11]. Why did they come round to you and not to other farmers?'

'Because my farm was, in those days, what it is today: the best-cultivated farm in the province. My land has always produced a better harvest than any other. After all, I am the farmer who received the principal prizes in the Battle for Wheat.'[12]

Someone jumped up in a fury:

'And you're even shameless enough to boast about it! The Battle for Wheat was an initiative of the fascist regime and you, by going for glory, have backed the regime to the hilt!'

Magnaschi spread his arms wide:

'In truth, my only intention was to increase wheat production: I didn't realise that it was a political crime to produce fourteen quintals of wheat per farm rather than seven or eight.'

Peppone turned red:

'The political point of the Wheat Battle initiative was infinitely greater than its economic value,' he shouted.

But Magnaschi was prepared for whatever they threw at him. He took a rolled up sheet of paper out of his pocket and handed it to the President of the People's Court, explaining:

'This is the Gold Medal diploma that my father received from the Itinerant Chair of Agriculture in 1913, for having obtained, on the Santa Lucia farm, an average production of fifteen quintals of wheat. My mistake, therefore, has not been to increase wheat production, but to have decreased it by one quintal. I actually undermined my father's work instead of, as you say, foolishly compounding it. However, let me demonstrate good faith by declaring that now I will endeavour to reduce production: I regret that my farmers, in addition

---

[11] The symbol associated with Italian fascism was not Peppone's derogatory pigeon but an eagle with spreading wings clutching a bundle of fasces in its talons, a symbol as old as the Etruscans (8th to 1st century BC). The Latin 'fasces' (plural of 'fascis') is the root of the word 'fascism'.

[12] The so-called Battle for Wheat was a propaganda campaign launched in 1925 by Mussolini, the idea to liberate Italy from the 'slavery of foreign bread'.

to their normal paid salary, have always earned a production bonus.'

Peppone chewed bitterly, then stated categorically:

'For the moment, you may go home and remain at our disposal. We will call you again when our investigation is complete.'

They didn't call him again and the matter stuck in Peppone's craw because his anger with Magnaschi was born not of politics but of personal enmity. He was not the only one in town to hate the man. Magnaschi annoyed a lot of people because of his self-satisfied, patronising airs. Unjustified airs, everyone agreed, for if the Santa Lucia farm was what it was, it was down to his inheritance – the money and land that old Magnaschi had left to his son.

'It's easy to be a farmer for sport,' his critics muttered. 'It's easy to get two crops a year out of the ground when you have money to burn. Machines, fertilizers, selected seeds, irrigation, labour, high-quality livestock, feed: it is easy to get 100 from a farm by spending 150. But the rest of us have to live on what we produce and we can't spend a cent more than a certain amount. Give us Magnaschi's money and we will make our farms yield far more than his!'

Above all, a lot of people liked Magnaschi no more than they liked smoke in their eyes because of his arrogance, and many would have gladly seen him go bust. But the people's tribunal concluded before Magnaschi ever went bust and, since from that time he became even more reserved and kept himself even more out of the lives of ordinary mortals in the countryside, the people's hatred of him only gained in proportion.

That is why, for his part, Peppone, every time people spoke about Magnaschi, grimaced and spat upon the ground. And one morning at the Town Hall, as the Mayor had just finished spitting on the ground (because people had been talking about Magnaschi in the context of the repair of the Strada Vecchia), Smilzo came to call upon his boss with some urgency.

Peppone went out into the piazza to see what was up and found a wonderful touring coach full of young men. Two very distinguished looking gentlemen stepped forward, and the less elderly one, the tour guide, after the other had shaken Peppone's hand and uttered a few incomprehensible words, explained with a smile:

'Here, on a tour of various European countries guided by our professor, are students of the most important agricultural school in France. They wish to make a study of the various types of agriculture in this area, working from actual on-site statistical data, as opposed to the usual more theoretical records in academic books. This area interests them because it is the centre of production of tomato sauce, cured meats, parmesan cheese, etc: would you arrange for them to access some farms, visit stables, granaries, barns, crops and so on?'

Peppone didn't think twice, he called Smilzo and instructed him:

'Fly to Torretta and explain to old Beletti that in half an hour we will be there to visit his farm: tell him that we need to make a good impression abroad and that he should endeavour to put everything in order.'

Then Peppone had those on the bus informed that the Mayor wished to offer them refreshments and welcome them formally to the Municipality. And shortly afterwards, in the Council Room, he raised a glass to the health of the mutual understanding of all free peoples and the triumph of peace. The tour guide responded with an appropriate speech and the students underlined the words of the Mayor and their professor with great applause.

When Smilzo returned to advise Peppone that everything was going according to plan, Peppone said that if the guests wanted, they could make their first visit.

The young people and the professor took their places in the bus again and Peppone escorted them, preceding the bus on his motorcycle.

Smilzo was with him, huddled inside the sidecar.

'This is the moment that pig Magnaschi dies of rage!' said Peppone suddenly. 'When he finds out that I brought the French to Beletti's farm, it'll make him sick! Gone are the good times when every two days a gang of fascist bigwigs came to town and went to pay homage to Magnaschi's wheat! Now no fascists and no Magnaschi! Now we're going to visit all the farms except Magnaschi's!'

Smilzo sighed: 'Right, boss: though it's a shame that the only really good farm is his.'

'Let's not talk nonsense!' Peppone shouted. 'Santa Lucia is not a smart farm. It's not even your average farm in the area! It's a kind of wonderland organised along the lines of the fascist concept of the general who, during an inspection, is shown a magnificent real cannon, and he replies: "Very good!" But he doesn't know that all the other cannons are fakes, wooden replicas! In a democracy we look at *substance*!'

Smilzo said the boss was right, but he had an objection to make:

'We must face our own reality so as not to be led into creating illusions, and that is as it should be. But is it useful for *outsiders* to come in and look at our reality in the face? If we make them visit Beletti's farm they will think that it will be the best of all our farms, and since Beletti's farm is not that great, they will consider that we have a rather depressed agriculture.'

'This is fascist reasoning!' Peppone shouted, as Smilzo stuffed himself all the way into the sidecar.

They had arrived at the Pioppo crossroads: to the left, the road led to the Beletti farm, to the right the road led to the Magnaschi farm.

Peppone took the right road and, when he realised it, it was too late to turn back because he had taken the bus with him. Seeing it, Peppone, furious, shouted at Smilzo: 'You damned pig, you made me make a mistake! When we get home we'll do the math on this!'

Magnaschi behaved like a gentleman and completely ignored Peppone. Only at the end, when, having completed the visit to his fields, the foreigners were received in Signora Magnaschi's shady garden, did he grant the Mayor the grace of admitting to his presence.

One of the tour group asked Magnaschi how many quintals of wheat he was able to reap as a normal average production per hectare. Magnaschi turned to Peppone and asked:

'Mr Mayor, can I tell them the truth, or should I say less?'
Peppone ignored him.

'Forty-five quintals per hectare,' he explained to the guests. The teachers smiled incredulously, which Peppone didn't like. He then addressed Magnaschi:

'Show them the diplomas, medals etc! So they know we are not telling lies!'

Magnaschi looked at him curiously:

'Even the ones with the *fasces*?' he inquired cautiously.

It was then that Peppone uttered one of his memorable, not to say, historic declarations:

'Here, we don't do politics, we do statistics!'

*

Magnaschi had only one son, Gigino, who was twenty-five years old at the time of the visit of the French students. He had a middle school diploma, but for a long time he had forgotten it because for a long time he, alongside his father, had been concerned exclusively with making the 100 *biolche* of the Santa Lucia farm prosper. He had learned everything there was to learn from his father and, at home, they treated him like a man.

But Gigino had a secret, which he hadn't confided in anyone, not even his mother, for he was a reserved type, even more self-possessed than his father. But one day, at the table, he spilled the beans.

'I met a girl who is dead right for me,' he said, 'and I intend to marry her.'

Signora Virginia was struck dumb by shock. The father simply spread his arms and said: 'Everyone follows the path they believe is the right one. And who would this girl be?'

'Bigoni's daughter.'

Then it was Magnaschi Sr who remained speechless.

'Bigoni?' asked Signora Virginia in amazement. 'Bigoni di Fiumetto?'

'Yes,' replied the son.

'But Bigoni used to be one of our cowherds!' exclaimed Signora Virginia in anguish. 'He is an ignorant … a coarse man.'

'I won't be marrying him,' the young man explained calmly. 'I'll be marrying his daughter. She's a nice, good girl, she has studied a little, she's nobody's fool.'

The father said nothing; it was a huge thing for him: Gigino was marrying the daughter of one of his cowherds!

'If you have nothing against it, I'm going to ask permission from her father tonight,' Gigino announced.

Magnaschi shrugged his shoulders:

'It's up to you.'

Signora Virginia cried all night and Magnaschi couldn't sleep a wink. Then, in the morning, there was another shock, the biggest.

Old Bigoni arrived in a car, and Signora Virginia, as soon as she saw him, went and locked herself in her room. Bigoni was the same as he always was and, dressed for his holidays, he seemed even more brutish and vulgar.

He got straight to the point:

'Your son came to tell me that he wants to marry my Pauline: if it's fine with you, it's fine with me.'

Magnaschi muttered: 'If my son has so decided... He is the one getting married, not me.'

'Well!' Bigoni exclaimed. 'This being the case let's wrap this up quickly. I have four sons and a daughter: to each of the four I leave a farm. I give my daughter a cash dowry of twenty million. You fork in twenty more, which makes forty, and you'll have exactly what you need to conclude a good deal: they are selling the Camporosso estate. It is made up of 100 *biolche*, a tidy farm and a beautiful homestead. The young couple move there and run the farm just like you run things here. I think it's a real good solution.'

Magnaschi approved the idea: 'It seems like a good thing to me.'

'Then let's get on with it because there's a lot of people sniffing around Camporosso and we shouldn't miss the opportunity.'

Old Bigoni went away pompous and sweating, and Signora Virginia came down to hear the news.

And all was soon said.

'I still can't believe it,' moaned Signora Virginia. 'But whatever, God's will be done.'

Magnaschi clenched his fists:

'He came to humiliate me with his money!' he exclaimed. 'Filthy villain!'

Signora Virginia was a little more accommodating:

'Twenty million dowry is not to be thrown away. And Camporosso is a great deal. You've always said that it's a good farm. Give them the money and let them live their life. The important thing is that Bigoni never again sets foot here, in Santa Lucia! What the eye doesn't see, the heart doesn't grieve over.'

Magnaschi looked at his wife.

'Virginia,' he said anxiously, 'how do we do it?'

'How do we do what?'

'How can we give them twenty million? All that we own today is the Santa Lucia farm and three million in the bank.'

Signora Virginia fell into an armchair. It was the first time that her husband had spoken to her about financial matters: he had never talked about money, never permitted anyone other than himself to take care of business matters. His revelation took her by surprise and left her dismayed.

'I can't borrow twenty million: even if I managed to I wouldn't take it,' he said. 'In the banks they ask for ten, fifteen percent interest. I would never be able to pay. There is only one way to raise twenty million: sell Santa Lucia.'

'Never!' the woman shouted. 'It would be a disaster. It would mean destroying everything irretrievably. It would mean having lived in vain. You cannot betray your father! Santa Lucia has always been the pride of the Magnaschis and must remain so. There is another way: oppose the marriage. If Gigino wants to marry her, marry her without expecting any financial support from us.'

Magnaschi shook his head:

'Gigino has the right to marry whoever he wants and we cannot oppose it. Furthermore, the Bigonis and all the others would say that we found this excuse because we don't have the twenty million. It would be a triumph for the rabble.'

Signora Virginia returned to the usual Signora Magnaschi, impassive and impenetrable.

'Decide what you want to decide,' she said. 'I'm for whatever you want to do.'

The next day Magnaschi sent for Bigoni:

'I thought about the matter all night,' he explained. 'The Camporosso deal is good but we are not up for it.'

Bigoni looked at him:

'Twenty million – you're giving up quite a score!'

'I don't care about that at all,' Magnaschi replied harshly. 'My grandfather created the nucleus of Santa Lucia, my father made it the most beautiful farm in the region and passed it on to me, who made it the most beautiful farm in Italy. Santa Lucia must pass to my son who will make it the most beautiful farm in Europe.'

Bigoni sneered: 'Let's not exaggerate! You're saying that here we play in the world championships! I don't think so.'

'I won't even agree to discuss this with you. I am the best farmer in Italy and I chased you away because you were the worst cowherd in the universe! Remember that.'

'And yet today I have made enough money to give a farm to each of my four boys and a twenty million dowry to my daughter!' Bigoni shouted.

'Money earned on the black market does not ennoble your low origins, nor does it diminish your ignorance!' Magnaschi stated. 'I won't give a cent to my son. I am ill and have to retire to the Riviera. I can't take it anymore: if I continue I'll die. I am retiring and leaving Santa Lucia, as it is, to my son because I cannot allow anyone other than a Magnaschi to run this farm. With your twenty million the betrothed will be able to buy another fifty farms and enlarge this one: Pattini is willing to sell the part of his land that borders Santa Lucia. That's the deal, take it or leave it!'

*

Once the marriage between Gigino and Bigoni's daughter was celebrated, the deal of the neighbouring land was concluded and Magnaschi and his wife packed their bags and left.

In Rome, they went to visit Giorgio, the only great family friend they had:

'Giorgio' explained Magnaschi. 'I left everything to my son. Don't ask me why I did this. I did it because I had to. We have nothing left and I need to get a job. Send us somewhere. You know that I know my craft.'

*

Leaning on the stern railing, Magnaschi and Signora Virginia looked back at their homeland which was slowly receding. When it had disappeared and they found themselves between the sky and the sea, Magnaschi sighed:

'It is all over. This is the journey of no return. It seems like being dead and watching the world of the living move away as we fly into the sky. And yes, basically, we are dead...'

'But we died *well*!' exclaimed Signora Virginia.

And there was, in her voice, an immeasurable pride.

The Bust of the King (1952)

'THE KING!' EXCLAIMED SMILZO, very agitated, darting into the Mayor's office.

Peppone raised his eyes from his papers and looked at Smilzo in amazement: 'The King?' he asked. 'Which King?'

'The dead one!' stammered Smilzo, leaving and signalling Peppone to follow him.

The attic of the town hall served as an archive, but was, more than anything, an immense warehouse of dust and cobwebs. Peppone had entered it only once, staying just long enough to mutter: 'What a pigsty!' Now he set off with very little enthusiasm after Smilzo, who was climbing the staircase, narrow and dark, three steps at a time, before, with obvious disgust, he crossed the threshold of the Kingdom of Municipal Paperwork.

Making his way quickly across the filthy room, Smilzo stopped before a large bookcase on the back wall.

'Here,' he said, pointing to shelves full of paper bundles, black with dust.

Peppone looked at the mess, then looked at Smilzo.

'Are you stupid or what?' he asked.

'Boss,' replied Smilzo, 'try pushing this upright... No joking!'

Peppone placed a paw on the wooden upright suspiciously and a whole section of shelving opened as if it were a door. Indeed the section was fixed on hinges and functioned *as* a door.

Peppone was non-plussed: he didn't warm to this kind of detective mystery business. But Smilzo had slipped through the narrow portal and now he too entered and found himself in a small room lit by a window at floor level. A very clean little room with no bundles of paper and with walls so clean that they could have been whitewashed a few days ago.

'Boss, look at this!' exclaimed Smilzo.

Peppone turned. And there was the King. Right in the middle of the tallest attic wall, an enormous bust of white plaster, resting on a wooden column painted to look like fake marble, and with its own plaque.

'Bah,' muttered Peppone. 'That this stuff wasn't destroyed is a disgrace. But I don't see anything extraordinary about it.'

Smilzo sneered: 'Boss, doesn't the secret door seem extraordinary to you? Doesn't the little room where there isn't a speck of dust seem extraordinary to you? Boss, let's be clear: there's someone here who comes every now and then to sweep the floor and dust the King! And if you don't believe it, take a look over there.'

Peppone approached the King's pedestal and, on the capital that was four inches taller all around than the base of the plaster bust, he observed some daisies.

'They can't have been put there more than two days ago,' observed Smilzo. 'Boss, there's no doubt about it: this is a royalist *lair*!'

Peppone clenched his fists: 'Stay here and don't move for any reason!' he shouted. 'I'll sort this out now, myself! This time I'll terminate it once and for all!'

*

The town clerk entered the Mayor's office and immediately opened with: 'The report on the state of the Molinetto bridge will be ready in half an hour. I am typing it up.'

'Forget about the Molinetto bridge,' Peppone snapped harshly. 'Let's talk about something more important.'

The town clerk spread his arms and waited patiently. He was an elderly man, a gentle man, accustomed to saying, 'Yes sir,' ever since he had done his military service.

'Here,' Peppone said, 'once upon a time there was a bust of the King, if I'm not mistaken.'

'Yes, sir,' the clerk replied. 'In every town there was a bust of the King.'

'Okay: but then in every town there was a monarchy, while now, in this village, as in the others, there is a republic. Had you noticed?'

'Of course.'

'It wouldn't seem so,' exclaimed Peppone. 'Otherwise you wouldn't have done what you did and continue to do.'

'I don't understand, Mr Mayor,' stammered the town clerk.

'I understood perfectly when I saw what's in the secret room of the archive!' shouted Peppone.

The town clerk spread his arms:

'I don't know anything. I haven't the slightest idea what secret room you're talking about.'

Peppone pounded his fist on the desk:

'All right: I'll open an investigation immediately,' he shouted. 'Only two people ever go into the archive: you and the custodian. We'll see who's responsible. We'll see who took the bust of the King into the secret room! We'll see who dusts it and brings it flowers!'

The town clerk shook his head. 'I had the bust brought here in 1943 when *la Repubblica Sociale* came into being. No one can blame me for having done that. I then thought no more about it. Equally, no one can blame me for having forgotten about the King.'

'And the cleaning of it? And the floral tributes?' Peppone shouted.

At that very moment Smilzo entered, dragging the old custodian behind him:

'I caught him at it,' Smilzo explained. 'He entered the secret room with a duster in his hand.'

The old custodian shrugged. 'Well?' he muttered. 'What's wrong with me dusting off a monument that's in the Town Hall? If it's in the Town Hall, it has to be kept clean like everything else.'

Peppone pounded his fist on the desk:

'Town Hall, my arse! This is in a secret hiding place that only you two know about!'

The town clerk intervened very calmly:

'Mr Mayor, hanging on the wall there, behind your desk, is a picture of the complete plan of the municipal building and, as you can check, the little room attached to the archive is marked and also bears the qualification, "Number 27: accommodation for the possible night guard, fire prevention and archive surveillance."'

Peppone was foaming with rage:

'And the flowers?' he shouted. 'There were fresh flowers in front of the monument!'

'My granddaughter put them there the other day,' the custodian explained casually. 'She was with me when I was cleaning. She saw the white statue and took it for a monument to a dead person. She's three years old: she doesn't understand...'

'And you, who are not three years old, didn't you understand that that monument is a crime against the Republic?' shouted Smilzo.

'I only understood that it was about a dead King,' replied the caretaker. 'Historical stuff.'

'Kings don't make history, neither alive nor dead!' stated Smilzo.

The caretaker spread his arms:

'I'm not interested in politics. I know that in the main square, in Milan, there's a monument of a King on horseback and they left it there even though we're now a Republic.'

'They left it there not for the King, but for the horse!' shouted Peppone.

Peppone was furious: not even on this occasion of barefaced felony had he seemed able to get the town clerk. He vented his anger on the custodian:

'You're a doting old royalist!' he stated. 'Go get a hammer, go up, smash that piece of junk and throw the rubble in the garbage!'

The custodian shook his head:

'He who is dead lies dead and may his soul rest in peace,' he said. 'I don't take it out on the dead. And in any case I am in awe of that one up there.'

'In *awe*?' shouted Peppone. 'In awe, a bust like that?'

'Bust or not,' replied the keeper, 'a King is always a King... Break it up yourself … if you dare.'

Peppone nodded to Smilzo and then, after ordering the town clerk and the custodian to follow him, led the way out, up to the attic. When they entered the little room, Smilzo joined them carrying a large hammer in his hand, which he handed to Peppone.

Peppone stood with his legs wide apart in front of the large plaster bust and, after looking the town clerk and the custodian in the eye, he raised the hammer and struck the bust a tremendous blow.

But then something happened that froze his blood: under the blow the bust of the King did not crumble. It remained intact and emitted a sound like a submerged bell.

The hammer slipped from Peppone's hands and the dull resonance seemed to him like a powerful call from beyond the grave, a reverberation from across immense, boundless desert plains, struck by a stormy sky. And, at its call, the dead arose from the bare and devastated earth and formed themselves into compact ranks. And, soon, the ranks arranged themselves in a square and the bayonets and helmets shone and, in the centre of the square, was the little King on horseback, dressed in gray-green (as Peppone had seen him when he was a boy) and, in his fist, he was gripping … a flagpole.

The Secretary's voice roused him:

'It's made of bronze,' he explained. 'I didn't have people to move it and so I painted it white to make people believe it was plaster. I was lucky because when the Germans arrived they said: 'Make that piece of junk disappear.' If they had realised it was made of bronze they would have confiscated it and taken it away to be smelted down and used in their war machine.'

The caretaker picked up the hammer from the floor and handed it to Peppone: and Peppone was seized by fury. He pushed the hammer away and, clutching the bust in his arms, tore it from its pedestal.

It was frighteningly heavy, but no matter. The window at floor level looked onto a vegetable garden; Smilzo stuck his head out of it and said:

'Boss, there's no one about: let it go!'

The bust fell into the void with a thud.

Peppone climbed downstairs and ran into the vegetable garden: the bust was intact face up, as if arranged that way for a purpose.

'Load it onto a cart and take it to my workshop!' he shouted. 'I'll fix it myself – with oxygen! – *tonight!*'

*

When he had finished dinner, Peppone set off to destroy the monarchy scientifically. The bust of the King had been dumped in the workshop yard, among the wreckage, and since it had been raining cats and dogs all day, the plaster and glue had disappeared.

Peppone grabbed the bust of the King and dragged it indoors. Then he prepared the gas cylinder and the other tools, grabbed his blowtorch, pulled the smelter visor over his eyes, and knelt before the victim.

The blowtorch crackled. The oxyacetylene flame approached the King's chest and pierced him.

Peppone turned off the blowtorch and looked at the black hole that now opened on the King's chest, in the area of the heart.

Standing up, Peppone spilled a large hammer from the anvil onto the bronze bust and that call from beyond the grave was heard again and Peppone saw the image of the dead arise once more out of the bare and devastated earth, struck by a stormy sky.

Again, he saw the little King on his white horse in the centre of the square. But now the little King's chest was engorged with blood.

Peppone ran to turn on the fan of the forge and when everything was ready, he laid the bust of the King on its back and, with a small brass disk and a bit of tin, plugged the hole that the oxyacetylene torch had opened in the King's chest.

Then he smoothed the weld with a fine file and went over it with pumice, the job so perfect that now it seemed as if the King had a gold medal pinned to his chest.

*

Don Camillo had just arisen from his bed when Peppone came knocking on the presbytery door with a wheelbarrow carrying a large thing on top, covered by a tarpaulin. He went straight into the entrance hall with the wheelbarrow, removed the tarpaulin and showed Don Camillo the bust of the King.

'Reverend, I don't know what to do with this corpse,' said Peppone, wiping away his sweat. 'You priests specialise in corpses from the old regime. I'll give it to you. I tried to smash it but I couldn't.'

'You couldn't?' asked Don Camillo. 'How come?'

'It's hard to explain.'

'I'll take care of it,' said Don Camillo. 'I know how Kings should be treated.'

When he had celebrated Mass, Don Camillo went into the shed where he had hidden the bust of the King, padlocked the door and removed the straw that covered it and wiped the dust off it with his handkerchief.

'Your Majesty,' said Don Camillo in a low voice. 'I do not seek to judge you, I simply address this ardent prayer to God: "May it be that this man has been a good King."'

Then to the King: 'Your Majesty, it is not rancour that inspires me: if I hated you I would keep you hidden here among the faggots or among the cobwebs in the attic. If I respected you when you were alive, I will not disrespect you when you are dead. I will not allow your image to be secretly worshipped as that of a divinity, I will not allow it to be publicly despised. I am doing my duty as a minister of the King of Kings and as an old soldier of the King of Italy.'

A large club was nearby: Don Camillo took it and struck a tremendous blow to the bust of the King.

And the bust of the King shattered as if it had been made of plaster instead of bronze.

Don Camillo collected the pieces and carefully placed them in a box.

*

A few weeks passed and one day, Peppone, while returning home, heard something that gave him a little shiver.

The bells were ringing out loud and it seemed as if they were always the same bells that Peppone knew well but, every now and then, an unusual touch was added to the chorus.

Peppone strained his ears and soon he was sure: there was a new voice.

A thin, ringing voice that went to flush out echoes never before to be heard.

While Peppone was standing there with his nose in the air, Smilzo arrived.

'Hello, boss,' said Smilzo, 'the clergy is enhancing its acoustic repertoire!'

'A new bell?'

'A little one,' explained Smilzo. 'They hung it up this morning and now they're testing it.'

They walked away in silence. Then, suddenly, Smilzo turned to Peppone and said in a low voice:

'It's the King's bell.'

At the crossroads they parted and Peppone continued on alone.

When he reached the front door, the concert of bells gradually died away and it seemed, at a certain point, that it had ended completely, but, after a grave toll of the big bell, the new bell rang once more, clear and imperious. And, at that ring, Peppone turned around with a start as if someone had called him.

The fact that he had been taken by surprise annoyed Peppone. Grumbling, he slipped out of the kitchen door.

'Did you hear how beautiful the King's bell sounds?' his wife asked him.

'Nonsense!' Peppone replied. 'They'll notice when Stalin's bell rings!'

In the meantime, however, he was thinking about the hole he had made in the King's chest with the oxy-acetylene torch and he wasn't at all displeased with having soldered it with tin and brass confetti, which, after all said and done, had looked like a medal.

The Direct Route (1952)

PEPPONE HAD 'A THING' about getting directly to the point. Which, when applied to the singular map of the Municipality, couldn't really be criticised as wildly obsessive.

The territory of the Municipality was like a slice of cake: a triangle with its base resting on the main embankment of the Great River. The Municipal 'capital' was the village located about halfway along the base of the triangle, nestling along with six other villages – three upstream and three downstream – to which it was connected by the embankment road.

But the Municipality in fact possessed an eighth village, Castelletto, which was located at the apex of the triangle, at the point opposite the embankment, connected to the capital by the old Rovaccia road.

The road along the embankment was wide and beautiful, but people who wanted to go to the city without extending their journey by twenty kilometres or more needed to go via the capital, then from the capital to Castelletto via the Rovaccia road, after which they joined the provincial road.

As the crow flies, the distance from the capital to Castelletto was about six kilometres, but the road took you a good eleven kilometres. Why the Rovaccia road had turned out to be so bizarre and crooked as to become eleven or so kilometres long, is lost in the mists of time – perhaps to avoid passing through the woods, perhaps to follow the borders of some ancient enormous estate. Not worth investigating: if you want to find bizarre roads, turn into la Bassa!

In addition to being eleven kilometres long, the Rovaccia road was among the most uncomfortable roads to travel in the universe: full of curves and counter-curves, narrow, muddy or dusty depending on the season, it seemed designed to encourage people to neglect their business in the city and stay home.

So, calling Peppone's idea of building a *direct route* from the capital to Castelletto an obsession was at the very least unfair.

But, where politics are involved, any sensible reasoning goes by the board and if your political opponent warns you that it is raining, you, to spite him, will leave the house without an umbrella.

And then Peppone's mistake was to harp on continually about the issue of the direct route. He found a pretext to talk about it when and wherever he could.

'He's obsessive about the direct route!' people muttered. And they said it with the tone and spirit with which one says: 'He has a persecution mania.'

But Peppone was as immoveable as a cast iron object and, by dint of hard work, one fine day he managed to put the direct route project into practical implementation.

This created a real storm: in the opinion of the people there were a hundred thousand more urgent and important jobs, and wanting to bury a lot of money in his undertaking seemed tantamount to betraying the community.

It was an expensive project not least because of the Rovaccia River, a little river which flowed from Castelletto down into the Great River and would have to cross the planned new, *direct route* twice: at one kilometre after the capital, and at one kilometre before Castelletto. So, anyone wishing to join the two towns directly with a straight road, would be forced to build two bridges.

'It's all an outrage!' shouted the owners of the farms through which the direct route would pass.

The battle was long, but Peppone won it and the work began. The two bridges over the Rovaccia were quickly built and the workers began laying the ballast for the new road.

The people were furious, but kept quiet. However, when the tar caravan arrived, they could no longer contain their bile. Asphalt! He's building a highway!

Instead of using the money, for example, to fix the problem of the aqueduct and the sewer system, Peppone was building a monument to megalomania: his!

Still he didn't budge an inch: he simply erected a sign at the beginning of the road that read, 'We will pull directly ahead together!'

Towards the end of the work he had a moment of despair and, during discussions in the piazza, he needed to share out a number of slaps. But his faith in the importance of his undertaking and the certainty that, later, the various villages would be grateful, helped him overcome the crisis.

On the day of the inauguration, only the members of his gang were present, but Peppone didn't mind.

'The toad is hard to swallow,' he observed. 'But *it will be swallowed*.'

The following morning, the bus that went from the capital to Castelletto, having picked up the people in the piazza, instead of taking the old damnable Rovaccia road, happily took the direct route.

'Stop there!' the people in the bus said to the driver. 'Either you take the old road or we get off and we'll never use the bus again.'

The driver took the old Rovaccia road: it was a hundred thousand times more uncomfortable, but he too preferred it to the new one. That evening, Peppone called the man to the Town Hall:

'Either you use the direct route or I'll take away your licence!' he told him.

The next morning the bus did take the direct route: but completely empty. And completely empty it returned.

After five days of this refrain, the driver went to Peppone and asked him what he should do:

'Go to hell, you and those wretches!' Peppone replied.

But they must have been very wretched because no-one ever took the direct route, even when it was pouring with rain and the Rovaccia road was a river of mud.

And even those coming the opposite way, from Castelletto to the capital, used the old Rovaccia road exclusively. And Peppone had to send a special service team to Castelletto because, at the fork of the new bridge, there was always some damned person who left signs in front of the entrance to the direct route with words like: 'Warning: dangerous road'; 'Work in progress'; 'Road closed.'

Visitors were also always directed along the old Rovaccia road when asking in Castelletto. One oil and soap salesman, who didn't give a damn about the warnings and arrived in the capital via the direct route, never managed to do another cent's worth of business in the area.

Peppone couldn't take people by the throat and force them to journey along the direct route. He would have done so willingly, in truth. But he understood that the only way was to cash in with a smile on his lips.

'There's no need to rush!' Peppone observed, pretending to be very calm. 'All will pass! All will pass!'

One morning he found the whole village covered in graffiti 'No-one will pass!'

He continued to take it on the chin: but one day, finally, he pounded the table and said:

'No more!'

*

A certain Brichetti had died in Castelletto and, like the dead in all the other villages, he had to be taken to be buried in the municipal cemetery in the capital. Now, considering that the transportation service for the deceased was provided by the Municipality, there was no way the hearse could pass by any road other than the direct one.

So, when the head of the motorised undertakers came to tell Peppone that the hearse would travel along the Rovaccia road, it was only logical for Peppone to jump out of his seat.

'Have you lost your senses too?' Peppone shouted at the boss of the undertakers.

'I am simply here to receive orders,' replied the little man, spreading his arms.

'There's no need for orders!' replied Peppone. 'It's logical that you have to take the most direct route, the express route!'

'Logical up to a certain point,' explained the little man. 'The fact is that the relatives of the dead person don't want to.'

'Since they can't keep the dead person at home,' shouted Peppone, 'and since the service is the Municipality's, either they bring the dead person here, taking the express route, or they take him to another cemetery! You can and must only take the express route.'

An hour later the relatives of the dead person arrived:

'We can't take him to another cemetery,' said the relatives. 'We have to bring him here and take the Rovaccia road.'

'And why?' asked Peppone. 'What is there in the direct route that you don't like?'

'Nothing as far as we're concerned,' replied the dead man's eldest son. 'For us, direct or not direct, it's all the same. The fact is that my father has it in his will that he wants to be buried here and that the cortege must pass along the Rovaccia road. Otherwise, we will lose our inheritance.'

The relatives showed Peppone the will and there was, indeed, a clause like that.

Peppone replied that he didn't care about the will: either the cortege goes direct or it goes to another cemetery.

'As you wish!' exclaimed the dead man's son. 'But you have to put this in writing because if we lose our inheritance we will sue the Municipality.'

The dead man passed through the Rovaccia road.

It took Peppone fifteen days to regain his cool and get over it. But he did regain it and one evening, entering the café that functioned as a den of reactionaries, he began to chat cheerfully about this and that, then, suddenly, he looked at his watch:

'It's late!' he said. 'I have to get up early tomorrow morning. I have to move the petrol station.'

Peppone had a petrol station in front of his workshop: everyone knew about it, but no one could figure out why the hell he wanted to move it.

'In this neck of the woods, if you don't get ahead of yourself, you'll end up stranded,' he explained. 'Now that all the traffic is to be directed onto the direct route, it will end up that no one will pass in front of my garage anymore and since, no matter how little petrol you have in your tank, you'll always have enough to go six kilometres on a straight, asphalted road, there's a risk that everyone will wait to fill up until they arrive in Castelletto. It used to be different: in eleven kilometres of disgusting road full of curves and braking, you use up a lot of petrol! So, I'll move the petrol station to the bridge of the express route. I'll put some of my guys on the job there while I prepare to move my workshop too.'

Putting the petrol station on the bridge, almost a kilometre past the entrance to the Rovaccia road, when all the traffic was on the Rovaccia road, and not a soul, either living or dead, passed by the bridge of the express route, meant that Peppone had surely gone crazy.

No one took it seriously and, as soon as Peppone had left, everyone said that it was obviously just another aspect of his power-driven delusion. But it was not, and two days later the petrol station was standing sentry on the deserted bridge on the direct route.

A month later the tanker of petrol at the station was still full to the brim.

*

The *Madonna Pellegrina*[13] had arrived in Castelletto, and from Castelletto it was to pass to the capital of the Municipality. Those from Castelletto would escort it to the border and people from the Municipal capital would go to the border to receive it.

Don Camillo went to visit the parish priest of Castelletto to make the necessary arrangements.

'There is little to arrange,' the parish priest of Castelletto replied. 'The border is what it is. It follows the course of the Rovaccia river, starting two kilometres before the new bridge and continuing to halfway along the Rovaccia road. At the Mulino Vecchio the border cuts across the road. So I'll wait for you at the new bridge.'

Don Camillo shook his head: 'That's not fair,' he observed. 'You know how things are and you're getting me into trouble, making me go along the Rovaccia road.'

'No trouble,' replied the parish priest of Castelletto. 'I'll stop at the crossroads where the Rovaccia road joins the direct route after the bridge. I'd be getting you into trouble if I waited for you at the other accessible border point, on the Rovaccia road. Because you, for example, might arrive not from the Rovaccia road, but from the direct route. If I stop at the crossroads, no matter which way you arrive from, we're fine. Besides, if I were to take the Rovaccia road I would be assuming a position that I am not allowed to assume.'

'Well, that's sorted then…' Don Camillo muttered.

'Every man for himself and God for all,' replied the old parish priest of Castelletto.

Having agreed the arrangements, Don Camillo returned home along the road he had taken on his way there: which was the Rovaccia road. Shortly before reaching the village he found himself confronted by Peppone.

'Reverend,' said Peppone, 'why, to go to Castelletto, didn't you use the shortest and most beautiful express road?'

---

[13] The Pilgrim Madonna, a specific religious devotion centred on a statue of the Virgin Mary, a nationwide 'thank you' for the end of World War II.

'Habit,' replied Don Camillo. 'Force of habit.'

'Right,' replied Peppone. 'Force of habit makes you do things that are contrary to logic. However, while you may be used to taking the Rovaccia road, the Pilgrim Madonna is not used to it. In your opinion, Reverend, which road will *she* take to come from Castelletto?'

'I have no idea,' said Don Camillo. 'In any case, it doesn't seem to me that the Pilgrim Madonna needs permits issued by your party.'

'The Party has nothing to do with it. As mayor, I would like to know from which direction the Pilgrim Madonna will arrive. Mayors must always worry about when and where significant personages will arrive.'

'Is the Madonna now significant for you too? Politics *is* a strange thing!'

'Politics has nothing to do with it, nor should they. The Madonna does not do politics. Be careful, Reverend, not to direct her down the wrong path...'

'I don't understand what you mean.'

'I mean that the straight road is the shortest and the least dangerous.'

Don Camillo spread his arms:

'He who leaves the old road for the new, knows what he loses and does not know what he will find.'

Peppone shrugged: 'Do as you please, Reverend. Forewarned is forearmed.'

*

The procession formed in the churchyard. All the opponents of the Reds were there, and it did not cross anyone's mind that they might go to meet the Pilgrim Madonna by any other road than the old Rovaccia.

It was eleven kilometres, but they would have travelled thirty to avoid going by the direct route: and the very long procession travelled along the winding and dusty road and finally arrived at the outlet onto the main road, immediately after the bridge. The flower-bedecked truck on which the sacred image was enthroned was ready and waiting there, surrounded by the people of Castelletto.

The new procession formed in front of, around, and behind the truck. And Don Camillo took the lead:

'When we are on the Rovaccia road,' he said to his most trusted men, 'leave a good gap between me and the rest of the procession. I know what I'm doing.'

The procession moved off and travelled 300 metres before the bridge, where the fork in the road was just a few steps away.

'Jesus,' Don Camillo said, 'forgive me, but I would consider myself an unworthy soldier of yours if I gave in to an obscure threat. Make sure that if something painful is to happen, all damage will fall upon me.'

A car emerged from the Rovaccia road, pulled to the side and stopped. The Marshall of the *carabinieri* got out:

'Reverend, I happen to know that someone is planning to cause you a bit of trouble,' the Marshall said in a low voice to Don Camillo. 'But you may proceed safely. We have received reinforcements and the Rovaccia road is completely under our control...'

At the fork, to the left the Rovaccia road was completely controlled; to the right lay the bridge of the direct route: and, on the bridge, stood Peppone alone.

He was dressed for the party with the Tricolour mayor's scarf and had his hat in his hand.

A murmur was heard behind Don Camillo, but by now the archpriest had crossed the bridge and was walking on the asphalt of the direct route.

He walked with his head held high and with a determined step. Someone tried to catch up with him, but Peppone had placed himself between Don Camillo and the head of the procession and the Mayor's immense presence seemed an insurmountable barrier.

The march continued and, since the distance between the head of the procession and Don Camillo was considerable and since the singing had not yet resumed, Don Camillo felt his heart filled with dismay and said in anguish:

'Jesus, let them follow me!'

At that moment the singing resumed and Don Camillo whispered: 'Jesus, grant me the grace that I may always *go before*.'

The asphalt, clean and intact, seemed like a large carpet of black velvet. By and by, the six kilometres of smooth asphalt ribbon had been covered and the flower-bedecked truck of the Madonna was crossing the next bridge, when a murmur was heard and Don Camillo, turning, realised that the procession had come to a halt.

'Nothing to worry about, Reverend,' Peppone whispered in his ear, as he arrived, 'the truck stopped simply because it has no more petrol. We'll fix that in a moment.'

The petrol station was two steps away and Peppone's son was there already, with the hose in his hands.

It was a matter of a few moments and the engine started to mutter again and the procession started moving once more.

'As a first customer, I cannot complain,' observed a subdued voice.

Don Camillo turned and, with an atomic look, glared at Peppone.

*

Don Camillo and Peppone next met a month later, halfway along the old Rovaccia road, and the mud was up to their knees.

'It feels like we're on a road in Russia!' observed Don Camillo.

'In Russia there we also have magnificent roads, asphalted like the direct route!' replied Peppone.

'Yet the Pilgrim Madonna can never pass through.'

Peppone spread his arms and then muttered:

'If there were priests like you there, I think she would make it.'

'Even if there were mayors like you, comrade.'

Peppone lit a half-Tuscan and then declared:

'Priests like you are dangerous for the triumph of the people's cause: we will have to hang them all.'

'*Giusto*,' Don Camillo replied.

La Rosa Rossa (1952)

'Boss,' said Smilzo as he entered the Mayor's office, 'there's something wrong down in the piazza.'

'What do you mean something wrong?' Peppone asked.

'Hard to explain,' muttered Smilzo. 'You need to see.'

Peppone left his papers and followed Smilzo.

In the piazza everything seemed to be fine at first, but under the portico people were gathered in front of a little shop.

'It's Jofino,' explained Smilzo, as Peppone marched resolutely into the target area.

'What did he do?'

'Ten minutes ago, as soon as news arrived, he closed up shop and nailed a sign to the door.'

By this time they had joined the group and Jofino's sign was perfectly legible:

'Closed for national mourning.'

It was completely out of character that Jofino, the watchmaker, should have acted so impulsively. In his sixties, small, skinny Jofino had never said a word more than was necessary in his life, he had never meddled in politics, limiting his activity to taking care of sick watches and fishing with a line.

And yet Jofino, as soon as the news of the Queen's death reached the village, had closed up shop and nailed this sign on the door, which people were now staring at in silence and with not a little concern.

Now that Peppone was in among the group he had to act like a Mayor.

He lit a half-Tuscan.

As a position it wasn't bad: but it wasn't especially good either. The Republic expected something more substantial from him. The group parted, the people moved aside, opening up a clear passage to the door of Jofino's shop: this meant that the Republic was inviting citizen Peppone to approach the very door of Jofino's shop.

Peppone did as he was bid and, once there, realising that he could not simply remain and just look at the sign, he knocked on the door.

Jofino's head appeared at the mezzanine window.

'Come back, I'm not working today,' the watchmaker muttered.

'Just because you don't work, the nation doesn't come to a standstill,' Peppone replied.

'Then go and have the nation fix your watch,' Jofino replied.

'It's not a question of watches,' Peppone explained. 'The fact is that if you don't want to work, you are completely free to close up shop. However, it is very clear that you are making something of a personal statement by so doing.'

'The death of the Queen is not my personal affair, it concerns the entire nation.'[14]

Peppone shook his head: 'Depending on where you are: in England, for example, yes, because in England there is a monarchy. Here, no, because here there is a republic. And you are not in England, you are here.'

Jofino was not at all convinced by Peppone's rigorous reasoning:

'Republic or monarchy, a Queen is always a Queen. And if she dies there are people throughout our nation who will grieve. So there is national mourning.'

'National mourning when the entire nation agrees on the exceptional importance of the person who dies. Here, for example, the death of the Queen does not bother me any more than when any woman has died.'

---

[14] Queen Elena of Montenegro, wife of King Victor Emmanuel III, has died in exile. Nostalgia for the monarchy and reverence for the Risorgimento, the great unifying force in Italian culture, has been re-awakened.

Jofino was discovering his inner rebel: 'The Queen was not any woman and everyone knows it!'

'It does not matter that she was different from other women,' declared Peppone who was starting to sweat. 'In a republic, except for the President's wife, all other women, even if they are different, are equal!'

Jofino had already said too much: 'For me it is national mourning. Everyone is free to think as they wish.'

Having said this, Jofino withdrew and closed the window.

Peppone wiped the sweat from his forehead and turned to the assembled throng:

'It is useless to correct people who do not want to understand!'

'If they do not want to understand, it is up to you to make them understand!' replied the pharmacist, who was a passionate republican. 'That sign is a provocation and, without wanting to be too contentious, you should take it down.'

'True,' agreed Peppone. 'When reasoning does not lead anywhere, one has to take action.'

'Then take down the sign and let's not talk about it anymore,' said the pharmacist.

Peppone shook his head: 'In my capacity as Mayor I cannot go around tearing down signs or posters,' he explained. 'Every action of mine must be legally justified, otherwise it becomes an arbitrary act. Rather, *you* should remove it, doctor. Your reaction chimes with public opinion.'

The pharmacist remained hesitant, then shook his head.

'The Mayor is right,' he concluded: 'the matter is delicate and could lend itself to political speculation. Let us act within the strictest limits of the law. Let a commission report the matter to the Marshal of the *carabinieri*.'

The commission was then composed of the pharmacist, Peppone, Smilzo and Bigio, because, as soon as they heard about commissions, everyone ran away and only the pharmacist, Peppone and the other two drinking buddies remained on the spot.

They walked in silence towards the *carabinieri* building and, having arrived at the turn of the main road, where stood the pharmacy, Peppone stopped and turned to the pharmacist.

'By the way, doctor: do you have any good remedies for liver disease?'

'I have two or three very good ones,' the pharmacist replied.

'Then why don't you take advantage of it to sort your liver out?' Peppone muttered.

The pharmacist shook his head and then snorted: 'That damned old man made me lose my temper. If he hadn't been so volatile I wouldn't have spoken. If you come in for a moment, I'll let you sample the tipple I make. It's extraordinary.'

They all went into the pharmacy and, thence, into a little room, where the pharmacist filled four shot glasses.

The tipple was excellent and the pharmacist did a second round. And then he did a third.

The third glass took away everyone's desire to speak. They were silent for a long time, looking at the tablecloth, then Peppone sighed:

'Huh!'

'That's life!' said Smilzo.

'The world is no longer what it used to be!' muttered Bigio.

The pharmacist grabbed the bottle of hootch and filled the glasses for the fourth time. Which signified that he was basically in agreement with Peppone, with Smilzo and with Bigio.

All four raised their glasses and toasted in silence to who knows who.

And old Jofino's sign remained where it was and the whole town filed past it, but no one stopped to comment. As if they didn't see it.

*

That evening, Peppone couldn't sleep because he had something in his head that he couldn't get round.

Let's be clear: it was a thought that had suddenly come to his mind, so it was all his own personal stuff. But a thought that ended with a question mark.

Bad business, because it was something urgent and there was no time to waste on cerebral contortions.

Finally, he came to the most logical conclusion: do the thing and then, later, try to understand why he had done it.

He jumped out of bed at four, went to rummage among the scrap metal in the corner of the workshop and found the piece of iron that he needed for the job he had in mind.

He rekindled the fire in the forge and stuck his piece of iron in it. Then, when the iron was red, he began to hammer it on the anvil.

What the hell he wanted to get out of it was his to decide. He hammered away until noon, then hid the iron in the hot ashes of the forge and went to eat.

He didn't even finish eating before they brought him the newspaper and, in the newspaper, he found a story that made him nervous.

'I'm not here for anyone today!' he said to his wife.

'If you start hammering away again they'll hear you,' the woman replied.

'Whether they hear me or not doesn't matter: the important thing is that no one bothers me.'

Peppone's wife knew when not to insist. When Peppone spoke with that kind of voice, the only thing to do was to obey to the letter.

He returned to the workshop, closed the iron shutters on the windows and went back to work by the light of an electric bulb.

They had to hurry because everything had to be finished by the next day: the newspaper had the exact time. They couldn't be a minute late. In fact, they had to finish early to have time to think about the reason for all the work.

If Peppone hadn't found a logical conclusion to that, everything would have remained a dead thing, without meaning.

But, in the village, Peppone wasn't the only one living through such agitated hours. Even if he wasn't struggling to hammer away at an anvil, Don Camillo was having trouble of his own.

Because, during dinner, he too had found in the newspaper the same news item that had alarmed Peppone, and now he was walking up and down the deserted church without finding a possible solution to the problem that was occupying his brainbox.

'Lord,' he said suddenly, turning to Christ above the High Altar, 'I know I'm going to do something, though I don't know what it will be.'

'Do not worry, Don Camillo, you will know when you have done it.'

'Jesus, I am worried. Because I don't know if this thing I'm going to do will be good or bad.'

'If it is bad, do not do it.'

'Jesus, will I have time to realise whether it is bad before I've done it?'

'If, in the meantime, you have not renounced your quality as a sentient being, you will have time.'

'This reassures me completely,' sighed Don Camillo. But it was a big lie that he told, a lie not to deceive God, but to deceive himself.

*

Meanwhile, Peppone continued his furious hammering. In the evening, they passed him something to eat through the window. He devoured a few mouthfuls of food and then went back to work. With the windows closed and the light on, he lost all track of time. The hours flew by, but he didn't keep track of them. His only concern was to complete his work as quickly as possible.

And, in the end, the thing was finished.

Peppone looked at it in amazement: it was a large, magnificent rose made of wrought iron. The piece of iron had become a flower with thin, delicately crafted petals.

Peppone grabbed the rose by the end of its long stem: yes, 'the thing' had worked, but had it worked in time? He opened a window a crack and saw that it was day. The clock in the bell tower told him that there were only a few moments left. He closed the door and was overcome with dismay: he had done the thing, but it was as if he had not done it, because it was a grey, cold thing. A useless dead thing: a piece of junk, an artisanal 'masterpiece' to be put in the family museum. So much hard and feverish work thrown away...

He looked at his big, cold, grey rose which, born within those walls, would remain there, the useless little corpse of a piece of iron.

Meanwhile, Don Camillo, after spending an hour with his eyes glued to the clock, realising that the moment was about to arrive, had thrown himself desperately up the stairs of the bell tower.

And shortly thereafter, when Peppone heard the bells tolling for the dead, he came to his senses and found the solution.

He grabbed his extraordinary rose by the stem and plunged it into the flames of the forge and turned the fan furiously. Then he took it from the coals and the rose was no longer gray, but red. It was alive!

He placed it, so red and sparkling, on the black anvil and stood there looking at it. It was so alive that it seemed to him to be throbbing. And when the red started to get darker, Peppone said:

'Now the Queen's casket is before me!'

And throwing off his hat, he grabbed the big hammer and whispered, 'Hail, Your Majesty,' and struck the rose with a tremendous blow. And the tears of still red-hot iron shattered and splashed all around.

A handful of red petals on the casket of the Queen who had died in exile, in a foreign land.

Don Camillo's bells continued to ring for a long time. Then they fell silent and people forgot that the bells had rung.

Peppone reopened the shutters of his window and began to work on the engine of a tractor. Calm, with no more problems to solve, because the red rose had graced the occasion as, and when, it was supposed to have done.

The Sharecropper's Heart (1952)

IN THE SUMMER, when drought dries up the wells and the hot sun scorches the leaves of our elm trees black and sucks the life out of the meadows, the clover-like alfalfa at la Badia – fresh and full – reach up to 2 or 3-feet in height.[15]

This happens because the land of la Badia is high-altitude 'Ladin land', where the air is thinner, but above all because the longest side of the farm that we have in focus – a strip of 700 by 500 metres, which takes the name of the region – lies at the foot of the embankment of the Rovaccia canal, and in the Rovaccia there is always water to refresh deep down the fields through which it passes.

The farm was called Badia, which means 'abbey', because of its unusually imposing farmhouse. Way back when, this arrogance was probably justified: but up until recently if you had taken a moment to look inside the house, you'd soon have realised what a parlous state of repair it was in.

Notwithstanding this and despite general appearances, a good half of the farmstead was in fact in fine working order, having been restored to perfection in 1938: although the farm animals alone could rejoice, as the restored part comprised only the stable and the barn.

---

[15] Badia is a municipality in northern Italy, a Ladin-speaking community in an area surrounded by the Dolomite mountain range. Ladin is a minority language in 54 Italian municipalities. The clover-like alfalfa plant, a forage plant rich in antioxidants, is also called 'lucerne'.

The rest, the part reserved for Christians, had a history of decay going back at least 200 years – decay accelerated by war, which had transformed the place into quarters for soldiers, a conglomeration of two or three nationalities.

Before that, the son and grandchildren of the late Cristoforo Gabassi had lived at la Badia, having come to settle there as Bocci's sharecropper in 1888.

Just to give an idea of what type of Christians these Gabassis were, it will be enough to remember that people had renamed la Badia the 'Kremlin'. Altogether, the Gabassis numbered only twelve: two old men in their sixties, plus a married son of thirty-five with two bad boys aged fifteen and fourteen, plus three other sons aged twenty-seven, twenty-four and eighteen, plus two daughters aged twenty-five and seventeen, and a five-year-old dog. People placed the dog among the members of the family because, they explained, it was the most civilised Gabassi, being the only one not to be a member of the Party.

Village people exaggerate and it is always necessary to weed out the tares from everything they say: in any case the eleven two-legged Gabassi, politically speaking, were worth at least as much as thirty-four of the best men of Peppone's gang. And this because, if the male Gabassi were worth two, the female Gabassi were worth four.

Bocci, the Gabassis' landowning master, lived in the city: once upon a time he came at least weekly to la Badia, but he had not shown up since the war.

One fine day, the Gabassis saw a manager appear instead of Bocci, and he immediately went on the defensive:

'I'm here simply to go over the books: if you agree, that's fine; if you don't, I personally don't care about it one way or the other. The owner is Mr Bocci, not me.'

Old Gabassi simply pointed to the door: 'When Mr Bocci has tidied up the house, then we'll talk about our accounts.'

The young man left and returned a month later to bring Bocci's response:

'Mr Bocci says that, before talking about anything, you must give him what is his due from the farm.'

The manager left la Badia with a dry mouth, naturally, and it was clear that the story would run and run. Eventually, Bocci sent his ultimatum:

'I cannot possibly do the repairs to the house because the expense would be enormous. If you want to stay as sharecropper of my farm, you must pay what you have contracted to pay and then we'll see. If you don't want to stay, keep the share that belongs to me as an equable parting of the ways and leave the farm free for me to develop.'

Little by little the storm had abated and a date for the proletarian revolution seemed to have been postponed: the Gabassis realised that they would never be able to find land like that of la Badia anywhere else and had to bite the bullet. They argued interminably about bills and rebates, but, in the end, they paid their dues.

Revenge took the form of their becoming even 'Redder' and, seeing that talking to the estate manager about repairs to the house was like arguing with a wall, they stopped talking and their bitterness increased. In truth, the house was in a disgusting state and, if the Gabassis had brought the animals into the house and lived in the stable, they would have been better off.

Peppone, in his speeches, always cited la Badia as an example of the selfishness of landowners, while the Gabassi situation had become a symbol of sharecroppers exploited ignobly by landowners everywhere and treated worse than beasts. Photographs of some of the farmhouse interiors were even published in Party magazines and there were those who took care to send a copy of the articles to Bocci on each occasion. This did nothing to improve the situation, on the contrary it made matters worse, because it served only to poison Bocci.

Some more time passed and then, one Sunday afternoon, something extraordinary happened: a Fiat 1400 appeared in the Badia farmyard, with a lady, a young man and a beautiful girl on board.

'So this is the farm known as la Badia?' the young man asked two or three Gabassis, who had approached the car.

'Yes,' replied old Gabassi suspiciously.

'Good,' the young man rejoiced, going down and holding out his hand. 'I am Bocci, son of Bocci. This is my sister and this is our mother.'

The Gabassis looked at each other in amazement without knowing quite how to respond.

'Come on in,' said old Gabassi, touching the hands of the young man, the girl and the lady. 'Follow me.'

'Thank you, perhaps later,' exclaimed the young man. 'Would you allow us to take advantage of this little bit of sunshine to take a look at the lake. I saw it once when I was ten and still see it in memory as a wondrous thing.'

'I was seven, I was with you!' the girl added, 'and I haven't forgotten it either. I want to see it again too. Let's go, Mamma!'

The lady turned to the Gabassis:

'The children are in charge,' she explained, smiling. 'We surely cannot deny them.'

Old Gabassi set off and the Boccis followed. It didn't take them long to reach the poplar grove within which the 'wondrous thing' was hid.

Alas, on a Sunday afternoon in December, the 'wondrous thing' appeared to be more of a large pond of rank water. But the young man and the girl found many a beautiful thing to see in it. And, since the Rovaccia canal was nearby, after looking at the lake they expressed a desire to go up the embankment. Then they aspired to explore a small abandoned church, which could be seen beyond the Rovaccia. Thus did evening creep up on them and 'Mamma' became concerned: they must surely return to the city at once, so as not to get stuck in the fog.

Back in the farmyard, after greeting the Gabassi gang, who were all present, they got into their car. The young man behind the wheel pulled the starter knob: but, after a brief splutter, the engine stalled. Young Bocci tried again, but each new attempt served only to drain the battery.

One of the Gabassis lifted the car's bonnet and then, helped by one of his brothers, tried to crank start the car.

'It's not just the battery,' he said finally. 'There's a bigger problem with the distributor and the coil. We need a mechanic.'

Meanwhile, the first wave of fog began to sail across the fields and la Signora Bocci became more and more concerned. Old Gabassi ordered one of his nephews to fetch a mechanic from the nearest town and the boy set off on his bicycle.

'It's seven kilometres away,' explained the old man. 'Locally we have only a blacksmith. We hope to get the mechanic to come, but I'm afraid today is a Sunday.'

Multiple waves of fog were now chasing each other and the evening was increasingly growing dark and cold.

'Please let us now gather in the house,' said the old man. 'Nothing to be gained standing around out here.'

The Signora and the two boys followed the old man into a large room lit only by the flickering light from a wood fire. One of the Gabassi women lit an oil lamp.

'There is no electricity I'm afraid, but we manage,' muttered the old man.

The room was squalid, the floor uneven, the large beam on which the ceiling joists rested was bowed and was propped up midway between the walls, while the window frames couldn't have been more dilapidated had they been gnawed by mice. And the cold night air came hissing in.

The Signora looked around in dismay.

Old Gabassi put some glasses on the table. He then called one of his women and said: 'Grab a napkin and wipe these glasses!'

Turning towards the Signora, Bocci reassured her: 'They've been washed but since we don't have a sink we have to wash all the dishes under the tap in the yard and it's all too easy for a little muck to stick.'

The young Bocci man looked at him amazed: 'No sink?'

'No.'

'Why on earth not?'

'It's just the way it is,' Gabassi replied, starting to pour white wine into the glasses that the girl had wiped with a napkin.

'I would prefer a glass of water,' murmured the Signora. 'I don't drink wine.'

'It is sweet and light,' said Gabassi, 'you can surely drink it and maybe you should, for here the water is really not very safe to drink: the old well only just reaches the surface of the water table.'

The boy, who had gone to town to fetch the mechanic, took a long while to reappear. When he did he explained that the thick fog had delayed him and alas the mechanic hadn't been in...

'Did you at least say that they should tell him to come immediately, as soon as they did see him?'

'Yes, I told his wife. But he is out of town for a service. He'll be back in the morning.'

Signora Bocci was becoming a little agitated: 'We cannot remain here doing nothing! You have to sort this out, find me a vehicle that will take me to the city. The village is big enough to have transport of some sort!'

'It is,' agreed old Gabassi, 'but the public transport is run by the mechanic and the mechanic is actually out of town with his car ... for a service.'

'But there will be private cars!' the lady moaned. 'We will pay for whatever the inconvenience entails.'

'In this fog it will be difficult to find someone to take you into the city,' muttered old Gabassi.

The lady turned animatedly towards her children:

'It's all your fault that we're in this mess, and it almost seems like you couldn't care less! You are totally irresponsible.'

'Mamma,' exclaimed the young man, 'we're not lost in the middle of the Sahara desert.'

The old man intervened:

'If you're up for it, there's room for you all to sleep here for the night.'

'We don't want to put you...!' replied the Signora. 'We'll go to the village: there'll surely be a hotel.'

'There is,' explained the old man. 'The trouble is getting there. I can only provide you with bicycles and a scooter.'

The fog was dense and now it was also dark.

'Don't worry, Mamma,' exclaimed young Bocci, 'we will sleep here. There's no need to even tell Dad because he's in Rome and he won't be back until tomorrow evening.'

The Signora calmed down and, together with her children, went to sit in front of the fire to allow the Gabassi women to set the long table for dinner.

During the meal, old Gabassi tried to brighten the atmosphere by talking about the weather, but the young Boccis were too hungry to listen to him, and the Signora had no specific knowledge on the subject. So, since the other ten Gabassis simply stared at her without saying a word, the gathering turned out to be rather depressing.

Finally, mercifully, dinner came to an end and Signora Bocci felt able to say that she was very tired and could happily go to sleep.

'We have prepared a double room for you and the young lady,' explained old Gabassi. 'The young master's room is next to yours.'

Old Gabassi's wife lit a small oil lamp and set off towards the stairs followed by the Signora, the young lady and the young master.

'Be careful,' she warned, when Signora Bocci reached the stairs. 'The steps are worn and a bit dangerous.'

As she mounted the staircase the Signora had the distinct impression that rather than approaching normal sleeping quarters she had somehow found her way into a barn, for she found herself in a large room with an enormous bed, freakishly contorted due to the presence of a priest, a hot-coal bed warmer stuffed between the sheets:[16]

'The bed is smoking!' the Signora noticed. 'It must have caught fire!'

The old woman smiled: 'No, it is steaming on account of the humidity. We put coals in the bed not so much to heat the sheets and blankets but to dehumidify the bedclothes. I hope you have everything you need. Good night.'

---

[16] Widely and mischievously known as 'a priest', the structure misshaping the bed was no Don Camillo, but a large wooden trellis or frame keeping the bedclothes off a pan of hot coals, something more usually to be found in the coldest, harshest climate of settlements in the Apennine mountains.

After removing the priest, placing the pan of hot coals in a corner and putting the oil lamp on a bedside table, the old woman made to leave the room.

'Please take the pan away!' the Signora moaned. 'It is still full of embers and the smoke could asphyxiate us in our sleep!'

The old woman picked up the pan: 'There is no danger, Madam. Between the ceiling and the windows there are so many cracks that sleeping here is like sleeping in the open air anyway. But I will take it away.'

Mother and daughter quickly undressed and slipped between the hot sheets.

'Mamma, turn the lamp off. I want to go to sleep right away,' the girl whispered drowsily.

'No!' her mother exclaimed. 'The darkness of this place scares me. Suppose something were to happen, there'd be no ready light. What would we do?'

'Nothing is going to happen,' the girl muttered, snuffing out the lamp and crawling under the covers.

However, something was destined to happen just an hour later, when the Signora, still unable to sleep, jumped up and clung desperately to her daughter. 'Put the light on!' she moaned. 'Light it or I die!'

Easier said than done because no matches could be found and the girl had to go into the next room to rouse her brother.

Once the lamp was lit, their mother had no intention of turning it off again: 'It was a mouse!' she gasped. 'I felt it … walking … across the bed!'

A couple of hours passed, apprehension simmering, then something particularly distressing brought the Signora to the boil once more. She could not find, either under the bed or inside the cupboard of the bedside table, a certain thing that she was bent on finding. So she woke up her daughter once more and despatched her to search her brother's room.

Not there, either.

The situation became more and more desperate, but how can you find your way around a dark unfamiliar farmhouse without, in the process, risking opening six or seven doors first, alarming the people asleep on the other side needlessly?

Bocci's son was asked for his advice.

'I know where you'll find what you want,' he said. 'The car will have been wheeled overnight near the *barchessa*, on the right.'

'The *barchessa*?' said the lady. 'What is the *barchessa*?'

'It's that arcade strewn with straw on the far side of the courtyard.'[17]

To the Signora, gaining access to this was scarily problematic: leaving the house at that hour, not knowing the way out. And the cold? And the fog? And then there was the dog!

Faced with his mother's despair, young Bocci made a courageous decision.

'I'm going to wake someone up.'

'No you don't!' exclaimed the lady. 'You young people don't have the slightest idea what dignity is!'

'It's not a question of dignity...' stammered the young man.

But his mother pushed him back to bed.

Then the lamp went out with the oil and she was left suffering in the dark, watching and waiting sleeplessly until dawn, listening to the wind whistling through the thousand cracks and catching the soft shoe shuffle of mice scuttling around the attic.

At four o'clock old Gabassi arose from his bed and, a few moments later, was startled to see the Signora appear before him.

'Already up? May I help you?'

'If you would please call the dog so that I can get to the car to fetch a bag of tablets I left on the seat with my handbag. I have a tooth that is driving me mad.'

The old man called the dog and put him on a chain under the dead-door to the barn. And so, at last, the lady marched, with her dignity intact, towards the car, which was, thank goodness, under the *barchessa*.

*

---

[17] A *barchessa*, typically fronted by an arcade with high round arches, is the working area of the homestead and includes sheds, stables, barns, etc.

They had to wait until ten before they could take their leave, and, with the benefit of that time-lag, the Signora and her children could not help but notice that, seen during the day, the farmhouse looked far more dilapidated than it had the previous evening.

'Come visit us again sometime,' said old Gabassi, as the Boccis climbed into their car. 'Have a good trip and best regards to our lord and master.'

Which master, when he returned home later that evening, found not the usual wife and two children, but three hard faces:

'For the first time in my life I was ashamed of being your wife!' the Signora stated indignantly.

'And we your children!' added the young man and the girl.

The lady, trembling like a Saragattian socialist[18], reported in detail on the horror of that night and of that house, supported by the silent but complete approval of her children.

'The Gabbassis disabled your car on purpose and made sure you couldn't find what you were looking for in the bedroom!' Bocci cried. 'Those scoundrels wanted you to spend the night at la Badia. They set you up!'

'And by so doing,' replied the Signora, 'they forced us to face reality. You have an obligation to fix that house: what you have to do is, quite simply, your duty!'

'No, no, no!' Bocci shouted. 'If that scoundrel leaves la Badia and we get new tenants, *then* I will tidy up the house. Otherwise, the house will remain as it is! They don't deserve it: in '45 they made it clear where they stood! Let them have their house repaired by Stalin!'

The young man spread his arms:

'As you wish: you are the boss,' he said. 'But you are doing Stalin a great service.'

---

[18] Reference here is to a post-war split in the Italian Socialist party. Petro Nenni led the party to participate in the Popular Democratic Front with the communists, while Giuseppe Saragat launched the more centrist Italian Workers' Socialist Party in alliance with the Christian Democrats.

Bocci thought about that for a whole day, then capitulated: 'Fine: I'll put the house in order.'

*

Winter passed, spring broke upon the land, and one beautiful sunny day, the estate manager re-introduced himself to Gabassi:

'If you are willing to put up with two months of disorder, the landowner will tidy up the house for you. If not, he has no intention of talking about it anymore.'

'The day the builders arrive, we will leave the entire property, from the cellar to the granary, for them to get on with it.'

And so everyone was satisfied with what was, to all intents and purposes, a superb victory for communism against the agrarian exploiters.

Fifteen days later the Gabassi family cleared out the farmhouse, making efforts to settle in the shed, in the woodshed, under the *barchessa*, and a large team of workers from the city threw themselves into the assault on la Badia.

The builders were all people who spoke little and worked a lot. They must have been chosen from the ranks of men unsympathetic to the Reds because they never consorted with the Gabassi and, when asked about the work, they replied:

'Each of us does his job and knows nothing about politics.'

In sixty days the restoration was complete, down to the last detail, and the house, plastered from top to bottom and painted yellow and with pastel green roller shutters, looked like it had been transplanted from Milan.

The interior was amazing – everything redone according to the rules of modern construction and design. When the Gabassi women went in, they gasped at the dazzling lead-polished marble floors. And electricity had of course been incorporated, and a new well dug with an automatic submersible electric pump and compressor, which made drinking water available at a pressure equal to that of any city aqueduct.

And there was a fully equipped bathroom, gleaming with greenish tiles, and a dressing room with sink. And even the gas, where deployed throughout the house (including in a full central heating system), didn't cost anything, as it exploited methane collected via a gasometer in the manure heap.

All the Boccis came to the opening of the house: the Signora gave the Gabassi women a pack of little flower curtains to put on the windows. Her daughter gifted doormats and a large carpet, and her brother gave the men a radio.

Bocci didn't give anything away: he looked, touched, checked, took notes and, before leaving, called old Gabassi to him and said:

'We will also have to redo the contract. We will take into account all the benefits that you owe me, according to law, for the so-called "spend" on the farm. The estate manager will bring you the new contract.'

The new contract arrived an hour after Bocci's departure and was filled out according to all possible and imaginable laws. It also contained this clause:

'The landowner undertakes, every year, to send the tenant a *panettone* at Christmas and a *semifreddo* cake at Ferragosto.'[19]

The Gabassis were all gathered in the farmyard around the old man and listened to him in silence while he read the new contract. When the old man reached the notoriously condescending clause, he looked up at Bocci in amazement. Remaining for a moment as still as a stone, he then spat upon the contract.

*

Fifteen days later the Gabassis abandoned la Badia with all their belongings and the old man, before leaving forever the new house in which no one had yet dwelt, wrote with a piece of coal on the yellowish wall:

'You damned pig, you don't fool me!'

---

[19] The Motta *panettone* means 'home' to all Italians at Christmas and is a tradition dating back at least to 1599. *Ferragosto*, 15 August, is a national holiday marking the feast of the Assumption, *semifreddo* cake an elegant frozen Italian desert that features in a multitude of recipes.

The '99 Boys (1953)

THAT YEAR, AS EVER, Barchini arrived at the rectory to give Don Camillo the invitation:

'Reverend, it's November 4th and, tonight, we old fighters will meet for the usual dinner. We would all be very pleased if you were among us.'

And Don Camillo gave the usual answer:

'Thank you, but I can't for a number of reasons. Pray *pretend* that I am present.'

Barchini shook his head:

'No, Reverend: this time you must be present, not only in spirit.'

The first dinner, or 'Victory Meal', the village fighters had organised for the evening of November 4, 1919, and so, on the morning of that same November 4, 1919, Barchini and five or six others from the gang had arrived at the rectory to bring the invitation to Don Camillo, and to them Don Camillo had explained, one by one, the reasons why he could not attend the event.

These were reasons so obvious that Barchini and his associates had considered them valid not only for that year, but for the next thirty-three. But now, suddenly, on the occasion of the thirty-fourth meal and the thirty-fourth invitation, the reasons given by Don Camillo no longer seemed convincing.

Don Camillo was surprised: 'Barchini, what's new about this?'

'Reverend, you have to come this year because Peppone will also be at the dinner.'

Don Camillo let out a loud yell: 'That lout there! Very well: one more reason why I won't be.'

Barchini didn't give up: 'We didn't invite Peppone, he invited himself. He's coming to make propaganda, to upset our whole company. Only you can keep him at bay and stop him from causing trouble for us.'

In 1919, when they had spoken to him about the first Victory meal, Peppone had replied that they shouldn't bother him because he had already gulped down too much of it during the war. He had added that, instead of organising patriotic dinners, they would have done much better to organise the revolution against the damned capitalists who had enriched themselves on the blood of poor soldiers. In 1919, Peppone was already the ringleader of the young, wild Reds of the Municipality: so they did not insist and, in future years, they were careful not to repeat the invitation.

Peppone had not bothered the old fighters until the eve of November 4, 1945: until, that is, in his capacity as mayor and leader of the local proletarian masses, he had published a proud proclamation in which he explained how the 'People' did not appreciate the repetition of rallies or veteran association celebrations:

'The only victory valid for the purposes of both history and progress is the one won by the People against tyranny,' explained Peppone. 'Which, if the honest fighters intend to celebrate the Victory, they should join the heroic mountain fighters of the Resistance, under the banner of democracy and not bother them with nostalgia.'

The old fighters gave up the restaurant and met for rations elsewhere. And it worked so well that, even when they could have done it, they no longer had their Victory dinner in the trattoria.

And now Peppone resurfaces: no longer threatening as he had been when he published the proclamation of 1945, but cordial and accommodating:

'I am also an old fighter like you,' he had told the organisers of the meal. 'I hope that, if I come to the dinner with you, you will not send me away.'

Peppone had a plan: he had not suddenly felt in his blood nostalgia for the old gray-green.

'I have to go and work on these people a bit,' he had explained to Smilzo. 'We have to form a popular front of fighters by cementing the old and the young into a single democratic block. If I see that something good can come of it, fine, otherwise I will sow discord in their house and throw their society into disarray.'

Smilzo had not opened his mouth to anyone but the townships are organised in such a way in the Municipality that people even hear what no one says. And so Barchini and the other old fighters' leaders were alarmed and asked Don Camillo for help.

'All right,' said Don Camillo when Barchini had brought him up to speed. 'I'll come.'

'Thank you, Reverend,' exclaimed Barchini cheerfully. 'See that you bring your old mess tin.'

'My mess tin?' chuckled Don Camillo. 'Do you still have this nonsense in your head thirty-five years after the First War? Imagine if I still had my mess tin! I threw it in the garbage as soon as I got home.'

'You did wrong,' replied Barchini seriously, 'we all kept ours.'

*

The Cascina Vecchia had once functioned admirably as a warehouse for maturing the cheese produced in the Lolli dairy. Then, when the dairy went to ruin, the Cascina had not ceased to be a large and solid building. And here, on the evening of November 4th, the group of old fighters had gathered since 1945 for the famous meal. There were benches, trestles and boards of food galore.

There was no need for plates because of the mess tin, and given that each guest had to bring a fork, spoon, knife, glass and (optional) napkin, it is easy to see how, having procured a few pots and a few pans, the organising committee had quickly completed its task.

The menu for each ration was simple: salami and culatello, pasta, chicken cacciatore or veal stew, two or three pies as big as wagon wheels, pieces of parmesan cheese and a universal flood of bottled wine. The meat arrived cooked and it was only necessary to keep it warm, the rest arrived ready to use: the kitchen simply had to provide the pasta.

And, when Peppone arrived at Cascina Vecchia on the evening of November 4, the pot with the water to cook the pasta had just been put on the fire and they were waiting for the trays with the cold cuts to arrive at table.

The group consisted of about seventy people and they all shouted and laughed, banging their fists on the trestles.

They were having fun as if they were kids again and even the old farts were making a racket, loudly demanding their 'entitlement'.

But when Peppone entered and greeted the company loudly, the uproar ceased and the people, after a moment of almost absolute silence, started chatting again, but in a less audible tone.

The large cutting boards with piles of cold cuts appeared and this improved the general carburation considerably. Wine did the rest.

The assembly became cheerful and noisy again: but Peppone – even if the people at the table next to him were talking to him – felt even more alone and isolated than when every voice, upon his appearance, had fallen silent.

It went on like this for a long while and then, suddenly, Torelli arrived in the large room.

'*Silenzio!*' he shouted. 'We threw the pasta down at eight twenty, so we have to organise the kitchen fatigue duty detail to wash up and dry. It will not do if, when the time comes, the detail is not ready.'

'Good!' shouted the band. 'Out with the kitchen chores detail!' Remo Tondelli stood up:

'It's easy,' he explained, 'you pull the strings and whosever's turn it is, it's his turn.'

'No way!' replied Torelli. 'You have to go by seniority. The kitchen chores are down to the lower ranks.'

'Hurray! The raw recruits to the kitchen!' shouted the assembly. 'Out with the rookies!'

'Present and able!' replied a guy, standing up.

And it was Antonio Nosbelli who, having fought in the war at forty with the Territorials was now almost seventy-seven.

Nosbelli's intervention made the whole gang go crazy with joy and the wine filled glasses were raised along with enthusiastic shouts:

'Long live the "Terrible!" Long live the grandfather of the regiment!'

Then, since the kitchen chores threatened never to come up again, Torelli, an old infantry sergeant major and therefore authoritative, precise and positive, silenced those unruly people and brought the matter back on track:

'Let's hurry up and not try to screw the battalion: out with the lower ranks!'

Cleto Morini, the shoemaker, stood up and shouted:

'Present and able!'

'Class of?' asked Torelli.

'One thousand eight hundred and ninety-nine.'[20]

Morini was fifty-three years old and had a moustache under his nose that made him look at least sixty.

The assembly let out a volley of shouts:

'Rookie!... Stumpy! Look at him there, the infant holding his moustache to show that he is already a man!'

Then a group of wild men started the chorus:

> *'If you go around all of Italy*
> *you won't find any more pipiòle*
> *they've requisitioned them*

---

[20] In 1899, Italy saw a new conscription or First World War call up of the 1899 class, a group of men born in that year who would have been called up for military service as they turned 18 in 1917. This class was specifically mentioned as the 'Ragazzi del '99' (the 1899 Boys).

for the ninety-nine
bim, bom bom
to the roar of the cannon!...

Many, many years before, in those gray days of war, when the boys of 1899 were called to arms, that song belonged to the defeatist repertoire: but here, sung by people who had fought the war and well, it had a completely different flavor.

Morini tried to dominate the uproar to defend his class:

'We of the ninety-nine...' he began. But he had to stop because they buried him under an avalanche of shouting.

Then another voice was heard, but it sounded like thunder, it was so powerful:

'We of the ninety-nine,' roared the second representative of the newbies, 'we of the ninety-nine are capable of doing *this...*'

Everyone turned toward that voice and saw a kind of devil who, leaning over a heavy chair and biting the back with his teeth, with the strength of his teeth alone pulled it up from vertical to horizontal.

It was clear that the kind of devil was Don Camillo and the people were speechless with amazement.

But Don Camillo had not yet loosened his jaws to let the chair fall, when another voice came:

'And we are also capable of doing this!...'

All of a sudden all eyes turned towards devil number two, third representative of the newbie class. Devil number two, grabbing a piece of oak beam that was lying nearby, banged it on the ground in order to demonstrate the perfect efficiency of the wood, then grabbed it by the ends and, stretching his arms upwards, lifted it. Then, suddenly, he pulled it down so that the middle of the beam hit the top of his head.

Peppone's head did not split: the beam split in two pieces.

The assembly went crazy and vented its enthusiasm by trumpeting and roaring: and, in the midst of that triumphant uproar, the class of 1899 headed proudly, gloriously, victorious towards the kitchen.

And Morini, who was following Don Camillo and Peppone, passing in front of Torelli, said to him with ferocious sarcasm:

'You, who are a sergeant major, try to do what we of the ninety-nine can do!'

Once the chore in the kitchen was over, Don Camillo and Peppone returned to their designated quarters and immediately afterward, the distribution of rations began.

'Everyone take their mess tin,' Torelli ordered, 'and get in line. When they get to the pot, they'll get the pasta. Are we clear? And let's remember that the dues are a mess tin of pasta, full to the brim but without the lid and without any extras. No confusion and no Camorra.'[21]

The gang of wild men began to file slowly past the pot of pasta and each one handed over his mess tin. The old mess tin that had kept them company on the Carso, at Caporetto, on the Piave.[22]

Suddenly a ferocious cry was heard:

'No! No! Camorra! No differences! The military service is the same for everyone!'

The distribution was interrupted and all because of Don Camillo's mess tin. Which was, yes, a mess tin, but one of those big ones, for an Alpine soldier.

'It is my mess tin!' Don Camillo affirmed, 'and you can check it from what's written on it. Furthermore, when I say that it is my mess tin, no one can doubt my word.'

'No one doubts your word,' they replied. 'But you were not an Alpine soldier, so that is an illegal mess tin.'

'Okay,' replied Don Camillo. 'Now you fill another mess tin and then pass the pasta into mine. That way the ration is fair.'

'Use this one!' exclaimed Peppone, stepping forward and offering his mess tin.

A new cataclysm broke out because Peppone also had an Alpine soldier's mess tin.

---

[21] Skulduggery: the Camorra, a mafia-style organisation, emerged in southern Italy in the 18th century.

[22] The Battle of Caporetto (24 October to 12 November, 1917) had threatened to knock Italy out of the war. After terrible losses, British and French troops were deployed to join the Italians and remained together as a fighting force until the Armistice.

Given how things were, the ration commission decided to consider the two mess tins as if they were regular mess tins.

'For special merits.'

When everyone had their mess tin filled with pasta and had taken their place at the long table, Torelli stood up and shouted:

'A moment of silence. The chaplain will give the commemorative speech.'

They all fell silent and Don Camillo, rising, said:

'Peace to men of good will. The floor is given to the Mayor.'

Peppone stood up and said:

'*Viva l'Italia!*'

'*Viva!*' replied the assembly.

'Now enough with the speeches and let's eat our rations while they are hot,' concluded Torelli.

*

Late in the evening the assembly broke up and everyone went home. Don Camillo and Peppone walked together to the Crociletto and did not open their mouths.

Before parting, Peppone said:

'Well…'

'Well…' replied Don Camillo, spreading his arms.

The Great River, swollen with muddy water, glistened among the poplars and, after hearing all that talk, whispered her pleasure at 'how well these people speak'.

Part Two

Letter to the Reader (1955)

D EAR READER,
   By now, you may realise, it has become a habit of mine
to tell you everything about myself and so, for years, you have
known perfectly well everything I have done.

Well, among the various good and bad things I have done,
I have also put together a screenplay, which serves as a pretext
for making the third film about Don Camillo and Peppone –
the one entitled *L'onore Peppone*, which they will soon begin to
show here too.[23]

I am writing this letter to tell you more or less what it is
about.

*

Don Camillo came to a halt, panting in front of the High
Altar and showed the Crucified Christ the newspaper that had
brought him some incredible news:

---

[23] *Don Camillo e l'onorevole Peppone* (1955).

'Lord!' he shouted in horror. 'He's on the list! They want to send him to Parliament... He is a Member of Parliament!... Peppone!...'[24]

Christ smiled:

'Well, Don Camillo: what is strange about that?'

Don Camillo widened his eyes:

'Lord, what would you say if I put myself on the list to become Bishop?'

'That would be strange,' replied Christ. 'Not so in Peppone's case. If they can make him Mayor, they can also make him a Member of Parliament. The substance is the same.'

Don Camillo shook his head.

'The substance may be the same, but the form is different. This time Peppone and his accomplices want to triumph with fraud, with deceit. Their *Il Fronte della Patria Unità* is playing false!'

Christ sighed, then said:

'Perhaps, Don Camillo. But it will never be as false as the 5,000 lire note that you gave to Peppone a little while ago.'

Don Camillo spread his arms: 'That note was false?' he exclaimed, apparently sincerely surprised.

'Without a doubt,' Christ clarified severely. 'And you know it too.'

In fact, Don Camillo knew it perfectly well: that damned 5,000 lire note, which some dishonest person had perfidiously stuck on him, had been circling around his pockets for at least two years and, every time his hands fell upon it, Don Camillo suffered further.

Five thousand lire, for a poor country priest, is something. But, to be honest, the idea of making up for his suffering by passing the swindle on to others had never crossed Don Camillo's mind... Until one day he found himself in front of Peppone handing out copies of the *Fronte della Patria Unità*,

---

[24] Peppone was elected to the Senate by his regional constituency. The Senate is one of two houses in the Italian parliament, the other, larger house being the Chamber of Deputies, where the majority of seats are allocated through proportional representation at a national level.

whereupon Don Camillo did not hesitate passing him the fake bill, because then it was not a question of cheating a poor man, but of damaging the Communist Party.

In politics things work in a special way and not only does the end justify the means, but the means actually justifies the end.

But Christ, being apolitical, did not think so, and he did not like Don Camillo's undertaking at all.

Don Camillo feebly tried to excuse himself by explaining that it had been a distraction, concluding: 'Lord, in any case, I paid false money for falsehoods. It all adds up.'

'It would add up,' Christ pointed out, 'if the 4,975 good lire that Peppone gave you in change were not left unaccounted for...'

Don Camillo sighed, and having laboriously taken the 4,000 etc. lire out of his pocket, went to put the money through the slot of the donation box for the children's hospital.

He explained to Christ that he would send Peppone a letter of thanks for the spontaneous donation of 4,975 lire.

'Four thousand four hundred and seventy-five,' Christ corrected.

Whereupon Don Camillo took out the 500-lire note that he had 'forgotten' and, putting it also in the box, exclaimed:

'There, Lord! There are no tricks here... Peppone and his friends play tricks... Wolves dress up as lambs to deceive naive sheep. But they do not deceive the shepherd!'

Don Camillo clenched his fists and concluded:

'Lord, they will not pass muster! God cannot allow their triumph!'

'If Don Camillo has established it so,' Christ replied softly, 'let Don Camillo's will be done.'

'No, Lord,' said Don Camillo, bowing humbly. 'Let *God's* will always and only be done...'

*

Thus begins the third cinematic adventure of Don Camillo and Peppone, and I put the script together in my cell in the prison of San Francesco, writing on sheets of paper diligently numbered and stamped by the Higher Authority.[25]

The funniest part of the whole adventure is that no frame of the film has portrayed the spectacle offered by the author in the act of its composing.

In point of fact, I worked wrapped up – from my slippers to my waist – in a blanket held up by a towel tied around my stomach (the prisoner cannot have ropes or straps in case he causes the director trouble by hanging himself): from my waist to my moustache I was immersed in a vast collection of shirts and sweaters.

On top of this large bundle of rags was a blue and white striped woollen lid, tilted so as to leave my eyes and nose free (the Republic allowed prisoners to keep their mouths closed and breathe through only one, two or three nostrils).

The total effect was an object so massive that the guard on duty came every now and then to make sure I was actually inside the bundle.

The least funny part of the affair, however, is represented by the effort it took to get Don Camillo and Peppone *into* prison.

At a certain point the characters I call Don Camillo and Peppone in my stories have a way of becoming stronger than their creator, and this time they did not show the slightest intention of coming to keep me company in cell No. 38. The air of the prison did not seem suitable for their lungs, their being accustomed to the clean air of la Bassa.

So, I banked on human ambition and told Peppone: 'If you come, I'll make you a Member of Parliament.'

Peppone took the bait. And, of course, Don Camillo also arrived shortly after, as he would have gone to the ends of the earth to prevent Peppone from becoming a Member of Parliament.

But even this not very funny but telling story is not seen in the film. In the film you see other stories, more or less funny, that

---

[25] In 1953 Guareschi was imprisoned in Parma's San Francisco jail, serving a sentence for libel. See *Merry Christmas Don Camillo* (Pilot Productions, 2022).

concern Don Camillo and Peppone, stories stitched together by the words of the usual guy who, in films, speaks without being seen. Together these tales form a single story that can be summarised as follows: Peppone becomes a Member of Parliament but, in the end, the one who wins is Don Camillo.

Actually, in the end, in essence, both of them win and everything goes back to how it was before, while Comrade Cleonilde Isetti returns to base.

*

I no longer remember what Comrade Cleonilde Isetti is called in the film. I think she is called Clotilde (like 'Destiny'[26]): in any case they gave her a different name because someone apparently pointed out that Cleonilde Isetti could make one think of 'I don't know what' character in active politics.

In any case, the fact remains that, even in the film, this Comrade Cleonilde is a magnificent piece of girl.

And, naturally, even though the Higher Hierarchies of the Party sent her to Peppone's village to reorganise the women's Section and galvanise the election campaign, she ends up galvanising the men's Section and disorganising the women's Section.

And so comes the moment when Peppone opens his comrade heart to Comrade Cleonilde.

Peppone is depressed: he 'eliminates' the chickens which Don Camillo fattens up to celebrate Peppone's love life. The affair is discovered and Peppone has to answer for his actions to the magistrate. He is saved *in extremis* by Don Camillo: but in the process he makes a fool of himself.

As he returns to the village by motorbike, with Cleonilde in the sidecar, Peppone is gloomy.

'Why are you downhearted, Comrade?' observes Cleonilde. 'You have been acquitted!'

---

[26] Saint Clotilde was a Burgundian princess and Queen of the Franks. Her marriage to Clovis I, and her influence in his conversion to Christianity, significantly impacted the religious and political landscape of the Frankish kingdom. Some sources suggest that her actions and her life story are seen as a manifestation of a divine plan or a predetermined path, hence 'like "Destiny"'.

'Acquitted, but ruined!' replies Peppone. 'That damned priest made me look ridiculous! He made me look like a caricature!'

'He did you a favour, Comrade... Mayors who go to church at night... They are votes!'

Peppone stops the motorcycle and gets off. Comrade Cleonilde gets out of the sidecar.

It is spring and spring is beautiful and sweet, even there in rustic la Bassa.

Peppone becomes languid. He looks at the trees in bloom, the streams.

He sighs: 'Comrade... Will we see this land purified and fertilised by the proletarian revolution?'

Comrade Cleonilde is overcome by the sweetness of the moment and even her words in response are languid and subdued:

'Everything depends on the *cadres*, Comrade... We need to train efficient cadres...'

A subtle anguish takes hold of Peppone:

'The cadres!... My nightmare every night!... The young people disappoint me...'

The subtle anguish becomes desperation: Peppone stops. He has something very important to confide in Comrade Cleonilde. It is at this point that he makes up his mind and opens his comrade heart to her:

'Comrade!... I have to confide in you a secret that is eating my heart out!... Sales of *L'Unità* are decreasing!'

Comrade Cleonilde gently shakes her head and on her lips is a sweet and inspiring smile:

'What does it matter, Comrade? As long as it doesn't diminish our faith!'

'Faith! But is faith enough?'

Comrade Cleonilde's voice becomes serious:

'Comrade, think of Him... He too was alone and had nothing but his faith: and he was victorious! And today the USSR is the first country in the world in both heavy industry and nuclear research!'

*

That's how Comrade Cleonilde turns out in my story: however, it was logical that not everyone could see her simply as a proud comrade in Peppone's struggle.

So much so that, one evening, Don Camillo discovers something very interesting. In the church, in the little chapel of the Madonna, we find Peppone's wife kneeling.

'Jesus!' Don Camillo whispers. 'I haven't seen her here for ages! The last time was for the baby's baptism. And now the baby is three years old...'

Suddenly the woman stands up and tries to open the chancel gate to enter and offer the Madonna the candle she has brought with her.

She cannot shift the latch. Don Camillo comes forward.

The woman hands him the candle:

'Light it for me,' she says.

Don Camillo takes the candle, opens the gate and is about to enter the chancel. But immediately, he stops. 'Excuse me,' he asks the woman, 'am I wrong or are you the wife of the new vet?'

'Forget it, Reverend,' the woman replies brusquely. 'You know very well that I am the Mayor's wife.'

'Curious!' exclaimed Don Camillo maliciously. 'But isn't the Mayor's wife that young girl with brown hair?'

The woman bursts into a fit:

'Reverend, I didn't come here to listen to your malicious gossip.'

'Malicious?' Don Camillo mutters, shrugging his shoulders. 'I go along with what people say... And then: isn't it customary in your party that when someone becomes a big shot, the management assigns him a new wife?'

Peppone's wife tries to explode, but her tears well up and stop her. She begins to sob furiously.

'Calm down! I was joking!' exclaims Don Camillo.

'You're joking!' the woman shouts, 'but I'm really suffering. Since that one arrived, I've had no peace.'

Don Camillo looks stern:

'That is bad, Comrade. The representative of the people belongs to the people, not to his wife! Do you not want him to be in the House of Deputies? Then bear the consequences with discipline!'

'I can't stand anything anymore!' the woman shouts. 'I'm going to run home now, take my bike and run away to Torricella, to my parents. I just wanted the Madonna to give me the strength to do this.'

Peppone's wife leaves: Don Camillo watches her go out then shakes his head.

He goes into the chancel, lights the candle the woman had given him and puts it on a candelabrum on the altar.

'That's because you gave her the strength to leave,' he says, turning to the image of the Madonna.

Then he takes another candle, lights it and puts it in a candelabrum next to the first one, explaining:

'... and this is to give her the strength to return soon.'

Don Camillo goes to the presbytery and, shortly after, Peppone thunders in. He is looking for his wife: he's been told that she had gone to church.

'She came, but then she left,' Don Camillo replies brusquely.

'She's not home! She has disappeared,' Peppone shouted, handing Don Camillo a note.

Don Camillo read the note: 'Now that you have a secretary, you no longer need a wife. Goodbye forever. Maria.'

Don Camillo opens his eyes wide in horror:

'I,' he stammers, 'thought she was joking... Oh, Lord, help that unfortunate man, make sure he doesn't carry out his insane plan!... Just think that she told me!'

Peppone grabs Don Camillo by the shoulders.

'What did she tell you?' he shouted.

'That she was going to throw herself into the river...' Don Camillo explains.

*

Of course the story doesn't end there. Peppone, desperate, goes to look for his wife, and Don Camillo accompanies him.

The searches, which spread along the banks of the river and the Canalaccio, are in vain. In the end, Peppone puts his head in his hands:

'She drowned! And if she drowned, I'll kill myself too!'

Then Don Camillo decides it's time to stop and, climbing into Peppone's motorcycle sidecar, calls out:

'An idea! Come on. Let's try this one.'

The race into the night begins and, at one fine moment, the beam of Peppone's old Guzzi headlight discovers a woman pedalling, a hundred metres ahead.

It's her, the runaway.

Peppone turns the throttle: he reaches the woman, passes her, cuts her off.

The woman is forced to stop and get off her bike.

'What are you after?' asks the woman.

'Get home!'

'No, I'm tired of making the village laugh.'

'Don't talk nonsense.'

'Nonsense! I'd like to hear what you have to say about it if I get a young and handsome secretary!'

Peppone starts shouting: 'What do I have to do with that? It's the Party that sent her to me.'

'And you can keep her! I didn't marry the Party... Keep her... And then, when you're a Member of the House of Deputies, marry her... But if you hope to become a Member with my vote, you'll have to wait some time!'

The woman's voice becomes increasingly angry:

'My vote is for the priests!...' she shouts. 'Jesus, let me die if I don't vote for the priests!'

'Vote for whoever you want, but get home and stop this!' replies Peppone, dragging his wife towards the motorbike and shoving her into the sidecar.

Then Don Camillo intervenes, smiling.

'Go,' he says to the woman. 'It's not a given that he'll be elected. Maybe he'll stay Mayor, and mayors are not obliged to reduce their wives' weight.'

Peppone lets off the gas and the motorbike shoots away. Don Camillo realises he's stranded:

'What about me?' he shouts.

Peppone doesn't even turn around: 'You'll get by! Did you win a vote? Pay for it!'

The motorbike disappears: Don Camillo picks up Peppone's wife Maria's bicycle, mounts it and starts pedalling into the night.

'Lord,' he mutters, 'the ways of Providence are infinite... But why did one twenty-five kilometres long have to happen to me?'

The road goes around a great wall and, on the wall, it is written in coal: 'Come on Bartali, you are on your own!'[27]

*

This is one of the stories of the story and it does not end there, but continues in the little scene of 'the tailor'. Once elected to the House of Deputies, Peppone has a new suit made. And the tailor insists it be double-breasted. Peppone doesn't like the idea: 'Why a double-breasted suit? I've never worn one. It won't suit me.'

'It is suitable for the Chamber,' explains the tailor. 'You shouldn't model yourself on mayors anymore, but on qualified parliamentarians. Look here...'

The tailor shows Peppone some photos cut out from newspapers: the photos of Molotov in a double-breasted suit, a photo of Thorez in a double-breasted suit, one of Togliatti in a double-breasted suit.

'Are you not convinced, *Onorevole*?' concludes the tailor. 'You need a double-breasted suit like theirs to make a good impression.'

Peppone's wife, who is watching the scene, intervenes:

'You will also need the mind, not just the suit, that those guys have. You can't be a member of parliament with the mind of a mayor.'

'Stick to your own business!' replies Peppone, annoyed. '*I* have to be a member of parliament, not you!'

'Of course,' replies the woman. 'But now that you have a double-breasted suit, you will also need a double-breasted wife...'

---

[27] Gino Bartali, renowned cyclist, won the Giro d'Italia twice, in 1936 and 1937, and the Tour de France in 1938.

The story of Cleonilde doesn't end there either. And, in my opinion, and also in the opinion of Peppone's wife, it ends in the best possible way.

In point of fact, Peppone was elected a Deputy and, having to choose between the office of mayor and that of deputy, he gave up being mayor and, one fine morning, with his double-breasted suit and the corresponding hat, he left for Rome. He left with a lump in his throat and his comrades followed him as if they were following a funeral bier.

He got on the train and found Cleonilde sitting in his compartment. She had finished her mission and was returning to base: Rome.

The train leaves and there are a few kilometres of anxiety. Then the train stops at Boretto station.

And here, waiting for the Honourable Peppone, is Don Camillo.

Peppone appears in a furious frame of mind at the door:

'What do you want?' he shouts.

'I haven't forgotten that you were here to say goodbye to me when I was going into exile,' Don Camillo explains.

'I'm not going into exile! No one is sending me away.'

'Ambition is sending you away.'

'What ambition!'

'Party discipline, then. The fact is that you're going.'

'I'm leaving because I won, not because I lost!'

Don Camillo shook his head:

'Poor Peppone: you lost even if you won because your wife voted against you...'

'Leave those who have nothing to do with it out of this!' Pepponc shouted.

'They do have something to do with it and you well know it... Poor Peppone: here you were the Mayor. You were someone. There, you'll be one of many... A little white or black ball, according to the boss's orders... Your conscience and your *will* will no longer count. That's why you have lost...'

Peppone clenched his fists:

'I'll always be me!'

The train whistles and moves slowly away. Don Camillo holds out his hand to Peppone:

'Goodbye, *Onorevole* "Nothing".'

Peppone closes the door angrily and Don Camillo remains there with his hand outstretched, while the train moves faster and faster.

The carriages pass and when the last one has passed, the platform opposite comes into view.

And, planted on the opposite platform, is the Honourable Peppone, together with the honourable suitcase.

'Porter!' Peppone shouts to Don Camillo, just as Don Camillo, on another occasion, had called Peppone "News vendor"[28].

'Porter!' repeats Peppone impatiently.

Don Camillo crosses to the platform.

'Was it you, your Honour, who called?'

'No,' replied Peppone grimly. 'It was the Mayor.'

Don Camillo takes his suitcase and sets off.

When he reaches the station forecourt he puts the suitcase on the ground. Peppone arrives and, fetching his wallet out of his pocket, takes out a 5,000 lire note and hands it to Don Camillo.

It is the famed fake note.

'I don't have any change,' exclaims Don Camillo, spreading his arms.

'Keep it, gentleman,' replies Peppone, putting the 5,000 note in his hand and emphasising the word "gentleman".

Shortly afterwards Don Camillo is pedalling happily along the road that leads to the village, when, suddenly, a cyclist in shirt sleeves and with a large suitcase on his handlebars overtakes him.

It is Peppone, and Don Camillo cannot let Peppone overtake him, not even when it comes to cycling.

---

[28] 'La Festa' in *The Little World of Don Camillo* (Pilot Productions, 2013).

Don Camillo presses down on the pedals and, having reached Peppone, overtakes him.

But neither can Peppone bear that the clerical reaction rides faster than the proletarian revolution. And he presses on the pedals again and, having reached the clerical reaction, overtakes it.

Don Camillo does not take the insult in his stride and presses even harder on the pedals and again reaches Peppone.

But Peppone stands up on his pedals and begins to struggle on like a madman, forcing Don Camillo to pedal with his bottom in the air instead of on the saddle.

Then the voice of that guy who, in films, speaks without being seen, is heard, and the voice says:

'Here, once again, begins the eternal race in which each of the two desperately wants to be first... However, if one should delay, the other will wait for him... The road is the same even if Don Camillo drives on the right and Peppone on the left... And together they will continue their journey... May God go with them...'

Now, it is a matter of seeing whether God will receive permission from the Higher Authority in the Producer's Chair to accompany the two. Not so much because, by marching to the left, Peppone will incur excommunication, but because, by marching to the right, Don Camillo does not march to the left, which contravenes fashion now.

*

Dear reader: what I have told you is not the film. It is about some of the many stories that make up the film.

I could not tell you the whole story: if you go and buy 2,000 metres of canvas do you expect to have it shown to you all inch by inch? Isn't a little sample enough for you?

And I have given you a little sample. I must tell you that the theft of chickens suffered by Don Camillo is not worth four cents. Not from a cinematographic point of view, but from a technical point of view. Don't let my fellow chicken thieves judge me harshly for organising a chicken theft so poorly. I did it only for cinematic purposes. If I had to organise a real chicken heist, I would do much better. At least I learned that much in thirteen months in *onorevole* prison.

Smilzo's Intervention (1957)

BRUSCO'S IDEA WAS elementary: summon all the comrades to the piazza, line them up and march them to the Great Hall in the People's Palace, where a distribution of membership cards for the New Year can take place with due solemnity.

'Of course,' Brusco explained, 'before the ceremony we'll retrieve membership cards already renewed and return them as the others get their new ones, just to put everyone on an equal footing and release comrades who haven't yet got their act together from any embarrassment.'

Bigio objected that he didn't see what advantages could result from such a demonstration.

'At least three,' Brusco replied. 'First: give a push to the wavering comrades. Second: force traitorous comrades out into the open to take a firm position. Third: organise a show of force that will give our enemies a liver this big.'

Peppone, who had been listening attentively, shook his head:

'It's a chancy business,' he muttered. 'It could be that the "liver this big" will come to be ours. I don't like it.'

Smilzo's idea was more ingenious: 'We all know how they do it, the radio people, how they persuade people to subscribe or renew their licence: "Among all new and old subscribers who are up to date with the fee, a car, a television, a refrigerator will be raffled weekly," and so on. Why don't we use the same system? A circular is sent to each member: "Among all comrades who have renewed their membership, a prize box containing this, this and that, will be drawn weekly, until such and such a day..." Isn't that a better idea?'

Peppone shook his head decisively:

'No. 1, comrades must renew their membership out of faith, not out of greed for a prize box. Ours is a Party, not a toothpaste factory.'

'Boss,' replied Smilzo, 'there are times when faith needs to be given a helping hand. I'm not going to specify how many comrades have not yet renewed their membership, but let's simply say that X comrades have not yet regularised their position. Among these X comrades there are four or five who, for one reason or another, have a notable influence over all the others. We must work on these four or five. If they renew their membership, all the others will renew theirs too.'

'That's fair,' grumbled Brusco, 'except the four or five influencers aren't the sort to rush to renew their membership just because they can compete for a prize box!'

Smilzo smiled: 'My idea is made up of two parts: the first is to put the box up for grabs. The second is to make sure that the box goes to one of the four or five famous comrades each time... Are we not the ones who draw the lots?'

Peppone was starting to get interested and asked for more details.

And Smilzo explained his plan so clearly that he convinced the entire general staff.

The gang immediately got to work: the circular was produced, passed to the mimeograph machine[29] and the letters were sent to their destination.

---

[29] The duplicating machine of the era, which reproduced multiple copies of a document by creating a stencil and forcing ink through it onto paper.

So, the next day, all the comrades in Peppone's Section learned that anyone who renewed their membership could be favoured by luck with a box containing: a kilo of salami, a kilo of butter, a litre of oil, a kilo of parmesan cheese, five kilos of pasta, five bottles of wine, twelve handkerchiefs and two pairs of women's socks, five packets of 'Nazionali'[30], five nougats, a *panettone* and a 'large silk handkerchief with the Party symbol.'

There was enough there to please the whole family: indeed, that was its true value.

Of course, even though it was a highly confidential circular, on the evening of the same day Don Camillo, finding himself face to face with Peppone, was able to tell him:

'I am pleased with the happy assortment, Mr Mayor. 'The idea of including a large silk handkerchief to stifle the consciences of the comrades was excellent. The prize box is a great idea.'

Peppone looked at Don Camillo with a bored expression: 'You should think of something like that from your point of view too. The idea of promising a prize to be received after death seems a bit exploitative, if you ask me. Especially since no one has ever come back to tell us whether things are good or bad in your Paradise.'

'On the other hand, a lot of people *have* come to explain to us that things in your Paradise are in fact not so good. For example, those 150,000 Hungarians who managed to escape.'[31]

Peppone made an angry gesture: 'The usual song. When you have no more arguments, you bring up Russia. You priests have little imagination!'

---

[30] A famous brand of cigarettes with a popularly high tar and nicotine content.

[31] The Hungarian Revolution of 1956 followed Khrushchev's removal of the country's Stalinist leader Mátyás Rákosi. A popular uprising, the revolutionary regime disbanded the communist secret police and pledged free elections and withdrawal from the Warsaw Pact. Between November 4 and 10, seventeen divisions of Soviet troops and tanks suppressed the uprising, killing or executing thousands, arresting, imprisoning and deporting others. More than 150,000 fled the country.

Don Camillo shrugged: 'Have pity on us, Mr Mayor: we are arid materialists and give importance only to facts. The Hungarian revolution is a fact. And the universe is a fact. That is why we do not believe in communism, while we do believe in God.'

'Amen,' Peppone said through gritted teeth.

*

The letter had been received by all comrades on a Friday, but the general staff deemed it appropriate not to postpone the extraction of the first box until Saturday of the following week. The matter could not be dragged out beyond the end of January and, in January, there were only four Saturdays available. All in all, since there were four comrades to be "drawn", it was regarded as essential to move immediately into action.

The entire general staff gathered at headquarters around eight o'clock on Saturday. The session was reserved for the leaders only, but the programme was regularly posted on the People's Palace noticeboard: 'Agitation of agricultural workers: detailed study of the action to be carried out. Coordination of various directives. Drawing of the first prize box.'

Peppone opened the session by taking stock of the situation:

'We must act with the utmost caution: the four we are interested in are Tognacci, Bigoni, Mazzabrina and Rampini. Let's take the first: Tognacci. While we remain here discussing the agitation etc., Smilzo, Bigio and Lungo leave by the courtyard and get on with it. The box is all ready on the van. As soon as they return with confirmation of receipt, we will announce the name of the winner of the first box. Not before.'

So it was that, a quarter of an hour later, Comrade Romualdo Tognacci saw Smilzo arriving at his house, followed by the other two members who were carrying the famous box.

'Comrade,' said Smilzo, 'did you receive the circular about the prize to be drawn among those who have renewed their membership?'

'I did,' admitted Tognacci.

'Well,' continued Smilzo, 'this evening we did the draw and the box went to you.'

Bigio and Lungo lifted the lid of the box and the sight of all the goodies took Tognacci's wife's breath away as she passed nearby.

Even Tognacci himself was speechless: he was a bricklayer and had not worked for two months because of the bad weather and the cold. So, since he had three children to feed, in addition to his wife, he was surviving by the skin of his teeth. An injection like this really wasn't going to hurt him!

'All top-notch stuff,' explained Smilzo, 'and we're happy that fate made it your turn. You know: we put together the names of all the members and, when yours came out, someone said that we had to redo the draw because you hadn't renewed your membership card yet. But the boss and all of us insisted that the box was yours and that you should have it. Now, it's simply a matter of regularising the situation. We brought the register: you sign, we'll give you the card and it's *buona notte al secchio!*[32]

Tognacci raised his eyes from the box.

'I understand,' he stammered, 'but right now I...'

'We know you're not in work!' Smilzo interrupted him. 'Don't worry about the money. The Federation has given us the right to pay in instalments. All you need to do is pay a few lire, enough to be able to issue a receipt and settle the matter administratively.'

Tognacci shook his head:

'I can't for the moment. I have to think about it a bit more. In short: I want to see how things develop.'

'What things?' asked Lungo.

'Well, you have to admit that the situation isn't clear,' exclaimed Tognacci. 'Within the Party, there are those who think one way and those who think another. It's a bit ... confusing at the moment.'

---

[32] Here this ancient expression means the same as our 'All done and dusted', although the translation, 'It's goodnight to the bucket' points more to the modern expression, 'End of', either because the bucket is lying at the bottom of a well after the rope has broken, or because the bucket was the last thing one saw at night in the bedroom in the days before indoor lavatories.

Smilzo shook his head: 'There's no confusion. Everything is very clear now. Congress has eliminated all doubt.'

'I'm not so sure,' Tognacci said, picking up a newspaper from a chair and showing it to Smilzo. 'There are plenty of comrades who publicly disagree with Party policy...'

Smilzo chuckled: 'Ah, you read that stuff?'

'I read it because I find facts in it that aren't to be found in *L'Unità*.'

'If they aren't to be found in *L'Unità*, it means they're bullshit!' Lungo stated flatly.

'Maybe,' Tognacci admitted. 'But maybe not. That's why I decided to wait for things to become clear.'

'The soldier who abandons his comrades engaged in battle is a deserter and, therefore, a traitor,' Smilzo pronounced.

'I'm not abandoning the battle,' Tognacci replied. 'I just want to see who I'm shooting at.'

Smilzo and the other two realised there was no point in insisting: they took the box back and left.

Five hundred metres from headquarters, they stopped the car and Smilzo ran to report to the boss, while Lungo and Bigio remained guarding the van.

When he saw him appear, Peppone looked worried: 'Is everything okay?'

'Everything is not okay,' replied Smilzo. 'Tognacci said he was waiting for the situation to develop. What do we do, boss?'

Peppone pounded his fist on the desk. 'We simply do this!' Peppone shouted. 'We despatch Tognacci to hell and move on to Bigoni. And we don't come back here until the operation is concluded. Or, if we come back without a positive result, we'll be kicked out of that window!'

Smilzo turned pale: the idea had been born in his brain and the onus on him was massive.

He ran out and, having reached his lurking associates, started the van and took off like a rocket towards Bigoni's house.

But Bigoni had also decided to wait for the situation to be clarified and it was a waste of petrol and words to try to persuade him.

The third to receive a visit from the 'box' team was Comrade Mazzabrina Alvaro, who was going to bed and expressed himself more or less in tune with Tognacci and Bigoni.

And so it came to the turn of the fourth official, Comrade Elgo Rampini.

Rampini was already in bed and, to persuade him to come down, took all of Smilzo's patience. When, finally, Rampini found out what it was about, he dismissed the matter without further ado:

'When I have made my decision to renew my membership card I will come to you as I have done for the past eleven years. The box is full of wonderful things, but there is not one thing that can explain to me what's happened in Hungary.'

They met at eleven o'clock at night, a cold January night, on a deserted and muddy country road.

'I don't feel like repeating this old story any more,' Smilzo said. 'On the other hand, if I don't get anything done, Peppone will tear me to pieces. We must move forward with confidence. Here is the house of Comrade Benito Pasotti, who renewed his membership card on January 2nd. Fortune favoured him by making his name come up.'

They arrived at Pasotti's house and stopped the van in the middle of the farmyard, making a hellish racket, sounding the horn.

And, when Pasotti cautiously stuck his head out of a window on the first floor, Smilzo explained to him how fortune had favoured him, etc., etc.

'Good!' Comrade Pasotti Benito rejoiced. 'But you shouldn't have bothered bringing me the box. I could have come and picked it up tomorrow morning.'

'No,' replied Smilzo. 'It's better this way because, now, if you have an ounce of respect for life, you're going to give us something to drink!'

Pasotti came down with his wife. A bundle of firewood soon blazed in the large fireplace and bottles and salami were brought up from the cellar.

Smilzo, even more than his two partners, had an enormous amount of sorrow to drown and it took some quantity of wine.

The Grand Council saw the three of them again around one the following morning and Smilzo was dragging along a hangover as heavy as a sheet of lead.

'All good, boss!' he shouted. 'Operation concluded. Fortune favoured Comrade Pasotti who, having been one of the first to renew his membership, had more than anyone the right to a prize.'

Having said this, Smilzo collapsed and Brusco wisely pointed out to Peppone: 'Boss, you'll have to wait at least until tomorrow evening to beat him. For now, all you have to do is write up a report of the draw.'

*

While Peppone (bellowing) wrote the report, Pasotti took inventory of the box.

'There's so much wonderful stuff,' he exclaimed when he had placed all the merchandise on his large kitchen table. 'There are even twelve handkerchiefs and a pair of socks for you.'

His wife, who was trying to tidy up the room devastated by the orgy, stopped sweeping for a moment and said:

'I don't even want to see that stuff. You renewed the membership, not me. I certainly wouldn't have renewed it!'

'I wouldn't have renewed it either,' Pasotti replied. 'But I didn't want to make a point. You know what kind of people they are.'

'Whatever,' the woman snapped at him, 'you renewed the membership and the prize is yours. The prize of fear!'

Pasotti took it in silence. Little by little he diligently put all the merchandise back in the wooden box, onto which, finally, he nailed the lid.

Then he wrapped himself up, pulled his hat down over his eyes and, having taken the box up so as to hide it under his cloak, left the house and headed for the fields.

In consequence, the next morning, Don Camillo, opening the door that led to the garden, found himself confronted by a box on the lid of which had been written with a piece of charcoal: 'For the collection in support of Hungarian refugees.'

Don Camillo took the box into a large room where all the stuff collected for the refugees was stored and, opening the register, took note of it contents:

'A kilo of salami, a kilo of butter, a litre of olive oil, five bottles of wine, twelve handkerchiefs and two pairs of women's socks, five packets of 'Nazionali', five nougats, a *panettone*: it's all there,' he muttered to himself. Then, taking it with the tips of his thumb and forefinger, he pulled the 'large red silk handkerchief with the Party symbol' from the bottom of the box and went to put it in the appropriate chest, walled into the floor of the most well-hidden room in the presbytery.

'This stuff is too indigestible even for you,' Don Camillo explained to his dog, who gave a delicate yelp of approval because, even though he was a dog, he was able to understand things that many a man still cannot.

So the matter ended there, and had ended well.

Clementina's Gift (1957)

FOR CLEMENTINA, A car trip was an exceptional event: the classic Fiat Giardinetta was used by her father for his work and when the poor guy had a bit of holiday, he didn't really feel like grinding out another damned road, driving his wife and daughter around. Furthermore, his work was paying less and less, while petrol was costing more and more.

It was a dazzling day in March and Clementina's father had removed the canvas hood from the Giardinetta and folded down the back seat so that she could enjoy the show while standing and looking out through the roof of the car, as if she were on a travelling terrace.

Having crossed the city and passed the outskirts, Clementina lost interest in the world around her, sat down again and said:

'Last year, in the middle of a hedge, I found a very small bird.'

'Last year we went there in May,' her mother replied, 'with the greenery and the flowers.'

'The hedge is wonderful even without leaves,' Clementina stated firmly. 'And in any case, now there are violets.'

La Cascinetta was a small farm of ten hectares, an elongated rectangle with the longest side to the south, skirted by a dirt road of about 500 metres. And, between the dirt road and the boundary line, there was a strip of grass about ten metres wide and the aforesaid hedge: large, about two metres thick. Giving inner substance to this tall, massive green wall were pillars of oak, black locust, elm, poplar and walnut.

For Clementina the hedge was something immense, like something out of a fairytale: she was now twelve years old but still held it in the mind's eye of a four- or five-year old.

In the hedge there was everything: birds' nests on the very high branches of the poplars (even a nest of magpie), red creepy crawlies, red berries, blackberries, elderberry flowers and berries that make wine, mushrooms, and the purple-blue bloom of the blackthorn to sting the palate and make her mouth water. Here, too, were willows, their soft branches good for weaving baskets, also small wild plums and crab apples, sorb apples, walnuts, scented black locust flowers, ivy and moss for the Nativity scene...

Clementina began to talk excitedly about her hedge. The whole meaning of the trip simply revolved around seeing her hedge again.

Just her gossiping away like this cheered her father up no end: 'Maria,' he whispered, smiling at his wife, 'as you can see my idea wasn't so bad. Don't you hear how she likes Cascinetta?'

The woman sighed: 'Thank goodness,' she muttered, 'given what the place brings in... Up to this point you have done nothing but bury money in that land.'

'The land is not disloyal to us,' replied her husband. 'Land is honest and always gives back what you give it. And in any case, the period of investment is now over. Everything is in order, everything is settled. There is nothing left to do or re-do. From this year the farm is starting to yield. It has been a good year and we will be able to put Clementina's first return aside.'

'Wait until you have done the accounts,' warned his wife. 'You're never happy when you do the accounts with the sharecroppers.'

'You mustn't generalise,' protested the man. 'The Giacomaccis are not like other sharecroppers. They're rustic but honest people and have always treated me with great respect.'

'And so I should hope, after all you've done and spent on them! It would have been better if you'd spent that money on us.'

The man shook his head: 'Maria, do I have to tell you again? We didn't spend that money on them, and we couldn't spend it on ourselves. We spent it – and we had to spend it – on the little girl. Clementina will have her dowry. A small but excellent farm, organised to perfection, will always be the safest capital investment. Everything else is subject to change: industries, like mines, which today are worth billions can be liquidated by technical progress, by the discovery of new materials... The only thing that will remain what it has always been is land.'

The woman didn't know what to say against that argument. Besides, they were in sight of Cascinetta.

*

As soon as the car stopped in the middle of the farmyard, Clementina slipped away like a little lizard.

'Let her go!' her father said to his wife who was about to hold her back. 'Accounts are no fun for kids.'

The Giacomaccis were all at home: the old man, his son Francesco, head of the company, his wife and Francesco's three children. All people of few words and with little good to say about anyone. They talked for a few minutes about the weather, then the head Giacomacci opened the drawer of the large kitchen table and took out a handful of papers.

'Here, Mr Rosi,' he muttered. 'If you want to check them, the receipts are all here.'

Mr Rosi noticed that Giacomacci had called him 'Mr Rosi' and no longer, as before, 'Master'.

He had always been annoyed by being called 'Master', and a hundred times he had said to Giacomacci: 'My name is Rosi.' But now, hearing himself called 'Mr Rosi', he felt a certain discomfort. Perhaps because of the tone of voice used by Giacomacci.

Rosi produced his accounts out of his bag:

'We'll check the receipts later,' he said. 'It'd be better first to see that our two records match.'

'If you don't take note of all the stuff I have here,' Giacomacci explained, 'we'll never agree. Extra stuff that I had to get urgently: injections for the animals, disinfectants, missing semen, etc. I've already paid for it all myself.'

Rosi began to sort through Giacomacci's ragbag handful of greasy, crumpled sheets of paper.

'It would be better for administrative purposes,' he observed, 'if in these "urgent" cases you issued proper receipts.'

'There's no need for revenue stamps among gentlemen,' the older Giacomacci observed bitterly. 'If trust is the price, it's worth it.'

'It's not a question of trust,' Rosi replied. 'Every accounting needs supporting documents...'

At that moment, Clementina came in, panting:

'It's gone!' she exclaimed, clearly anguished.

'What has?' asked her mother.

'The hedge!' explained the little girl.

'Don't talk nonsense and leave us be,' muttered her father impatiently. 'Go, look more closely, you'll find it.'

The youngest Giacomacci sneered: 'She'll be lucky!'

Rosi looked with concern at the scallywag's attitude, and then at Giacomacci.

'We dug it out,' explained Giacomacci. 'On a farm of thirty *biolche*, you can't throw away two on a hedge. Where there's shade, nothing good grows. The stable has increased and there is a shortage of fodder: without the hedge we can have a 6,000 square metre alfalfa plantation.'

'But you didn't say anything about this to me!' Rosi protested resentfully.

'You knew,' Giacomacci replied. 'We talked about it last year when you wanted to enlarge the stable.'

'Yes, we spoke about it,' Rosi acknowledged, 'but I said No, outright. The hedge was the most beautiful thing on the farm.'

'You can't eat beauty!' the old man exclaimed spitefully.

'It was Clementina's passion,' Maria protested with tears in her voice.

'We have to feed the animals,' the old man exclaimed, 'not Clementina!'

The head Giacomacci intervened:

'Forget it,' he said to the old man. 'If the owner doesn't do what's required for the farm, the sharecropper must step in. The hedge has been dug out and your share of the wood is at your disposal, Mr Rosi. If you want it all, you have to pay me for the labour.'

The lady intervened: 'And what do you suppose we can do with all that wood?'.

'That's your business,' Giacomacci replied, shrugging his shoulders. 'See that you send for it quickly because it's getting in the way here.'

Rosi wasn't interested in the wood: he was thinking about the hedge:

'Giacomacci,' he said, 'you can't dig up plants or change the layout of the farm without the owner's permission.'

'The owner gets the money,' the old man shouted, 'but we work the land and we know how to work it.'

'The management of the company is up to the owner,' Rosi replied. 'The law is clear about this.'

The boss Giacomacci shook his big head:

'Old law. Now the new law applies. Now, owner and sharecropper have the same rights.'

'The law is yet to be approved,' Rosi pointed out.

'It will be: in a matter of days.'[33]

Clementina had left and was walking slowly along the dirt road.

Giacomacci's boy was right: the hedge was gone. She felt like weeping. She left the dirt road, crossed the strip of bare land and stopped near the border ditch. The Giacomaccis hadn't noticed the violets – there were still some on the edge of the ditch. Indeed, something of the hedge was still there. She bent down and started picking violets.

The boy had also come out of the kitchen when his father and Rosi started doing their accounts again. He saw Clementina on the edge of the ditch and stood there watching her for a long time.

Then he called the dog and unhooked him from the chain.

'Go for it!' he ordered, pointing to Clementina.

The dog darted away, growling, and shortly afterwards, Clementina's heart-rending scream was heard, and Rosi and his wife jumped up and ran into the yard.

Immediately they saw Clementina struggling with the dog, and Giacomacci, who had followed, intervened with a loud yell:

'Bill! Here!'

The dog left its prey and returned to the yard.

Clementina was terrified: the dog had drawn blood on her leg with its paw, and had torn her dress with its teeth: it obviously hadn't felt like really hurting such a tiny girl.

While the mother disinfected Clementina's scratch with cologne, Rosi shouted angrily to Giacomacci:

'If he's a biter, why don't you keep him on a chain?'

---

[33] A sharecropper was a tenant farmer who paid the landowner with a share of his crops. Post-war, as the communists in Italy sought to dismantle capitalism on a ticket of improving social and economic conditions in the countryside, this system began to collapse. Sharecropping had political implications in terms of class, worker rights and landowner duties, and raised issues still being addressed today, such as heredity and the very nature of land-ownership. Here, Guareschi delves into the deeper values involved than the politics of the situation encouraged.

'The dog has done his duty,' explained the head Giacomacci calmly. 'The little girl was trampling on the lawn and he sent her on her way.'

'She wasn't trampling on anything!' exclaimed the lady. 'She was picking violets on the edge of the ditch and there's only bare earth there.'

'But sown!' croaked the old man. 'For alfalfa to grow, it must first be sown.'

Those damned accounts had to be done; Rosi accepted all the sharecropper's slips as good receipts and made a note of them in his little book: 'Let's get on with it,' he said to the boss Giacomacci. 'You read out yours and I'll check on mine.'

'Next year will be different,' the old man squawked. 'Next year we'll do the accounts ourselves because you'll have to rent us the farm. And when we're tenants the landlord will only stick his nose into our house if we let him!'

The old man, small, thin, twisted and wrinkled, might normally seem to be someone unsure whether it would be wiser to wait for the hearse or walk to his grave in the cemetery; but when offered the opportunity of pecking the landlord, he would perk up, his nerves twitching under his wrinkled skin and, in his eyes, the flame of hatred would light up:

'And the rent won't be set by the landlord,' he shouted, 'but by our unions!'

Rosi thought about Clementina's dowry and felt like crying.

*

When the accounts were finished and the Rosis got back into the car, the lady didn't even have the courage to speak, so depressed was her husband.

So they arrived at the village and found themselves in the square, coming to a halt at the edge of the churchyard. For many years they had always done this: after settling the accounts with the sharecropper, they would go to greet Don Camillo and make him a small offering for the church. Not once had they missed, as it was on Don Camillo's advice that they had invested all their money in that piece of land.

Guided by force of habit, they found themselves at a standstill in front of the churchyard, but the idea of having to get out to go and see Don Camillo seemed more foreign to them than anything in the world.

At last Signora Maria said: 'Now that we're here, we'd better get out.'

'No,' her husband replied. 'I don't feel like it. It's that lot that brought us to this point!'

'Don Camillo has nothing to do with it,' ventured his wife.

'He, like the others and even more than the others. It was he who recommended the Giacomaccis to us: "Good people, church people. They're one of us," he said.'

The church door was wide open and Clementina had a plan of her own: the sharecropper's dog may have filled her heart with fear, but he hadn't managed to take the violets away from her.

While her parents continued to argue, Clementina managed to open the back door of the Giardinetta and the little girl was already entering the church by the time her escape was discovered. The bunch of violets ended up in front of the image of the Madonna with a short heartfelt prayer:

'Madonnina, make the hedge grow again.'

Don Camillo, who was bustling around the High Altar, saw all this: the Giardinetta stopping at the edge of the churchyard, Clementina getting out and making her way to the little chapel of the Madonna. Seeing the Giardinetta leave again, he turned in amazement to *il Cristo*:

'Lord,' he said, 'this is the first time in ten or eleven years that something like this has happened. Why?'

Don Camillo was a good friend of the Rosis, whom he'd met during the evacuation. As soon as war broke out, the lady had arrived in the village, then, three months before the upheaval, her husband had joined her with a wounded leg and six months' convalescent leave. They had remained until the end of the war and, in March 1945, Clementina had arrived and Don Camillo had baptised her.

Why hadn't the Rosis come down to greet him as usual? He will not have been in doubt for long, for the old postman arrived with the usual newspapers and red-hot information of a particularly local kind:

'News, Reverend,' he explained. 'Half an hour ago I delivered a letter to the Giacomaccis. They were yelling at their master about the accounts. You could hear them half a mile away. I think they've made him lose the desire ever to show up at Cascinetta again.'

The postman left and Don Camillo went to confide in the Christ above the High Altar.

'Lord, Rosi is in trouble because of me. I encouraged him to trust the land and the land betrayed him.'

'The land does not betray, Don Camillo,' whispered the Christ. 'It is man who has betrayed the land.'

Land to the Bricklayers (1957)

BIGIO HAD NO involvement in agriculture because he was a bricklayer: he could, therefore, speak objectively about it and, for this reason, above all, Peppone chose him as official speaker for the Party at the upcoming rally, which was of supreme importance to sharecroppers.

Bigio was appearing in this role for the first time and, since everyone knew him as someone irredeemably sullen and used to expressing himself with short grunts, rather more than with any political passion, curiosity in how he would perform spread around the piazza.

So-called 'men of few words' often behave like bottles of Fortanella. If you leave them quietly in the corner, with their bottoms in the cool sand, they appear as what they are: bottles of a very humble wine that reaches, at best, the alcohol content of Coca-Cola. Pull them out of the shadows and, as soon as you start screwing the corkscrew into the cork, you find yourself involved in a kind of lightning-fast volcanic eruption. At that moment you will find wine on your clothes, on the wall, on the ceiling: everywhere except inside the bottle.

Once the cork was teased out of his neck, Bigio also exploded, releasing a tsunami of all the words he'd held in abeyance for his fifty years of life. It was such a hard-nosed and persuasive oration that it would have made even the toughest landowner break out in a cold sweat.

In the very front row of the Red-decorated grandstand, together with Bigio's son Athos, daughter-in-law Aida and grandson Libero, was Rosa, his wife. And after having listened with her mouth open to that volcanic speech, for the first time since she had met and married him, Rosa said to her husband:

'Bravo! That was spot on!'

Falchetto, the linchpin of the Red action squad, leader of the sharecroppers and a sharecropper himself, hearing Bigio conclude his speech by proposing the 'total destruction of the damned race of landowners', was moved and, even though he was the toughest of the tough, he hugged him with tears in his eyes.

Don Camillo had also followed Bigio's eruption from the living room window of the presbytery and made no comment. He turned instead to the elderly foreign gentleman who was right there, standing near him, and said simply:

'Look: the one who just made that speech is Rosa Bosoni's husband.'

The foreign gentleman looked at Don Camillo in astonishment: 'Don't tell me that the others in the family are of the same ilk!'

'I won't,' Don Camillo replied. 'I'll just point out to you that they are, to a man, PCI members and militants like the head of the family. Even Libero, the little one who is three years old: he is already an initiate and has not been baptised.'

The meeting in the piazza was breaking up: Don Camillo drew the curtains and withdrew from the window.

'Perhaps it would be as well to keep an eye on the churchyard,' suggested the foreign gentleman.

'Don't worry: on their way home, they have to pass by here,' Don Camillo reassured him.

'And how will you see them when they do?'

'There's no need to *see* them,' Don Camillo stated peremptorily, setting fire to his half-Tuscan.

Two minutes later, right under the window overlooking the churchyard, a thin little voice was heard shouting something and Don Camillo smiled:

'It's the child,' he explained. 'They taught him the Red Flag and, every time the little treasure passes by here, he sings these words to it:'

> '... *Capitalists*
> *agrarians and priests,*
> *Piazzale Loreto*
> *is ready and waiting for you...* [34]

'It may not rhyme, but the idea is clear enough,' Don Camillo went on, getting up and heading towards the front door.

As Bigio and the rest of the gang were about to pass, the priest hailed them:

'One moment,' he said. 'We need to talk.'

Bigio clenched his fists: 'The road is open to the public and everyone may sing what they want,' he challenged him.

'It's not about your songs,' Don Camillo replied. 'It's about your aunt, Desolina.'

'Let her die!' muttered Bigio's daughter-in-law.

'Already done,' Don Camillo replied calmly. 'She died this morning at six, in the hospital in town. They're transporting her here tonight and tomorrow we'll undertake her funeral.'

---

[34] The allusion is to the *Piazzale Loreto* in Milan, where, in August 1944, a massacre of civilians by fascist militia took place, and where, by way of reprisal, partisans brought the corpses of Mussolini, his mistress, Claretta Petacci, and sixteen fascist party officials, exposing them to public ridicule.

'I don't care,' Bigio grunted, indicating his wife with a nod. 'She's the niece. Desolina never could stand me when she was alive but I don't want to spite her by accompanying her to the cemetery. We take it out on the living, not the dead. We...'

Bigio was still energised by his speech and seemed to want to continue for a while longer, but Rosa interrupted him with a gesture and turned to Don Camillo:

'We don't have time to waste; we have to go. What time will the funeral be?'

'At five. But you will have to waste a little more of your time, as this gentleman here has come from the city to inform you of the deceased's testamentary provisions.'

The notary stepped forward: 'If you would like to come in, we can go through it quickly enough.'

The members of Bigio's gang chattered among themselves, then Rosa said:

'Give us your address in the city. We'll come by tomorrow.'

The notary shook his head: 'Your deceased aunt has decreed that the deed be read here and now. The Reverend also has an interest in her will.'

Rosa sneered: 'I would prefer to hear that the Reverend had no interest! He played that poor old woman for all she was worth, he made her leave the money to the Church, and now he wants the satisfaction of hearing it from the notary!'

'The satisfaction of not hearing you say stupid things would be enough for me,' Don Camillo replied with disinterest.

'Do as you think best,' the notary decided peremptorily. 'I'll wait for you inside.'

After a quick family consultation, Bigio's gang went into the presbytery, and the notary, taking a file from his bag, read from it as follows:

'I, the undersigned etc. etc., leave all my assets, and specifically the Argine farm and the sum of two million lire, to the son of my niece, Libero Busoni, aged three. He will come into possession of the aforesaid when he comes of age. In the meantime, my niece Rosa will become usufructuary of the Argine farm, provided that she runs it directly with the help of her family.[35]

In this case, the sum of two million lire may be used to purchase agricultural machinery and livestock necessary for the direct management of the farm. Otherwise, the two million will be donated to the orphanage, while all proceeds from the rental or sharecropping of the farm will be set aside and delivered to the said Libero Busoni only and exclusively when he comes of age. I appoint the very Reverend Don Camillo as executor of this will...'

*

L'Argine was not simply a ten-hectare farm, it was the best farm in the area. Thirty *biolche* of blessed land, plentifully fed by a canal always full of water, rich in minerals better than any fertilizer, with a vineyard, orchard, poplar grove and a lot of well-built and comfortable buildings, rustic but well-appointed.

Rosa had spent her childhood and part of her youth at the farm helping Aunt Desolina, her husband and their boy to manage it. Desolina had arranged for her son to marry Rosa: but, unfortunately, the boy had died and Aunt Desolina had made other arrangements for Rosa to marry a good young man with whom she would cultivate the farm.

But Rosa had lost her head over Bigio, a bricklayer who spoke only in order to swear, and Aunt Desolina, having become a widow, had to put the farm to sharecroppers to manage. She had never wanted to see her niece again and, when Bigio had become one of the leaders of the Reds, she had said, loud and clear, that, of her property, not a pin would go to Rosa and to that godless husband of hers.

Desolina had spent the last twenty years of her life suffering all the pains of hell at the hands of her sharecroppers.

'They killed her,' Rosa said to Bigio in the late afternoon of the following day, returning home after accompanying Aunt Desolina to the cemetery. 'Not sixty-four, she would have lived

---

[35] A usufructuary is a person who has the legal right to use and benefit from someone else's property, without owning it.

to 104 if she hadn't had to suffer the punishment dealt out by that rabble.'

Bigio muttered something, but Rosa was clear in her thoughts on the matter: 'It's no use trying to defend them: everyone knows what a cursed race Falchetto, his father, his mother, his wife and his son are! But if they think they can poison my whole line, they're wrong!'

At this point Aida, Bigio's daughter-in-law, who had been at the funeral with Rosa and had spoken to her at length, intervened: 'We have to live here in the most disgusting house in town: damp, without air, without light, without even a handkerchief of land to plant a couple of onions and a bit of parsley, while we now have a house that looks like a villa and thirty *biolche* of land with a yield like sixty. But we can't touch even a cent of the income that should be ours from it!'

Rosa doubled down: 'We cannot relinquish our interests and those of Libero to favour a family of bastards like Falchetto!'

Bigio rebelled: 'Falchetto is a smart man! Falchetto...'

'We know very well what Falchetto has been up to under the veil of war and politics. There's little more to be said: we will leave the hovel at San Martino and move into Argine. Either you explain everything to Falchetto right away, or I'll go and do it myself.'

Bigio's son, who uttered one word every six months, now thought it apposite to express his opinion calmly as follows:

'If he acts stupid, I'll put my guts around his neck.'

*

Bigio decided he'd think about what to do for at least a week, but that same evening his hand was forced.

At a meeting of the general staff at the People's Palace, Bigio found himself face to face with Falchetto, who, as soon as he saw him, went to shake him by the hand and said:

'Comrade, I hear that Desolina left Argine to you. I'm happy about that. We couldn't get along with that crazy old lady. I'm sure we'll all get along fine now.'

Bigio shrugged: 'I'm nothing to do with it, she left the stuff to the little guy. We're just usufructuaries until he comes of age. But we mean to cultivate the land ourselves. Otherwise, we'll lose the usufruct too. It's … a difficult situation'.

Falchetto began to laugh loudly:

'And what do you think you're going to do? Become a farmer?'

'My wife worked the land until she was twenty-three, me until I was twenty-two: we'll make do.'

Falchetto turned to others on the staff: 'This is extraordinary! Yesterday he made a great speech in favour of justice for sharecroppers and today he wants to throw me off my farm!'

'Justice has nothing to do with it,' replied Bigio coldly.

'Here we have a change of landowner and the new owner wants to run the farm directly.'

'You know we fight such wills,' shouted the Falchetto at him, 'we contest them and our challenge will soon be upheld! You know that very well.'

'I hear you,' admitted the Bigio. 'But right now wills of this sort are still allowed and I have the right to take advantage of them. I need you to give the farm in San Martino up.'

Falchetto tipped his hat back and, planting his fists on his hips, declared that the one capable of removing him even a millimetre from his farm had yet to be born.

He stressed too much on 'his' and Bigio, assuming a similar position, replied that he would gladly meet the son of a bitch who would put his feet on his neck.

At this point, Peppone intervened:

'In session we don't argue, we discuss,' he said in a serious voice. 'Everyone puts forward his point of view. Then, reasoning calmly, we arrive at the right solution.'

'My point of view is that no one is going to kick me out of my house,' explained Falchetto calmly. 'Even if it means using force, as in the good old days.'

'My point of view,' countered Bigio, 'is that we are discussing party affairs here, not personal interests.'

Smilzo jumped up: 'You're wrong: the Party is the body that deals with the personal interests of all comrades and, in so doing, protects the interests of the working class.'

'I, not the working class, inherited the farm,' Bigio pointed out.

'Property is theft and there is no money more misappropriated than inherited money!' Smilzo stated categorically.

'The land belongs to everyone and I am not stealing anything from anyone,' replied Bigio. 'I'm only taking the share that is mine.'

'Land must go to farmers!' shouted Falchetto. 'Not to bricklayers!'

'And why?' objected Bigio. 'Are bricklayers more stupid than sharecroppers?'

Peppone restored calm and invited Bigio again to state his case calmly.

'Boss,' Bigio said, 'I repeat, these are personal matters.'

'And I,' Peppone explained blandly, 'I repeat there are no personal matters for those who have the membership card you have in their pocket.'

Bigio was explicit: 'Between my membership card and a thirty-*biolche* farm, I'll give up the membership card if I have to. Is there anyone here who would do differently?'

'Millions of comrades have even given up their lives for that membership card!' shouted Smilzo.

'You have to understand,' Bigio replied. 'A drab life is worth much less than thirty *biolche* of blessed land like that of the Argine. Anyway, all I can say is this: for twenty years Falchetto has enjoyed the land, for twenty years I want to enjoy it. A little bit for each person doesn't hurt anyone.'

'Proverbs are the opium of the people!' shouted Smilzo indignantly.

Bigio had talked too much: 'Good evening,' he said, and left.

*

Bigio and his gang were determined and only Peppone's authority managed to keep things from getting out of hand.

But, after a month, Bigio informed him that nothing would turn him and so it was time to sort things out. Peppone sent for Falchetto and spoke to him clearly and roundly:

'Falchetto: do we want to be a laughing stock of half of Italy? The law is bad and unjust, but it is in Bigio's favour. We can go against the law in your favour, but can we go against the law to the detriment of another comrade? If I take an official position in your favour, I have to accept Bigio's resignation and expel him from the party. Wouldn't it be better if you settled amicably? Bigio is even willing to give you a golden handshake of 300 thousand-lire bills. That's money!'

Falchetto thought about it for a long time and then said his piece:

'Okay, and if I accept, where can I find another farm? Those cowardly landowners, before giving the land to someone, research them well. Boss, I've already tried: they leave things uncertain to gain time, then, when they research and find out that I'm a political activist, they answer me clearly and roundly with a No. How can they do that?'

Falchetto found the 300,000 lire convenient. Moreover, he didn't like having Bigio's entire gang on his back. On the other hand, he could only afford to leave Argine when he found another farm to sharecrop or rent.

He thought about it long and hard and concluded: 'Boss, there is only one solution to this. Throw me out of the Party for "serious indiscipline". Communists expelled from the Party are popular with the bourgeoisie. I'll be able to get back on my feet.'

Peppone hesitated, but Falchetto convinced him: 'Boss, why do you want to do me down?'

Peppone then took a sheet of paper, wrote out an expulsion notice 'for serious indiscipline' and handed it to Falchetto:

'Read it and tell me if that's what you want.'

Falchetto, having read the statement, gave it back to him: 'Chief: "for serious indiscipline" is not enough. Add "for lack of faith": it makes a bigger impact.'

Peppone added: 'for lack of faith.'

The statement was published by the Federation's weekly and reported, with appropriate commentary, by the independent provincial newspaper. But Falchetto did not need that much publicity: less than half a kilometre away from the Argine a clerical landowner entrusted Falchetto with an excellent farm of forty *biolche* just to spite Peppone and his Party.

Bigio stopped being a bricklayer and moved from industry into agriculture, while keeping his place on Peppone's general staff.

In practical terms, nothing had changed much, except for the three-year-old beneficiary Libero Bosoni, who had it explained to him with a slap that singing the Red Flag was inappropriate when passing under Don Camillo's window.

All purely and simply a matter of 'readjustment'.

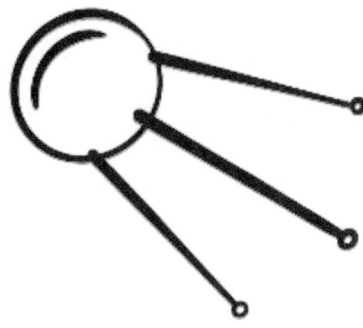

East and West (1957)

Rossetto was working in Ferotti's poplar grove and, suddenly, turning his gaze toward the river, something shiny caught his eye.

Between the last row of poplars and the river bank ran a strip of bare earth which, as it approached the water, turned into ashen mud: the reflection came from just where the mud began and Rossetto did not hesitate to climb down from the tree and walk the thirty paces that separated him from the mysterious object.

At first he thought it was a piece of mirror but, kneeling down to remove it from the mud, he realised that the more mud removed from around it, the more the surface of it widened, revealing a surprising dome-like surface.

Then he began to dig deeper in one spot just to make a probe but, having pulled up a few handfuls of mud, he stopped as if stunned. Quickly recovering, he picked up a bundle of brushwood and covered his find, returning immediately to work among the poplars. He determined not to lose his cool; he'd remain there calmly until midday, as if nothing had happened. But, after ten minutes, he could no longer control himself and, running to Ferotti's house, he fetched the bicycle he had left under the porch.

'Tell the boss that I'm leaving an hour early. I have to go see the union!' he shouted to the cowherd as he climbed on the saddle. A quarter of an hour later, a panting Rossetto appeared before Peppone and was so agitated that he couldn't get a word out.

Finally he did manage to say: 'Close everything!' And only when he was sure that Peppone had barred the doors and windows of the workshop, did he regain his composure.

Telling the Mayor the whole story, from A to Z, he concluded:

'Comrade, if it's not *it*, split my head open! I knew it right away, even before I saw the red star and the stamp.'

He then opened his arms wide: 'It's this big and it's completely stuck in the ground: it must be the second one.'

Peppone was clearly excited: 'We have to get it back at all costs. It mustn't fall into the hands of anyone other than us. Are you sure no one saw you?'

'Absolutely, Comrade.'

The little truck made from the glorious pre-war Fiat 514, realised unusually that there was no need today to be begged to get going: she took off like a rocket and, having crossed the village at full speed, reached the road on the Stivone embankment in one leap.

Only a foolhardy person would have driven at seventy on that narrow, muddy dirt track of a road. Peppone was going at eighty-five and only that because the 514 couldn't give more: moreover, when he came up behind a damned 1400 he didn't hesitate to press the horn and ask for the green light.

The people in the 1400 weren't crazy. They ignored him, but Peppone passed them anyway.

Only the Politburo knows how Peppone managed to overtake a 1400: the fact is that he did. He didn't even proffer a glance at whoever was travelling in it because only the right-side wheels of the 514 were in touch with the road and he had to be careful not to end up sliding down the embankment. But Rossetto took a quick look and, when the manoeuvre was complete, he said:

'In my opinion, it was Ferotti and the archpriest travelling in that 1400.'

'May God strike them both down,' roared Peppone.

Having reached the main embankment, Peppone took the descent that led to the sand and gravel deposits on the riverbank without slowing down and stopped the car a few metres from the water.

They hadn't been able to use the road taken by Rossetto on his bicycle that led through Ferotti's land to the place on question. They had to walk along the strip between the border of Ferotti's farm and the riverbank – State property, so no one could challenge them. It wasn't easy wading through that mud, but no obstacle was going to stop the particular revolution that was in progress.

'There it is,' Rossetto exclaimed at last, pointing to the brushwood cover beneath which he'd hidden the treasure that had fallen from the sky.

Once the branches were removed, the shiny object appeared, sunk in the mud, but Peppone couldn't revel in it because a muffled cry from Rossetto made him jump:

'Attenzione!'

Peppone turned suddenly and saw Don Camillo standing at the edge of the poplar grove, and now speaking in a low voice to Ferotti.

Ferotti signalled that he understood and ran away towards the dirt road that led to the distant farmyard, back over the embankment.

Peppone didn't hesitate for a moment:

'Rossetto, fly! Take the truck, get to town, load up the team and take them to the gravel depot. No explanation! Orders from the boss. As soon as you arrive, give two blasts of the horn. Wait without moving: if I need you I'll whistle.'

Rossetto disappeared and Peppone, taking a half-Tuscan from his pocket, calmly lit it.

'May I take advantage of your kindness, Mr Mayor?' Don Camillo then said, stepping forward. 'I don't have any matches and I'd be happy to have a smoke myself.'

'Don't bother, I'll come and light it for you,' replied Peppone, going to meet Don Camillo.

They met halfway and, once he had lit his cigar, Don Camillo, chatting about this and that, set off towards the pile of brushwood.

Peppone stood in front of him:

'Reverend, I advise you to change direction.'

Don Camillo evaded him and, reaching the brushwood, swept it away with a blow of his paw.

'My friend Ferotti wasn't mistaken,' he said. 'It really does look like something very interesting, looks like there's a brand name on it,' he observed.

The veins in Peppone's neck were as big as mooring ropes and, gritting his teeth, he threw away his hat.

Don Camillo didn't seem to take notice of Peppone, but before his hat touched the ground, he'd caught it.

'This stuff shouldn't interest you,' said Peppone. 'You didn't make it, we made it and it belongs to us!'

'But it fell on our land and now it's ours,' replied Don Camillo.

It's not known who fired first: probably they both fired at the same time and it was lightning-fast. A few but vigorous blasts: the intercontinental kind which dislocate a jaw or block an eye with just the movement of air.

They remained staring at each other for a long time without being able to understand what had really happened: then, from the direction of the gravel deposit, came the croaking of a horn.

'Just one whistle and the team will be here,' said Peppone, recovering. 'You'd better give up.'

'Just one more whistle and my team will be here too,' replied Don Camillo. 'You'd better retreat. Indeed: to avoid the onset of a mini revolution, it may be better for both of us to retreat and put everything in the hands of the authorities.'

Peppone fought desperately with himself and, in the end, threw up his arms: 'It is our property and must not fall into the hands of our enemies!' he shouted. 'Even if there is a massacre, if you don't give me a free hand, I will whistle!'

Don Camillo took a step back: 'I give in,' he said.

Peppone threw himself on the ground and began to scratch furiously with his hands all around the shiny steel sphere, which turned out to be an instrument of quite a size – at least sixty centimetres in diameter.

Then, when he was able to wedge his hands under it and grab it, he knelt down and gathered all his strength to give the tug that would surely pull the sphere out of the hole.

It came up with extreme ease, so much so that Peppone, not finding the resistance he expected, fell backwards and the sphere slipped out of his hands and crashed into a pile of rocks.

It couldn't have happened otherwise because it was a sixty-litre demijohn, the kind with the big mouth, to the bottom of which you can fish comfortably with your hand and which are used to pickle peppers, onions or something like that.

The work had been done conscientiously: the damned man who had had that brilliant idea, after gluing a star and a USSR cut out of red paper, had painted the whole inside with that aluminium coloured crap used to dye stove pipes, burying the contraption thus dressed in the sand, mouth down so that only a little bit of its shiny behind was visible.

'Perhaps you were right not to whistle,' observed Don Camillo after studying the wreckage of the demijohn.

'You too!' replied Peppone, picking up the shards and going to throw them into the water.

Don Camillo sighed and spread his arms:

'To think,' he said as he smoothed a dent on his forehead, 'that for a stupid thing like that, the Mayor almost punched the parish priest.'

'Worse,' added Peppone, stroking his sore jaw: 'the archpriest almost punched the Mayor.'

'All's well that ends well,' concluded Don Camillo. 'Let's forget the past.'

'Let us forget,' muttered Peppone.

They left without saying anything more.

*

Back home, Peppone found the soup cold and his wife very irritated. Not with him, but with their youngest boy:

'He's been bothering me all morning because he wants to go for a walk. I kept him home from school because he wasn't well, so how can I let him go out.'

'Just ten minutes,' begged the boy, turning to his father.

'And where do you want to go?' Peppone muttered, continuing to gulp down soup.

'Near Ferotti's poplar grove. A schoolmate of mine buried a demijohn there painted silver with a red star and so on, as if it were a Sputnik, and I'd like to see if anyone falls for it.'[36]

'Nonsense!' exclaimed the mother. 'Who would be stupid enough to fall for that?'

Peppone continued to gulp down cold soup and his jaw hurt like hell.

A couple of hours later, however, Don Camillo began to hear the confessions of the children who were to take Christmas Communion and the first was Ferotti's son. He had a small sack to empty but still he wasn't at peace:

'And then... And then I did something... Reverend, is it a sin to paint a demijohn silver and then bury it to make people believe it was a Sputnik that fell from the sky?'

---

[36] In 1957, Russia won a notable propaganda victory, by launching Sputnik, the first man-made object ever to leave the Earth's atmosphere. It passed over the stunned American continent once every 101 minutes and propelled the Soviet Union (the USSR) from backward state to superpower and pioneer of the Space Age.

'It depends, son,' Don Camillo replied. 'We need to see how you got this idea.'

'The idea isn't mine,' the boy explained. 'It's someone else's. I just helped him paint it and bury it on the riverbank. The one who did it all is Libero.'

'Which one?'

'The Mayor's son.'

'Then it is just a venial sin. Three Our Fathers, Hail Marys, and Glorias.'

Invaders Arrive from the City (1960)

S MILZO TURNED UP, pedalling like a madman, and having brought his bike to a halt two millimetres from the threshold of Peppone's workshop, jumped from the saddle and dashed in.

Panting, he mumbled something, and Peppone, who had stopped work to hear what he had to say, started hammering away again, muttering: 'Drunk already at nine in the morning?'

'Boss!' groaned Smilzo. 'I saw it with my own eyes and the others saw it too.'

Brusco and Bigio arrived and confirmed what Smilzo had said, and Peppone changed his tune:

'I'm not going to argue. I'm simply going to say that the most important agricultural strike in history is underway right now and I don't want anything to get in its way. Notify the Marshal. Make the necessary investigations and intervene, because what you tell me is shamelessly provocative and I am not responsible for the reactions it may provoke.'

Bigio shook his head:

'There is only one clerk left in the barracks. The Marshal and all his *carabinieri* are at the Ghiare farmhouse to protect the strike-breakers. There's no way they'll move from there.'

Peppone angrily threw his hammer into a pile of scrap metal:

'Those damned *carabinieri*!' he shouted. 'You only find them underfoot when they're no good for you. Where did "the landing" take place?'

'Two hundred and fifty metres from the dredge,' explained Smilzo.

'Where are they now?'

'Still there. They're pretending to mess around with the boat's engine, but it's clear they're waiting for someone.'

Peppone was a man of quick decisions:

'Gather together all the boys in the team. Let them show themselves around so as to make it clear that, if some strike-breaking wretch has it in mind to do some clowning at the Ghiare farmhouse and disturb the progress of this strike, he had better change his mind. In the meantime, I'll go and see what this is all about.'

While Smilzo and his comrades set off at full speed, Peppone took Sputnik out of the shed, and Don Camillo spotted it immediately.

The archpriest was, in fact, observing the situation from the top of the bell tower and, if he hadn't framed Peppone's car in his binoculars, he would have heard it start, because Sputnik was now the name of the most battered Balilla in the Po Valley, fished out from among the rustiest junk of a scrap yard and transformed into a pickup by a body shop mechanic, whose life depended only on his having a good back and an ability to dig, in an hour, the earth that a normal labourer could dig in two.

Don Camillo saw Peppone at the wheel of Sputnik start towards the embankment, and when, a few moments later, the Reds of the team began to arrive in the piazza, he abandoned his observation post and ran down. Passing by the High Altar, he tried to dodge any possible hindrance, but the Crucified Christ got him:

'Where are you running to, Don Camillo?'

'Lord, someone is about to find themselves in serious trouble and I must warn them before it's too late.'

His bicycle was outside, leaning against the wall, next to the door of the presbytery, and Don Camillo mounted it and took off like a rocket. But he couldn't help but hear the voice of Christ:

'Don Camillo, why are you carrying that ugly thing with you?'

'When public force is lacking, you have to make up for it with private force,' Don Camillo replied, trying to steady the section of a beam on his handlebars that he'd found in his hands while coming down from the bell tower. He then pressed desperately on the pedals but, when he reached the river, it was already too late.

*

The Reds had surrounded the invaders and, motionless, with their arms folded across their chests, were looking at them pretty grimly. The enemy didn't even seem to have noticed the storm clouds gathering above their heads and continued to mess around with an outboard motor, trying to restart it.

Don Camillo engaged low gear and began to advance like a Panzer splitting a wall, stopping only when he found himself behind Peppone.

'All this display of force for two little girls?' he queried. 'Couldn't the Mayor have solved the situation more economically by sending in the municipal guard?'

'Vipers are but small animals,' Peppone replied through gritted teeth without deigning to look at him.

At that moment, one of the two girls, the taller one, turned to the crowd and asked, smiling: 'Our engine doesn't want to work anymore. Please, where can we find a mechanic?'

Then everyone saw her face and that it was identical to the one in the newspapers.

Peppone clenched his fists and the veins in his neck bulged as big as one-and-a-quarter-inch pipes.

The girl's words sank into a heavy, menacing silence, then, suddenly, someone broke away from the curtain of flesh and advanced toward the boat.

He was wearing a blue mechanic's overalls and had the head of a communist card carrying mayor. He looked at the engine, tried to start it, then shook his head:

'A bearing is shot,' he muttered.

'Is it a long job?' the girl asked.

'It is what it is and will take the time that it takes,' Peppone replied grimly.

'Can you fix it?' the girl asked with that damned smile of hers.

'The job of a mechanic is to fix broken engines,' explained Peppone with appropriate seriousness.

The girl thanked him, then asked if the village was far away and if there was a way to make a phone call there. The father of her companion, who was staying with her, didn't know about the boat trip and he should be notified.

'The village is a kilometre and a half beyond the embankment,' said Peppone as he disconnected the engine from the boat.

The two girls set off up the embankment and the wall of flesh slowly opened to let them pass through.

As Peppone was about to overtake them in Sputnik, having loaded the engine in the cargo bed at the back, he threw open the door: 'There's not much room…' he said with just about sufficient rudeness.

'But there's so much room in the back!' the smiling girl exclaimed, obviously amused. 'We would both fit comfortably *and* keep the engine company.'

They were agile, light, and, in an instant, were onto the cargo bed of Sputnik. As Peppone put the truck in gear, he saw Don Camillo's face framed in the window.

'There's nothing to laugh about, Reverend,' Peppone roared. 'Engines don't engage in politics and, in the eyes of a mechanic, all are equal.'

'I understand, but how will the Mechanic broker an understanding with the Mayor and the Communist Leader?'

'Since the one who feeds the Mayor and the communist leader is the mechanic, when it comes to work, the mechanic reigns supreme.'

Sputnik started up with the best possible grace and began to move slowly along the embankment. Behind it, a long procession of bicycles and mopeds seemed never ending.

In the village, the few who had not gone to the dredge beach to catch sight of the invaders were waiting under their porticos or at their windows.

Sputnik stopped, as always politely, in front of Peppone's workshop and here the smiling girl and her companion got out. 'While you fix the engine for us,' said the smiling one, 'we'll go and make a phone call and then take a little tour of the village.'

The general staff immediately hailed Peppone:

'Is everything okay?' Peppone asked gruffly.

'Everything's okay, boss.'

'No reactionary clowning?'

'None, boss. All the reactionaries were monitored, one by one.'

'Double the surveillance and make it clear that we are not willing to tolerate any obstructive speculations.'

'They already understand, boss.'

The men on picket duty in the large agricultural estates of the Municipality arrived and Peppone got angry:

'What are you doing here?'

'Boss, what are we doing in the farmyards, given that the striking employees and the strike-breakers have all come here?'

'It's a formidable union success!' exclaimed Smilzo.

The smiling girl and her companion found a telephone nearby, in the shop of the consumer co-operative 'La Proletaria', and, after making the phone call, they stopped there to drink an orangeade.

Then they visited all of the little that there was to visit in the village, and tarried longest in the church.

Don Camillo received the smiling girl and her friend with dignified detachment and was an attentive but very controlled guide. He took them up the bell tower, but only and exclusively so that the smiling young lady could get an idea of the topology of the area.

He played some old tunes with the carillon like *Addio mia bella addio*, *La bella Gigogin* and *Il Piave*, but only to demonstrate the efficiency of the bell equipment.

*

Meanwhile, Peppone worked like a madman and Bigio acted as his assistant:

'We have to hurry' explained Peppone. 'The quicker we do it, the quicker we'll be rid of them.'

Then, when his wife came to gush about the beauty, grace, bearing and so on of the smiling girl, Peppone cut her short:

'Nonsense! There must be thousands of girls even more beautiful than her in the Municipality!'

'Beautiful, perhaps,' his wife replied confidently. 'But not one as beautiful as she.'

Peppone shook his head and vented to Bigio: 'If she didn't *know* who she is, she wouldn't find anything special about her. Since she does know who she is, she finds God knows what. It's the usual filthy, bourgeois cult of personality, Comrade.'

Peppone worked like a whole team of mechanics and, when the smiling girl reappeared, it was all done.

With the engine and the two girls back on Sputnik, Peppone headed towards the embankment: in a few minutes, having reached the boat, he mounted the engine.

When everything was sorted out, the smiling girl stopped smiling and explained: 'We left secretly for a little adventure and we didn't bring any money with us...'

'Don't worry,' Peppone interrupted her, 'just leave me your name.'

He didn't have any notepaper with him, so he handed her the first piece of paper he found in his wallet, along with a pen.

And, lo and behold, it was his party card. The girl signed her name and handed the card back:

'You are very kind,' she said, 'and I would like to know your name.'

'No matter. Anyway, they call me Peppone, but my name is Bottazzi … Giuseppe. Now get in and steer clear of that buoy: it's shallow here.'

The engine began to roar and the boat pulled away from the shore.

'Thank you!' shouted the smiling girl, waving her handkerchief.

This was the one and only moment Peppone lost control and, jumping to attention, shouted:

'Have a good trip, your Royal Highness!'

*

Justifiably satisfied, Don Camillo was giving the day's report to Christ above the High Altar:

'Everything is sorted, Lord. She's gone and before long no one will remember her. She passed like the glittering lizard that darts from one hedge to another and leaves only a light mark in the dust of the road. A mark that the first breath of wind will erase.'

'Unless it's a mark written with a fountain pen,' said Christ, smiling.

Don Camillo raised his eyes toward the Crucified Christ and said in a voice full of painful wonder:

'Lord, perhaps you want to insinuate that I, finding myself before the daughter of a King, could not resist the temptation to have her trace her autograph on the frontispiece of my Breviary?'

'I do really believe so, Don Camillo.'

Don Camillo spread his arms resignedly:

'Lord, would I even dare to contradict you?'

A Matter of Sport (1960)

'BOSS,' SAID SMILZO, 'OUR comrades have been waiting for the revolution for fourteen years and, in the long run, one does get increasingly fed up.'

'More so since this newfangled business of *détente* seems to be designed specifically to confuse us,' Brusco added.[37]

'Too right!' muttered Bigio. 'How can we expect our comrades to feel enthusiasm for the struggle if we continue to talk to them about peace, coexistence and other such rubbish!'

'We are not here to discuss the politics of the Soviet Union,' Peppone countered, 'rather to study the causes of the "general relaxation", and to help our comrades rediscover the spirit of yesteryear. In my opinion, the significance of Soviet conquests in the atomic, missile and space fields has not been emphasised enough…'

'Boss,' exclaimed Falchetto, 'Sputniks and so on are incredible, but what does the moon matter to a peasant who has to break his back on the same piece of land year in year out that isn't even his to own?'

'Are we not fighting to give the land to the peasants?' shouted Peppone. 'This raises another point: those responsible

---

[37] Premier and First Secretary of the communist party Nikita Khrushchev's policy of détente ('peaceful coexistence'), a huge reversal of Stalinist policy, opened up Russia to the outside world, even to an 'enemy of the people', a priest envoy in disguise. See *Comrade Don Camillo* (Pilot, 2017).

for propaganda don't explain enough to their comrades what the Party does for them.'

'They explain it all right,' replied Falchetto. 'And the peasants reply that they'll not get the land by writing articles in the newspapers or making speeches in the Chamber, but by pushing the owners against the wall, as happened in Russia. You take Boccia, hang him from a telegraph pole, divide his land among his tenants and then you will see the spirit of the struggle return immediately.'

'What's more,' observed Brusco, 'if we don't get on with it, no one will want the land anymore. One after the other the young are leaving the fray: young people don't want to know about farming anymore.'

'Well, there's another point!' agreed Peppone. 'The propaganda in the youth sector is way off the mark. We must intensify it!'

'You try!' said Lungo. 'There is not one young lad left who doesn't have a scooter and, if he doesn't have one, his friend does. As soon as they can, they take off. One evening they go to such and such a place to dance to some band or other, the next they run to God's house because there is such and such a singer performing, while yet another evening they have to see – I don't know where – the election of some beauty queen. Between fashion evenings, beauty queens, the rubbish on television, briscola competitions, prize competitions, sports matches, there isn't a free evening all year round. And these young people travel, Boss. You tell me where you'd fish for them.'

'Okay,' Peppone shouted, 'so will you tell me *why* we let them take off? Will you tell me *what* we do to bind the young people to the village and keep alive the old fighting spirit in their hearts? Comrade, the other evening, when the television at the People's Palace broke down, do you know where so many of your young people went to see the "Musichiere"?[38] To the parish priest's club!'

---

[38] An Italian game show based upon *Name That Tune*. It ran from 1957 to 1960 and ended with the untimely death of its host, Mario Riva.

Lungo, who was in charge of the youth section, threw up his arms:

'Boss,' he replied, 'it's not my fault. It's TV's fault.'

'Once upon a time,' replied Peppone, 'if one of our boys had just met by chance with one of the parish priest's monkeys, he would have at least slapped him. If this healthy antagonism no longer exists, it's not TV's fault. That's the point, comrades.'

They discussed the matter at great length and came to a decision that would remain under wraps until fifteen days later, when the village, upon waking up, found its walls covered with bright red banners:

'Team Dynamos wakes up and prepares to win the Provincial Championship! Premier stage of its victorious march: the resounding and definitive defeat of the Gagliarda. Assuming that the Gagliarda still exists and, if it does, has the courage to accept the challenge.'[39]

*

Don Camillo fell into the trap like an ingenue and called his emergency committee to order at the presbytery. These were serious people who gave a very relative value to sporting trifles, but everyone realised that this was a question of prestige and that such a provocation could not be ignored.

'The Gagliarda is alive and kicking,' proclaimed a tricolour poster distributed on street corners two days later, 'as the Dynamos will see when the medlars are in.'[40]

The technical committees of the two teams met to fine-tune the date of the match and the timing of training shifts at the municipal sports field. It was decided that training would be conducted in the strictest secrecy and that the Gagliarda would be first off the mark.

---

[39] The conflict between the Dynamos and Gagliarda was first introduced in 'The Defeat' (*The Little World of Don Camillo*, Pilot 2013).

[40] In Italy, medlars are traditionally harvested in late October/November, but concealed within the reference is a Chaucerian insult to Peppone's team. Since mediaeval times the ripened fruit of the medlar tree has been likened to a bare buttock in the act of mooning, an act used to express protest, scorn, disrespect, or as a direct provocation.

The next morning, on the pedestal of the famous monument to Hercules[41], eleven bottles of Proton were found: ten normal strength bottles and one quadruple, accompanied by a message measuring one by one and a half metres, written in capital letters: 'Given how things are, a tonic for the men of Gagliarda is more than appropriate. The quadruple bottle is reserved for their centre forward.'

In truth, the centre forward was the thorn in Don Camillo's heart and he did not know where to turn to find someone better. However, the next morning, at the first training session of Peppone's boys, a roll of wire mesh was found on the pedestal of the monument with an adequate explanation: 'Seeing how things are, we offer this net to Dynamos to nail in front of the goal.'

Spot on, because the Dynamos' weak point was their goalkeeper.

Peppone and his men did not take it well.

Meanwhile, the youth of the area were getting fired up about the match and one evening at the meeting of Peppone's general staff, Lungo had to concede that he had been right:

'Boss,' he admitted, 'you were bang on: our boys have already started to fight with the parish priest's boys and to tear off heads. The local doctor reports that, as the count stands, we are winning by twenty-five points to nil.'

Peppone was pleased and observed that, too often, mature men forget the importance of sport in the political education of youth.

'We must look at the naked substance of things,' he concluded wisely. 'One can discuss the validity of a reason for conflict, but the fact that our young people are beating up the clerics is indisputably positive.'

The secret training sessions continued, but the two teams remained exactly as they had always been: one strong in attack and weak in defence, the other strong in defence and weak in

---

[41] The marble statue of Hercules with his cudgel had stood, since time immemorial, upon a large, six-sided stone plinth in the village square.

attack. Overall, they were equal, and it was not clear why the Reds were so persistent in their bold assertions.

'If some new element does not find its way into the mix,' Don Camillo concluded, 'everything will end as before: in a draw.'

But just three days before the Sunday set for the match, the new element did appear in the mix. Piletti arrived at the presbytery and panted:

'We're screwed! They have a new goalkeeper! And he's better than ours.'

'Impossible!' Don Camillo replied. 'There is no goalkeeper in the entire Municipality who is on a par with ours.'

'They found him in another municipality, Reverend. And you know him because he is Gigiòla from Solagna.'

'They can't introduce foreigners into the team!' shouted Don Camillo.

'He is of local descent. Gigiòla's father is from Torricella. They bought him – found him a job in Torricella. The boy lives with his mother and has moved with her to Torricella. Peppone himself moved him in Sputnik two hours ago. We can't do anything about it. With a goalkeeper like that they will surely beat us.'

The head of the technical department expressed his dismay: 'Gigiòla is a phenomenon: to restore the balance we would need an equal phenomenon like the centre forward who plays for Castelbianco. But who can buy a guy like Folletto?'

'Everyone has his price,' replied Don Camillo.

'It's useless to think about it,' Piletti added, 'it would be necessary for Folletto, in addition to letting himself be bought, to be of Italian origin.'

'Everyone, in the long run, is of Italian origin!' Don Camillo decided.

A commission left immediately for Castelbianco: it was a fifteen-kilometre journey and a mission to be carried out in a town as big as the bottom of a tub. After three hours the commission was back.

'The situation is this,' Piletti explained: 'Folletto works in the workshop of a certain Benasca, but since there is often a lack of work, he would be willing to move if he found a permanent, secure position. He lives on his own, has no family commitments and, for him, living here rather than there is of no importance. The trouble, however, is that, as far as he knows, his family is from Castelbianco and has always lived in Castelbianco.'

The following day was a whirlwind for Don Camillo: by nine o'clock he had already convinced Filotti to hire Folletto as a tractor driver in his company and, at nine forty-five, he was already rummaging through the records of the parish priest of Castelbianco.

It was a tough job, but he managed to find that, in 1757, a certain Gozzini Desolina born in Castelbianco had married a Frambati Giuseppe, a native of Castellina and the fount of those Frambatis of Castelbianco in whom, probably, Frambati Amedeo, known as 'Folletto', has his origins.

In the records of the parish priest of Castellina, the baptismal certificate of Giuseppe Frambati was found and, since Castellina was a hamlet of the Municipality administered by Peppone's Reds, the game could be considered won.

'An eye for an eye, a native for a native!' Don Camillo declared at the evening meeting. 'If we have to put up with Gigiòla, they will have to put up with Folletto!'

It was a historic match because the indigenous natives and the displaced natives gave it their all. Folletto managed to fire at least six unstoppable cannon shots at the Dynamos' goal, but Gigiòla was there and he saved them all in the blink of an eye, and the match ended as usual, in a draw.

'Reverend,' Peppone said to Don Camillo at the end of it, 'as you saw, even without nailing your wire netting in front of the goal, we managed just fine.'

'And we managed just fine even without your tonic,' Don Camillo replied. 'In fact, we will return it to you. You will need it for the rematch.'

In the evening, at the presbytery, the Gagliarda management took stock:

'Nothing new,' the technical department asserted. 'Originally, the Dynamos weighed one kilo and the Gagliarda weighed one kilo. We added 100 grams to each, and each weighed one kilo and 100 grams.'

Don Camillo shook his head: 'Let's see,' he said.

On a shelf of the sideboard were the scales: Don Camillo took two old glasses with handles from the sideboard and placed them on the shiny brass plates of the scales.

The plates oscillated a little, then stopped because the weight of one glass was identical to the weight of the other. 'Dynamos and Gagliarda were perfectly in balance,' he confirmed. 'If things had remained like this, the two teams would always have balanced each other because they were two homogeneous blocks. The Reds,' he continued, taking a 100-gram weight from the box and placing it on one plate of the scales, 'made the scales tip in their favour. And we repeated the same manoeuvre.'

He took a second 100-gram weight from the box and placed it on the other side of the scale, re-establishing the balance.

'Result?' he asked.

'What I said, Reverend!' the technical man replied laughing. 'One thousand plus 100 is 1,100 and 1,000 plus 100 is 1,100.'

Everyone was of the same opinion.

'We are in the exact same situation as before,' Piletti exclaimed.

'But no,' Don Camillo stated categorically. 'The situation is profoundly different because, while before I only had two glasses that I had to leave where they were and as they were, now I can, for example, do this.'

He took one of the weights from one plate and placed it on the other plate.

'Now, if A is worth ten and B is worth ten, A will always be equal to B. And if X is worth one and Y is worth one, A plus X will always be equal to B plus Y. But A plus X plus Y is worth twelve while B is worth ten. In mathematics X and Y are called *unknowns* precisely because, when you introduce them into calculations, you never know exactly how things might end up.'

The technical man and all the others looked at Don Camillo not a little perplexed.

'I,' Piletti said, 'still remember something of what they taught me at school: I think the problem is to find the centre of gravity.'

'*Esatto*,' Don Camillo replied.

Piletti was stubborn and had a good disposition for mathematics; he showed up again a fortnight later:

'Reverend,' he said, 'I think I've found the centre of gravity and the value of Y.'

'Which is?' Don Camillo asked.

'A 175cc motorcycle with a cowboy saddle and saddlebags. All told, about 250,000 lire. Of course, he will also have to be guaranteed another job because those people, as soon as the bomb explodes, will have him kicked out.'

Don Camillo did not abandon his scepticism:

'And how will he be released?'

'We are lucky, Reverend. He hasn't signed the contract yet. They are dragging their feet to squeeze him over the deal. It has embittered him. He is a sensitive boy, and also he comes from a religious family and doesn't feel right among those godless people. He says that – deep down – they have been pressuring him to join the Party. I got him at a good moment: I asked him if he was okay and he confided in me. He spilled the beans and I, at just the right moment, threw the proposal at him.'

There was still a month to go until the Sunday set for the rematch and Don Camillo immediately got to work; the idea of screwing Peppone moved even the most tight-fisted: in an instant the money for the motorcycle and the new job for Gigiòla was underwritten.

To be on the safe side they met with the young man in the city and put their cards on the table. The negotiations took place with the assistance of a lawyer.

'You seem like a good boy,' Don Camillo concluded: 'however, know this: if you get any idea in your head about welching on this, we will send you back to Solagna after having kicked your backside all over the province. Don't worry about Peppone's lot because we will stand by you. As agreed, fifteen days before the meeting, the lawyer will have the motorcycle delivered to you.'

Deal.

And it was a big deal because a Dynamos team deprived of its defence would have been torn to pieces by a Gagliarda with a phenomenal centre forward like Folletto and a formidable goalkeeper like Gigiòla.

That evening, Don Camillo tried to slip away, past the High Altar, but the voice of Christ stopped him:

'Don Camillo, why the rush?'

'Lord, no rush, it's fatigue,' Don Camillo replied. 'I've been so busy lately.'

'Strange: I did not notice that there were more baptisms or weddings than usual. And all of your flock seem to be in rude health.'

'It's because of that blessed soccer match,' Don Camillo explained. 'If you want to keep young people away from temptation, you have to indulge them a little in their passion for sport.'

'We have spoken about this before, Don Camillo, and you have always put so much enthusiasm into your explanation that I too have become passionate about sport. Do you think that this time the match will favour our team?'

'Lord!' shouted Don Camillo. 'We will pulverise them! With a centre forward like Folletto, who will save Peppone from fifteen goals?'

'The same as last time: his new goalkeeper.'

'But how will he be able to do so *if he is playing for us*?'

It was too late: his very enthusiasm had betrayed Don Camillo.

'Don Camillo,' said Christ in a stern voice, 'in what conspiracy have you embroiled me?'

'None, Lord! The conspiracy was initiated by Peppone. If he had not plotted to buy the naturalised boy, we would never have hired Folletto. Now, if his mercenary wants to come to us, why should we reject the offer? Sometimes the dog runs and sometimes the hare runs: Lord, *it is the game!*'

Christ sighed:

'Don Camillo, even the dice game is a game. But the just man will never play with the Devil's dice. Even getting smoke out of a tobacco leaf is a game, but the just man will never light his cigar with the flames of hell. Don Camillo: the abyss of evil is found not only by way of the great road of blasphemy, violence, theft or murder, but also by way of the path known as cunning. No one is more foolish than the cunning man who deludes himself into thinking he is deceiving his God and only succeeds in deceiving his neighbour and himself.'

'Lord,' protested Don Camillo, 'You treat me as if I have committed who knows what crime!'

'Don Camillo, you can never use bricks made with the mud of hell to build the House of God. Not even one. Not even one in a thousand bricks mixed with good earth. Good and evil are on opposite shores and what is not good is evil… Now go and rest, Don Camillo: you still have many things to do for your team of footballers.'

'A little while ago you were saying "our" team,' Don Camillo regretted.

'Then, I did not know of your new line-up,' replied Christ smiling.

*

The bomb exploded about a week before the match. One evening, Peppone arrived dazed at the presbytery and, throwing a battered sheet of paper on Don Camillo's desk, roared:

'Reverend, do you want to tell me what this sleight of hand is?'

'I don't see any sleight of hand,' Don Camillo replied after unfolding the sheet of paper. 'It's a normal draft of a poster with the new line-up of the Gagliarda that will be posted the day after tomorrow, after you have received an official communication regarding the player Gigiòla's decision. The only dirty trick, if there is one, is that you have a draft copy of the poster.'

'No. The only dirty trick is what you did, Reverend, by stealing our doorman.'

'Comrade: a mercenary is someone who sells his sword and sells only to those who pays him the most. You, comrade, introduced mercenaries into the game, *you* brought disorder. What are you complaining about, if, playing with fire, you got burned? He who wounds by gamesmanship, dies by gamesmanship.'

'When we hired Gigiòla, you responded by hiring Folletto: that means you accepted the game. Now, by stealing Gigiòla from us, it is you who is cheating!'

'We didn't steal anyone,' replied Don Camillo. 'Gigiòla didn't like you and offered to come with us. Normal commercial undertaking: someone offers you something you need and you buy it.'

'Whoever buys stolen goods is not a merchant, he is a receiver!' Peppone decided.

'He hadn't signed a contract,' Don Camillo replied. 'He was his own free agent. Besides, our contract with him was concluded in the presence of a lawyer. If you want to discuss it, I can give you his address.'

Peppone became a little agitated, making mooing noises, then said:

'All right: we are willing to buy the goods back: how much?'

Don Camillo remembered the bricks mixed with the mud of hell, the Devil's dice, the just man lighting his cigar with the flames of hell: 'Not a cent more than what it cost us,' he replied. He took the invoice for the motorcycle out of the drawer and handed it to him. Peppone took the paper, glanced at it, then shouted:

'His motorbike also!...'

Don Camillo looked him over:

'His motorcycle as well as *whose*?' he asked.

'Gigiòla's,' muttered Peppone.

'Gigiòla is "his". Who does the "also" refer to? Comrade, put *your* cards on the table.'

Peppone fidgeted, embarrassed for a few moments, then, taking a piece of paper from his pocket, he placed it in front of Don Camillo and it too was an invoice for a motorcycle that differed from Don Camillo's only in one detail: the make. The engine capacity and price were identical.

'So *you*, comrade,' said Don Camillo, standing up threateningly, 'you came here to try to trap me...'

'He who wounds by gamesmanship, perishes by gamesmanship!' Peppone interrupted him. 'You said as much. Normal commercial undertaking: someone comes to offer you something you need and you buy it.'

'But you, after buying Folletto, want to buy Gigiòla back – to have them both!'

'Commerce consists not only in buying but also in buying back!' Peppone decided. 'Anyway, I've had enough of this: you take back your Folletto, we'll take back our Gigiòla and it's *buona notte al secchio*. Everything goes back to the way it was before, and let's pretend that none of this happened.'

Don Camillo shook his head: 'It is hard to pretend that you didn't pay 250,000 lire in cash!'

In the heat of negotiation, Peppone had missed the detail and it was a detail of some importance because he too had reeled off 250,000 lire. Remembering it, he turned red, and immediately calmed down:

'The swindle is the same for both of us: each one keeps his own. The important thing is that *balance* is re-established.'

'Let's see,' said Don Camillo, approaching the cupboard: 'Gagliarda,' he explained, placing one of the large glasses with the handle on one plate of the scales.

'Dynamos' he explained, placing the second glass on the other plate and re-establishing the balance.

'Gigiòla,' he explained, placing a 100-gram weight next to the Dynamos' glass.

'Folletto,' he explained, placing a second 100-gram weight next to the glass of 'Gagliarda' and re-establishing the balance.

'Okay,' exclaimed Peppone 'and with this, where do you want this to take us?'

Don Camillo placed Peppone's invoice next to the glass of Dynamos and his own invoice next to the glass of Gagliarda. Then, he removed the two invoices and the two 100-gram weights from one plate and the other, and only the two glasses remained.

Peppone pondered the 'trick' intently. Suddenly his eye flashed. Extremely excited, he took a coin out of his pocket:

'Heads for Folletto, tails for Gigiòla' he said, tossing the coin in the air.

And it came up tails.

*

It was a great thing that it came up tails because they found Gigiòla playing cards with Folletto.

Seeing Peppone and Don Camillo appear before them, the two young men suddenly fell silent.

'The idea wasn't bad,' Don Camillo said, taking off his cloak. 'Two brand new motorcycles came out of it. The idea wasn't bad, but it wasn't good either.'

Each one acted according to his strict competence: Don Camillo brushed Folletto's pumpkin and Peppone brushed Gigiòla's. Then, considering that the operation was duplicitous, Don Camillo combed Gigiòla's, Peppone combed Folletto's, and everything was smoothed out fine.

The two young men subsequently found no difficulty in taking the contracts and eating them down to the last bit of paper, including envelopes and revenue stamps.

Finally, Peppone warned them: 'If you are not out of the Municipality by midday tomorrow, we will kick arse.'

All in all, not many more words were said and, after less than an hour, Don Camillo and Peppone were able to climb back onto Sputnik and return to base. Their hands were sore, but in the trunk of Sputnik there were two brand new motorcycles worth two hundred and fifty thousand lire each.

When they arrived in front of the presbytery, the issue of the two motorcycles arose and Peppone, still caught up in his sporting enthusiasm, proposed an exquisitely sporting solution:

'Let's have a motorbike race, you and I. Whoever gets there first gets both.'

'I prefer to play for them at briscola,' Don Camillo replied.

They agreed on a compromise solution: the Municipality would hold a big lottery to fix the sports field and the 'Dynamos' and the 'Gagliarda' would contribute by offering, as prizes, a motorcycle each.

The bell rang at eleven in the morning.

'End of truce,' Peppone decided, making a stern face.

'End of truce,' Don Camillo approved with a grim face. 'But first, help me unload my motorcycle.'

Peppone helped him without arguing and this showed his sporting sense. Don Camillo, passing by the church, paid a visit to Christ on the High Altar.

'Lord,' he said 'the brick mixed with the mud of hell that was in the wall of the House of God has been removed.'

'With blows of a pickaxe,' whispered the Christ.

'Lord,' Don Camillo justified himself, 'I had no other instrument...'

'May God forgive you,' said Christ smiling.

*

Dynamos and Gagliarda met on the appointed day and played a historic match. They were equally strong but, at the last minute, a cannon shot, fired God knows how from the centre forward of Gagliarda, ended up in the Dynamos' net and the crowd went mad.

'Your tonic helped us a lot,' Don Camillo said, smiling at Peppone. 'It's a shame you didn't use our metal net.'

Lungo's boys were already fighting with Don Camillo's boys and this vision of healthy sporting antagonism sweetened the bitter pill of defeat for Peppone.

He didn't answer, letting the provocation drop, but Don Camillo insisted:

'Don't worry too much, Mr Mayor: sometimes the dog runs and sometimes the hare runs.'

'And one fine day the priest will run too!' Peppone replied through gritted teeth.

'But you, Comrade,' Don Camillo insinuated, 'will you be in front of or behind the priest? That is the question.'

And, thinking about it, it was a question of no small import.

Music (1960)

IN HER NINETY years of life, Desolina Camatti had never given anything for nothing and, feeling close to the end, she sent for Don Camillo and said to him:

'Reverend, if you could visit me, I will give you the money you need for the new organ.'

Don Camillo was breathless with emotion: 'Desolina, speak freely.'

'For three million I want 6,000 Masses.'

Don Camillo mentally calculated:

'Even if I said one a day, it would take me almost seventeen years. I am too old for such a long commitment.'

'You are right, Reverend. I will speak to the parish priest of Torricella who is a young priest and has time ahead of him.'

'Desolina, I have been dreaming of the new organ for a century: 1,200!'

'Five thousand six hundred.'

It was a long fraught negotiation: Don Camillo concluded the arrangement with 2,000 Masses, but he had to make a written commitment. The three million would be paid to him by the executor of Desolina's will, once the organ was completed.

Having thus concluded her final business on this earth, Desolina Camatti went to the other world satisfied and Don Camillo's organ fever began.

At first he let it be known that it was simply a matter of repairing the old organ. And, for the testing of the new instrument, he chose a day when it was pouring with rain against a wind that would take your breath away so that the people, holed up at home, were not aware of it.

They would hear the new organ in all its glory at its inauguration and no one, as long as they lived, was to forget that day. The programme was grandiose because the committee had contributed money and Don Camillo had been able to secure the services of a famous organist.

The inauguration date was kept the strictest secret:

'The announcement,' Don Camillo explained during the last meeting of the committee, 'will be made next Monday. The posters are all ready and will arrive from the city on Sunday evening. The teams will unleash themselves throughout the Municipality at four o'clock the following morning, and people leaving their homes will find the posters right there, in front of their noses.'

Everything was prepared: advertisements in the newspapers, flyers, banners, car radio. For six days straight it would be a tremendous hammering. People were to come from every corner of the Municipality and not only would the church be full, but also the churchyard and the piazza.

'We will place a loudspeaker on the bell tower,' announced Don Camillo. 'The Reds will die of rage.'

Don Camillo never knew if what happened happened by pure chance or if there was a betrayal: the fact is that, on the Sunday morning, the village was plastered with posters as big as sheets. The municipal administration had them stuck up during the night to warn the citizens that at four o'clock on the following Sunday in the renovated local theatre there would be a colossal Verdi concert. Something never seen before, given the fame of the orchestra, the choir, the conductor and the soloists. All with free admission and on the same day and at the same time as the organ concert.

Don Camillo celebrated his first Mass in such a way that God forgave him only because he admitted serious provocation and partial infirmity of mind.

Alone, he opened his soul to the Crucified Christ above the High Altar:

'Lord,' he said, 'isn't it an infamy?'

'No,' replied Christ. 'I would say it is normal competition.'

Don Camillo raised his eyes to Heaven in amazement:

'Lord,' he exclaimed, 'competition exists among shopkeepers. The theatre is a shop, but this is the House of God. A theatre must not compete with the House of God.'

'Just so, Don Camillo, as long as, in the House of God, you do not organise shows like those in the theatre. If you put yourself on the level of "the show", you transform the House of God into a theatre and you cannot complain if another theatre opens in competition with you.'

Don Camillo spread his arms in desolation. 'Lord, has the propaganda for détente now reached all the way to Heaven?'

'Don Camillo, have you forgotten that you are speaking with your God?'

Don Camillo lowered his head. 'Forgive me,' he whispered humbly. 'As a poor country priest, I had believed that the function of a church organ was very different from that of an orchestra that performs in a theatre.'

'As long as it serves to bring the thoughts of the faithful closer to God, your organ is useful for sacred rites. Not when it distracts the minds of the faithful from thoughts of God. It is a question of measure, Don Camillo: the priest pours a few drops of wine into the chalice, he does not gulp down a jug each time.'

Don Camillo celebrated the eleven o'clock Mass more calmly and gave a gentle notice to the faithful:

'Brothers, next Sunday, at four in the afternoon, that curtain that has piqued your curiosity for so long will fall. His Excellency the Bishop will bless the new organ, due to the generosity of the late Desolina Camatti. At the end of the service, as you will learn from further communications, a famous organist will perform a concert of sacred music with the participation of the choir of the Academy of Santa Caterina and well-known solo singers. At the same time, the municipal administration is offering a show in the theatre, which will be attended by a high-ranking politician, sent specifically by the Communist headquarters in Rome, and his entourage. Everyone can make their own choice freely: I tell you this only to warn you that, behind Verdi are the Reds, so as to disabuse anyone convinced in good faith that he is paying homage to Verdi, for actually he is paying homage to the Reds.'

Peppone, informed by his secret service, responded with a poster that was distributed the next morning, together with an announcement of the organ concert. He spoke generically of a 'clerical clique', of furious attempts at 'sabotage' and concluded: 'Behind Verdi there is only the soul of the people of la Bassa that has in "the Swan of Roncole" its most faithful interpreter.[42] While the democratic administration sacrifices itself for the cultural well-being of the working people, the clergy, in its medieval obscurantism spends money better spent on the orphans of the parish – (the old organ was in any case fine).'

Don Camillo replied that he had received three million lire to give the church a new organ and could only use the money for that purpose. Unlike Peppone and his companions who, having obtained the mandate to administer the Municipality from its citizens, were involved in politics. And, to mask their manoeuvres, now used Verdi just as they had once used Garibaldi.

'Poor Peppino,'[43] concluded Don Camillo's response. 'He too is forced to work for détente!'

On Thursday, Peppone destroyed Don Camillo with an unexpected blow, having a poster affixed to street corners showing a reproduction of a photograph of a bearded gentleman, wearing a fur hat and a long fur coat down to his feet:

'Giuseppe Verdi in Petersburg in 1862 for the premiere of *La forza del destino* – ninety-eight years ago Verdi worked for détente!'

On Friday a red banner was pasted over the poster:

'Times change! Ninety-eight years ago, Italians went to Russia to play, now they go there to *be* played!'

---

[42] Giuseppe Verdi, world famous composer, son of the innkeeper of Roncole and, as a young man, organist at the village church, maintained a strong attachment to the rural landscape of his childhood, proud that he would always be 'a peasant from Roncole'.

[43] Peppino, not to be confused with Peppone, was Verdi's nickname.

On Saturday evening, Peppone, meeting Don Camillo face to face, told him his story: 'Reverend, you don't have to go all the way to Russia to be played. Keep provoking me and you'll see that you can be played here.'

'We should find the player,' Don Camillo replied. 'Not easy.'

'You don't have to have studied at the Conservatory to play a guy like you,' Peppone sneered.

Together with Peppone were the men of his general staff and they immediately put themselves between the two.

'Boss,' Smilzo warned him, 'don't lose sight of the conclusions of the Ninth Congress.'[44]

That was the end of it and it was a real stroke of luck because both Don Camillo and Peppone were swollen to bursting.

'We live in a democracy,' Brusco warned, 'and the people must decide. Tomorrow the people will say whether they prefer the Verdi of the Reds or the *biancofiore* of the clerics.'

*

The next morning Spring broke and the sky was an intense blue, like a tourist poster. At the eleven o'clock Mass, the church was packed and people were crowding the churchyard outside. Don Camillo did not abuse his triumph and simply mentioned the afternoon's event without going into details.

At midday he ate with an enviable appetite, then, around half past three, while the most zealous of his flock were arriving at the church, he set off with the men of the committee to meet and escort the Bishop.

A convoy of at least twenty cars, having reached the boundary line of the Municipality, turned about and drew up on the edge of the road to await his Excellency's appearance.

At four o'clock sharp, the procession, led by the Bishop's black limo, entered the village but, contrary to what Don Camillo had predicted, the piazza and churchyard were deserted.

---

[44] Smilzo, in response to détente, is all for getting back to basics, the fundamental principle of revolution to overthrow the existing order and establish a dictatorship of the working class, expressed by Lenin at the Ninth Congress of the Russian Communist Party, March 1920.

It was a hard blow, but it was even harder when Don Camillo entered the church: the last three rows of pews were empty and the others were occupied, for the most part, by the same old regulars.

Unveiled, the new organ was revealed in all its splendour – truly exceptional.

Then there was the consecration ritual, followed by a short speech from the Bishop. And, finally, the organ made its voice heard.

'Perhaps now they will all come,' thought Don Camillo. But no one did.

The playing was outstanding, the choir unmatched, the soloists stupendous: but the last three rows of pews remained empty.

Don Camillo, his heart full of anguish, at one point could no longer resist: *how* was it possible that the whole town had flocked to the theatre?

The names on Peppone's poster were big time certainly, but that did not explain the lack of interest in the organ concert. The names on Don Camillo's poster were also big.

Peppone, at the last moment, must have had a tip from the Devil. God knows what he had thought up to attract all the people to the theatre.

Gracefully he made himself scarce and, hopping on his bicycle, he himself headed for the theatre, crossing a depopulated village and arriving to find little different.

The old man from the bicycle shed was one of his parishioners. 'Look here,' he said, pointing to a small group of bicycles and motorcycles in a corner: 'just a handful. And in the car park, there are only those of the bigwigs who have arrived off the street. The theatre is, more or less, half a joke. And it's about top-notch musicians and singers.'

Don Camillo climbed back into the saddle. The saying, 'a shared pain is half a joy' held no recompense and, pedalling slowly, he continued to mull over the inexplicable phenomenon.

'Maybe the reason is that we *both* got it wrong,' he thought. 'The controversy annoyed people. They don't want to hear about politics anymore and we've turned it into a political issue...'

'So ... what?'

A rude voice distracted him from his meditations and reminded him that he was pedalling on a public road. He barely had time to lock the brakes and avoid hitting the cyclist whose voice he had heard.

'What are you thinking?' shouted the man who, also, had stopped his bike at the last minute and almost hit the wall.

'Perhaps just what you are thinking, Mr Mayor,' muttered Don Camillo.

Peppone muttered something incomprehensible, then asked angrily:

'Now that you have seen what you have seen, are you happy?'

'And what about you?'

Peppone roared: 'If Messina cries, Spartacus doesn't laugh. Misery loves company, double the disappointment.'

It wasn't the time to quibble about Spartacus and Messina: the concept was not wrong. [45]

At that moment a motorcyclist arrived, and it was Smilzo:

'Boss, exactly as I said,' he said. *'Tutti là!'*

*

The old Bishop was very happy: for him everything *had* worked out in the best possible way. But his Secretary thought differently and, at the end of the concert, told Don Camillo that, for something like this, it would be better not to bother His Excellency in the future.

'I don't think we could ask for more,' Don Camillo replied. 'The organist is a celebrity, the singers...'

---

[45] An Italian proverb related to the Peloponnesian War - victory achieved at great cost, where even the victor suffers and cannot truly celebrate. Peppone actually says: 'Se Messina piange, Spartaco non ride.' But Messina, a city in Sicily, has nothing to do with it. The war was fought mainly between Athens and Sparta. Usually, the saying is: 'Se Atene piange, Spartaco non ride'. But in the original version it is said to have been Messen*ia*, a region of the Peloponnesian peninsular, which cried. Wisely, Don Camillo accepts the concept of what Peppone, famous for his malapropisms, is pointing out and doesn't bother to get into a tangle by correcting him.

'I'm not talking about the concert,' the secretary interrupted him, 'I'm talking about the congregation. A half-empty church: Reverend, it's almost a disgrace!'

Don Camillo's horses bolted: 'And how could I have known that the whole town would flock to Trecastelli to hear Tony Dallara sing?' [46]

'What kind of world do you live in, Don Camillo? Don't you read the newspapers? Don't you hear what everyone is talking about?'

The Secretary was very annoyed, but even more annoyed was the Federation's agent who, at that moment, was saying to Peppone: 'Comrade, what kind of joke is this? You persecute me for a whole month forcing me to bring the Honourable from Rome and then you perform something like this?'

'Like *this*?' protested Peppone. 'A Verdi concert with top-notch performers!'

'It would have been better if they had been third-rate, but with a few more people in the room. Politically, it's a slap in the face. Lack of organisation, lack of preparation.'

'It's not my fault if the whole town went to Trecastelli to hear Tony Dallara sing!'

'It is your fault: you have to take into account people's tastes. If you want to put on a show here and Tony Dallara is in Trecastelli, you have to hire, at the very least, Mina.'[47]

'I wanted to give a *Verdi* concert...'

'If the people want little songs, give them little songs.'

'But Verdi...'

'Verdi! When the people want Verdi, you'll give them Verdi.'

'We have to raise the cultural level of the people!'

'We have to raise, first of all, their political level,' the federal agent decreed. 'Then we'll think about the rest. Comrade, I don't like this discussion just as much as I didn't like this event.'

'I, on the other hand, did like it,' Peppone said through gritted teeth.

The federal officer turned pale:

---

[46] Famous popular singer of the day.

[47] Mina Anna Mazzini, 300 million records sold.

'Comrade,' he asked in an uncertain voice, 'what do you mean?'

'That we wanted to honour Verdi and we honoured him. If the Honourable doesn't feel honoured, haul off...'

He said exactly where the Honourable should have gone if he didn't feel honoured, and the federal officer asserted that it wasn't the most suitable place to continue a discussion of that kind.

'Comrade,' he concluded, 'I understand your admiration for Verdi: but you must care more about the Party than Verdi.'

Peppone looked at him. Ugly and so swollen with anger, he seemed even bigger than usual:

'I don't like the Party's music,' he stated in a dark voice. 'I prefer *Verdi's*.'

'Of course,' exclaimed the federal officer, trying to smile. 'Verdi is always Verdi. Here, we agree.'

Land to the Sharecroppers (1960)

'IT'S QUITE A SYSTEM,' Lorini muttered: 'they go on a demo protesting about their landowner using the landowner's tractor for which many of them haven't even begun to pay their share of ownership. Does that seem fair to you, Reverend?'

'Very fair,' Don Camillo replied.

The piazza, beyond the columns of the churchyard, was full of tractors that glittered in the sun, and each tractor had its own placard: 'Land to those who work it', 'No room for two owners on the farms!', 'We want 70% now and all the land tomorrow', 'The Middle Ages are over'. And so on.

This was the second wave of protests against landowners. The plan had been scrutinised by city 'experts' and the matter threatened to drag on, mainly because the sharecroppers enjoyed driving around on tractors cocking a snook at the landowners; especially on Sunday mornings, as they had nothing to do, for they didn't go to church and the land was rotten with water.

Every Sunday it was the turn of a different municipality. The sharecroppers would meet in the square of the capital township of a neighbouring municipality and any likely smaller villages along their way.

At that very moment, from the window of the presbytery dining room, Don Camillo was admiring tractors arriving from villages in the municipality of Solagna and, with his binoculars, trying to decipher the placards hoisted on the front of each tractor engine.

'I would say this is not fair at all!' exclaimed Lorini.

'On the contrary, it is very fair,' affirmed Don Camillo, withdrawing.

'When the Master is stupid, he should be treated like a fool.'

'And what, in your opinion, should the poor Master do?' persisted Lorini. 'Take up a gun and send the sharecropper back home?'

'No guns. The Master must simply enforce his rights.'

'Yes, well, "rights" is but a word, Reverend. It seems that sharecroppers have rights and the masters have only duties.'

'Don't you believe it,' Don Camillo cut him short. 'Grotti is Red as fire but you certainly don't see him here on *my* tractor.'

Lorini shrugged and went away rather dejected, but the following Sunday morning, he reappeared at the presbytery with the look of a lottery winner.

Don Camillo, who was preparing a Spring chicken *cacciatore* on the kitchen stove and was completely absorbed in his delicate task, sensed him coming up behind him, recognising Lorini by his panting:

'Today it's the ones from *our* municipality on duty,' the man exclaimed.

'I do know,' Don Camillo replied without turning around. 'So what?'

'All five of my sharecroppers are here with all five tractors!…'

'Of course!' Don Camillo chuckled.

'And Grotti is here with *your* tractor!' Lorini shouted, his voice triumphant and his eyes sparkling with joy because there is nothing in the world that cheers up a farmer from la Bassa as much as seeing another farmer in trouble like he was. Farmers were afraid that the Reds would take away their land, but the real suffering of the individual farmer was the thought that some landowners would manage to get away with it and not him.

Don Camillo owned a farm that his father had left him and it was very small: nothing compared to Lorini's 500 *biolche*, but he owned land and, therefore, he fell into the category of farmer.

He forgot about the cacciatore and made for the living room, grabbing his binoculars and taking up a position at the window.

The tractors were all already lined up in the piazza and the sharecroppers, having hoisted their placards into position, waited motionless with folded arms and with the grit of an October Revolution, legs planted wide apart on the pavement, each in front of his own machine.

'Grotti is right in the front row,' Lorini informed him. 'Fourth one from the left. As soon as that little truck passes, you'll see it, Reverend.'

The little truck passed and Don Camillo saw what he never wanted to see: *his* sharecropper leading the demo in front of *his* tractor.

He looked again in case he'd made a mistake, but he couldn't be mistaken because faces like Grotti's aren't mass-produced and, as for the tractor, it was the only 'Porsche' in the municipality.

'Words are all very well,' Lorini chuckled. 'But, in practice, you see that, in certain situations, being stupid rather than intelligent doesn't matter much.'

'Oh yes it does!' Don Camillo shouted.

*

Word had spread like lightning by Peppone's men, the news bouncing from mouth to mouth, causing the whole village to rush to the piazza:

'Don Camillo's sharecropper is here too!....', 'That one with the red tractor!....', 'Yes, the one with the placard, "Get the capitalist exploiters off our farms"!....'

Peppone was bursting with joy: he had gone to Grotti himself to invite him to take part in the parade and had also made him understand deep down that, if he ever burned his straw hat, no one would save him with a comb-over. Then, once he'd seen him appear in the piazza at the wheel of the 'Porsche', he had assigned him a position in the front row, where Don Camillo would be certain to notice.

Grotti was quick on the uptake and a man of few words. In difficult situations Peppone knew he could count on him: however, from the beginning he had spoken clearly about the possible downside:

'Boss, if you don't want us to get into serious trouble, don't put me in conflict with the priest because he is tough and I am tougher and, if we clash, it will end with one dead man.'

Nevertheless, Peppone's calm reasoning had convinced him, and he hadn't tried to duck out:

'Let him and all the priests in the universe die. On Sunday *I* will be there.'

Now he was standing there, gloomy, with his arms across his chest, waiting: but Don Camillo could not bring himself to stick his nose out of the presbytery.

When he did appear, the people had lost all hope of a confrontation.

With his sleeves rolled up and pushing a cart he headed straight for Grotti and, when he was within two of his feet, he stopped without even looking at him and took a jack and two pieces of elm down from the cart. He placed the jack under the rear axle of the tractor and lifted the left wheel just enough to position one of the two elm trunks so that it remained two fingers off the ground. Then he grabbed the wheel brace and began to unscrew the hub nuts.

Grotti went pale and, lowering his arms, clenched his fists, but Peppone put himself between him and Don Camillo.

'Reverend,' he asked, 'what are you doing?'

'This tractor is half mine and half the sharecropper's,' Don Camillo replied, without stopping his work. 'I do not intend allowing my half to be involved in politics and I'll remove it from the demonstration.'

The crowd had closed in around the tractor, and Peppone kept his cool:

'Reverend,' he said with a great show of sarcasm, 'have you not noticed that the world is moving to the Left?'

'No,' muttered Don Camillo, continuing to unscrew the nuts. 'I was lost in thought and it must have slipped my mind.'

The rear left wheel was now free: Don Camillo took it off the axle and loaded it onto the cart. A rear wheel from a thirty-five horsepower tractor is quite a weight, but at that moment Don Camillo would have lifted the entire tractor without saying, 'Bay,' such was the pressure he was under.

He took out the jack and went to lift the front left wheel, blocking the axle with the other piece of elm.

He took that wheel off in a few minutes, then dismantled the left headlight.

'Of course,' he exclaimed as if speaking to himself, 'now they will say that the clergy is in league with large-scale industry to seize control of energy sources. But really, can you expect a poor country priest to take the dynamo apart?'[48]

Instead, he loosened the clamps and removed the battery. Then he spread his arms and explained, turning to Peppone:

'You, who are a specialist technician, know perfectly well that it is not easy to divide a tractor into two equal parts because you would have to saw off the pistons, the connecting rods,

---

[48] In a 1950s tractor, as the engine turned, the dynamo's primary function was to charge the battery by converting mechanical energy into electrical energy, and so operate the tractor's electrical systems, lights, ignition, etc.

the camshafts and a lot of other stuff. However, given that it is, more than anything, a *symbolic* division, I believe that, by removing this part, the principle of what is happening here is clear.'

Grotti groaned and was about to spring forward, but Peppone stopped him:

'Let him do it!' he said through gritted teeth.

'But he's disassembling the cylinder head!' the anguished Grotti panted.

Don Camillo was dripping with sweat but it was clear that, if some nut had not loosened, he would have crumbled it by biting it.

The people watched the operation with bated breath and it was Peppone who broke the embarrassing silence:

'What a pity,' he exclaimed, shaking his big head. 'If, instead of being a priest, you had been a mechanic, you would today have an honourable profession.'

Don Camillo did not answer and continued to fumble with the nuts; then, finally, having removed the cylinder head, he turned to Peppone and showed it to him:

'Here is the basic difference,' he explained. 'While if you remove the head of an internal combustion engine it no longer works, a headless communist can yet function as Mayor.'

A guffaw rose from the crowd that made Peppone lose his home address.

Don Camillo, having placed the cylinder head of the 'Porsche' on the cart, turned to Grotti:

'I should also remove the gearbox, the differential, the cooling device, the starter motor, the injectors, the tank, etc. because, of the twelve instalments of your half, you have only reimbursed me the first two: but I don't want to be picky. Now, you can go wherever you like.'

Pushing his cart, Don Camillo walked resolutely toward the presbytery without turning around, and it was a triumphal march.

A roar from Peppone drowned out the squawking of people's reaction, engines roared and, when Don Camillo had unloaded his cart into the shed, he went to look out the window of the living room once more. Only Grotti's 'Porsche' remained in the piazza. As it were blind in one eye and with two wooden legs, it brought to mind the retreating Napoleonic army crossing the Berezina River in November 1812.

Never before had so many people been seen in the piazza and, within half an hour, the first tourists began to arrive from villages of neighbouring municipalities to enjoy the extraordinary spectacle.

For the eleven o'clock Mass, Don Camillo's church was packed to the rafters.

'Lord,' he said to the Crucified Christ above the High Altar, when, after Mass, he found himself alone in the church, 'if I made a mistake, forgive me. The flesh is weak even if it is the flesh of a minister of God. When I saw Grotti with my tractor among the others, a thick fog descended before my eyes…'

'What a pity!' whispered Christ.

Peppone's counterattack was inevitable and, in fact, it was launched early that afternoon: Smilzo showed up at the gate of the presbytery with a piece of paper.

'Municipal messenger in his capacity as a public official,' he began. 'Penalty Notice. Violation: illegal occupation of public land. Order hereby to vacate.'

Don Camillo was unmoved: 'It's not my stuff,' he replied. 'I brought the part that was mine here. Return to sender. Contact Comrade Grotti.'

'If you don't take that carcass away, we'll have it removed and send you the bill.'

'That doesn't bother me,' Don Camillo concluded, turning his back on him. 'If it bothers your Party, sort it out yourselves.'

In truth, the Porsche with wooden legs that was playing the clown in the piazza *was* bothering Peppone big time, and after Don Camillo had ignored the Notice he was scratching his head to find a way to get rid of the provocative wreck. Which was when Grotti surfaced.

'Boss,' the sharecropper muttered, 'what are we going to do about the tractor?'

He couldn't have appeared at a worse moment. Peppone thumped his paw down on the desk and shouted:

'And what do *you* want to do? Leave it there!'

'I can't. My cousin has to use it tomorrow.'

'Go to hell. The tractor is *yours.*'

'I wish! The tractor is his...'

Peppone looked at him in amazement and asked him what the hell he was on about.

'It's not a happy story, boss. I wanted to obey your orders and, at the same time, not get into trouble with the priest. My cousin who is a tenant in the municipality of Torricella has a tractor identical to mine. I borrowed it. If the priest had kept quiet and done nothing, no problem. If he had protested, I would then have replied that, with my cousin's tractor, I can do whatever I want... Don Camillo didn't notice the licence plate: it's small and I had camouflaged it with oil and muck. He fell for it like a blackbird, but when he came out, at the last moment, because you intervened and I didn't have the courage to speak up, I was in it up to my neck...'

Peppone, without more than a moment's hesitation, jumped to his feet: 'And so,' he panted 'that guy took apart a tractor that wasn't his and took the parts home!'

*

Peppone didn't even wait for anyone to come to the presbytery door: he marched straight in and surprised Don Camillo who, sitting in front of the window, was miles away, admiring the spectacle in the piazza.

'Reverend!' roared Peppone. 'It's four in the afternoon and the worst scoundrel in the village and the surrounding area is still disembowelling himself in front of Grotti's half-tractor. Now it's our turn: now we'll start laughing.'

'And why would that be, Mr Mayor?'

'Because in the next Act the priest goes and gets out the cart, takes the pieces back to the tractor and puts them back in place, *because*, I explain to the amusement of the working people, the priest made a silly mistake and dismantled not his own tractor but that of his sharecropper's cousin.'

Don Camillo started laughing: 'You're crazy, Comrade.'

Peppone showed him the registration document that Grotti had given him:

'Seeing is believing, Reverend. Check the licence plate number and then get going with reassembly. Today, *you're the double bill.*'

Don Camillo looked at the registration document, sent a boy to take down the licence plate number of the engine, listened to the story that Grotti had told Peppone, then gave the registration document back:

'You're crazy, Comrade.'

'You still don't believe that the tractor belongs to your sharecropper's cousin?'

'I believe it. But you're crazy just the same. No double bill. Paganini doesn't repeat.'[49]

'Well then, in ten minutes I'll run to Torricella, bring Grotti's cousin here, have him write up a theft complaint and send the police to your house. Yes, I know, you'll get away with it, they won't put you in jail. Priests never go to jail. But the newspapers will talk about it and the whole world will laugh.'

Don Camillo threw up his arms: 'God's will be done. Do as you wish, Comrade, but I won't give you the satisfaction of watching me go into the piazza and reassemble the tractor. This morning I won *as a landlord.* Now I'll not be defeated *as a priest.*'

'The usual story, Reverend: when a priest breaks down, we have to forgive the weakness of the man. When a priest has to pay, we have to respect his dignity. This time, both of you pay: the man and the priest. I give you half an hour: if you haven't started work by four thirty-five, I'll leave for Torricella and light the fuse.'

Peppone darted away and Don Camillo saw him, shortly after, running across the piazza.

He stood up, brought down the curtain and went to confide in Christ above the High Altar:

'Lord,' he said, 'you were right. It's a real shame that the fog fell before my eyes this morning. I was wrong and it is

---

[49] Niccolò Paganini, *Il violinista del diavolo*, was famous for not playing the same composition twice during the same performance, even after a request for an encore.

right that I pay, but not by putting on a public show in the piazza.'

'And this morning,' asked Christ, 'did you not put on a show then?'

'Yes, Lord: but I did so like a soldier who advances under fire. Now I would do it like a soldier who raises his arms and surrenders.'

'Don Camillo, is it perhaps pride that is speaking in you?'

'No, Lord, it is a precise sense of my responsibility. I will not allow anyone to make a minister of God look ridiculous. Not even myself.'

*

Peppone looked at the clock on the bell tower: it was about to strike midnight. It had to be considered that the half hour was up.

'That damned man hasn't shown up and there's no need to show mercy,' he said to Grotti, who had been keeping him company since four in the afternoon at a table in the restaurant in the arcade.

The piazza was deserted because, on top of everything else, it had started to rain and the wooden-legged tractor seemed even more unhappily abandoned.

'You go home. Tomorrow morning I'll go see your cousin and sort everything out. Sleep soundly.'

Grotti walked away and Peppone headed home.

He was dead tired and, as soon as he got into bed, he fell into a deep sleep.

That night he had a very strange dream: he was in bed and heard someone throwing pebbles against the lattice of his window.

He got up and, half-opening the shutters, he saw, in the street, a priest as black as coal.

'What do you want?' Peppone asked him.

'I have an urgent job to do...'

'You do it, it's two in the morning.'

'If they called me at two in the morning because you're dying, I wouldn't make a fuss and I'd run to bring you the Holy Oil.'

'I'd do it too, if you were the one dying!'

'At least tell me what I should do about the head.'

'What head?'

'I've already put the wheels, the headlight, the battery back in place, but I can't fix the cylinder head. Should I try to file it down a bit, or will it be enough to hit it with a hammer?'

Hearing such craziness, even though it was a dream, Peppone let out a shout:

'Don't do anything stupid!'

Then he got out of bed and, still in his dream, followed the priest. In the middle of the piazza they found a tractor and, struggling like slaves, they managed to push it to Peppone's workshop. There, after a lot of work, Peppone had managed to reassemble the cylinder head and get the engine of the tractor going.

A curious dream because the next morning when he left the house around six and arrived in the piazza, he found it completely empty – not even a shadow of the famous tractor.

'The bully had to swallow the pill!' Peppone rejoiced. 'He waited until night so as not to be a laughing stock.'

At that moment, someone arrived on a motorcycle. It was Grotti carrying a bundled-up Don Camillo on the motorbike's fender.

When the priest piled off, Grotti went away without a word and Peppone found himself face to face with his nemesis once more:

'Good work,' said Don Camillo. 'Send your invoice tomorrow.'

'Invoice?' Peppone muttered. 'I don't know what you're talking about, Reverend. I've never had dealings with a priest. When the time comes I will present you with the bill for sure and it will be hard to pay.'

'I can imagine,' replied Don Camillo. 'Fixing a priest's head is much more difficult than fixing that of a diesel engine.'

It had stopped raining and it seemed that the sky was clearing down there behind the poplars, where the sun, for God knows how many billions of centuries, has gotten into a habit of rising.

Peppone Has a Problem (1960)

T HE REVOLUTION BROKE out in the city and, among the teams
that fought with the *carabinieri* and the police, there was
– unfortunately – Peppone's youth athletic team, known as
Giovanile Atletica.

'Unfortunately', not because of their behaviour, but because
one of the team's athletes did not return to base.

The boys had been trained and commanded by Falchetto,
the toughest and most cunning of Peppone's gang, and they
fought like champions. That is, they did not allow themselves
to be so taken by the pleasure of smashing policemen's heads
with stones that they forgot that they had, in addition to a
heart, a brain. Thus, they concluded the only truly organic
operation of the day.

They fought in no particular order, of course, but within a
well-defined radius of action, moving forward, backward or to
the side only when Falchetto moved. He acted as the linchpin
of the affair. At a simple signal from him, the team was ready in
an instant for mass intervention.

In the city square, things were going badly for the police and a
group of *guardia*, called on duty as riot police, were on the point
of being eliminated because insurgents were squeezing them from
three sides, pushing them from the front to pin them against the
façade of a building, on the roof of which more insurgents were
preparing to bury them under an avalanche of tiles.

Reinforcements arrived; the *guardia* jumped off their
four trucks, ran to reach their comrades in difficulty and the

encirclement broke. The insurgents, in order not to be taken from behind, dispersed and even those on the roof of the building, having rained down their tiles, had to skedaddle to prevent being trapped up there.

The four trucks that brought the reinforcements had stopped at the edge of the square had been in the custody of a small detail of *guardia* who escaped the notice of insurgents caught up in the heat of battle, but not of Falchetto.

A whistle blew and Falchetto's team mustered. Three minutes later all but four lads were on the move. Once within range, they engaged those guarding the first three trucks head-on, with a furious launch of stones and Molotov cocktails.

Meanwhile, the four kept back and led personally by Falchetto, swept around and behind their position, pressing the guards of the fourth truck ever tighter and leaving with bloodied faces. Meanwhile another lad, having reached a truck on his hands and knees, jumped into the cabin and took off at full speed.

Like a lightning god he reached the square, dodging torn-up paving slabs, barricades of tables and chairs, and trucks that were burning belly up, and performed a gymkhana to give a champion pony club goose bumps. It was not clear what was in his head and where he wanted to end up, but he seemed never to be in doubt. At a certain point the fellow slammed the accelerator to the floor and headed straight for the group of *guardia* leaning against the façade of the building, then, locking the steering wheel, bailed out of the truck.

He should have broken his neck, but he didn't, he only twisted his leg, and Falchetto was already running to haul him out of trouble.

The truck crashed into the building emitting a tremendous report. That none of the *guardia* ended up flattened against the wall, was due to a concrete slab, placed there by the Eternal Father, causing the vehicle to veer a trifle to the right, an event that amply repaid Peppone for the trouble the idea of establishing a youth athletic team within the Section had caused him.

*

The idea, in truth, had not been Peppone's. He had been thinking of something completely different when he received the now legendary circular announcing that Central Management had decided to inaugurate an Inter-Federal Athletics Trophy, in which the representatives of all Sections were to participate, in order to encourage a healthy sense of antagonism in its youth.[50]

'The clericals are becoming more and more powerful, the comrades are becoming bourgeois and those of Rome are taking us for fools!' was Peppone's disgusted comment.

Then, since the circular invited the heads of each Section to go immediately to the Federation to obtain the necessary briefing, Peppone went to the city and, upon his return, was just dying of happiness.

'It's a great idea,' he explained to his general staff. 'The federations will provide the equipment and reimburse out-of-pocket expenses. Each municipal section will form a team, train it and straightway the contests for the provincial championship will be held in the city. As soon as each federation has selected its ten best teams, they will send them to compete with the representatives of the other municipalities in the region. Then, at a later date, the ten representatives of each region will meet for the title of national champion.'

Falchetto wrinkled his nose: 'So, in two years, when the tournament is over, the champion team will be able to go to the Vatican, accompanied by its Bishop, to receive the Pope's blessing and a holy card.'

Peppone shook his head: 'You're wrong, Comrade. The matter will be undertaken far quicker, because you, this very evening, will

[50] In 1960, Italy was still governed by the Christian Democracy party, with support from smaller parties. In March, the party faced a crisis when it received support from the neo-fascist Italian Social Movement (MSI). Protests led to armed police charges against anti-fascist demonstrators, some of which resulted in fatalities. Armed 'Red assault squads', disguised as sports teams, emerged as a result. Tensions arose throughout Italy, but Guareschi took his cue for this story from particular events in Rome – police charges against demonstrators of anti-fascist partisan associations, in which the police killed five people.

bring before me twenty of the Giovanile Atletica, and tomorrow morning you will go to the Federation to pick up equipment, and the day after tomorrow you will begin training. Then, in ten days time, you'll accompany your team to the city where it will meet with the other municipal representatives. Workdays missed by the lads will be reimbursed: there are no problems because everything is foreseen and sorted in the competition regulations.'

Falchetto went away muttering that he didn't even know where athletics and other such nonsenses were undertaken, but reading the rules cleared his mind and, that same evening, he introduced the twenty young athletes to Peppone.

These were boys who seemed tailor-made for just the type of sport envisaged: they immediately got down to it with fire in their bellies and, after a week of gruelling training, they left promptly for the city.

There they stayed for five days and fought like lions. Between one match and another, their comrades from the Federation took them around the city showing them the most important monuments: the Prefecture building and police HQ, the brick and stone warehouses, hardware stores, sporting goods and weapons shops, Party HQ, etc, not forgetting to gen them up diligently on the topography, place names and technical characteristics of the various types of road paving.

In short, the boys from Peppone's 'Giovanile Atletica' returned to the village so shrewdly deep-laid with their training that, when, in due course, Falchetto gave them a whistle, they jumped on their motorcycles and, travelling singly along different roads, all twenty of them found themselves in the city at the agreed place and time and undertook the aforesaid little bit of stuff.

Unfortunately, one of the boys did not return to base. At a certain moment the *guardia* and the *carabinieri*, in order not to get killed, made their machine guns sing and Rossetto took a bullet in the middle of his forehead and died.

*

In the city they gave him, together with another four unfortunates, a great funeral, attended by important political figures from Rome. In the front row were the big shots of the Party who had organised the Athletics Tournament, plus the representatives of all the federations, the unions and so on.

Peppone was there, of course, and when the funeral was over, he brought Rossetto's body back home to the village.

Before leaving, he had given strict orders to his staff: 'I want a historic demonstration. Not one of us will be absent. There will be representatives of all the Sections of the Municipality, with flags. Representatives of the democratic parties. Make the herd of non-Party members understand that anyone who is not in the procession will be blacklisted as an enemy of the people. I want, lined up on the embankment road, two kilometres of people, packed like flies. When I arrive with the hearse, the coffin will be unloaded and carried on shoulders to the cemetery, first passing through the village. The people will form a line as the coffin passes and then fall in-line. I want perfect order. I want drapes or flags in black at every window. And as soon as the hearse arrives on the embankment, I want the bells to begin to toll for the dead and continue for the entire duration of the funeral. No speeches: what the bells have to say will make the enemies of the people tremble with fear. I will allow no excuses: if you run into difficulties, smooth them out with slaps.'

His general staff got busy and, since the people sensed that they were capable any moment of playing dirty, they did not need to get heavy.

Smilzo, Brusco and Bigio went to Don Camillo: they found him in the presbytery garden and Smilzo confronted him with a mean face:

'The police under orders of your government have murdered Rossetto. As soon as you receive my order, ring the bell for the dead and continue until they tell you to stop. And when the funeral passes through the piazza, behave like the other shopkeepers: close the door of your shop.'

Don Camillo spread his arms wide: 'I'm sorry, but I can only ring the bells for the dead who attend church. If you don't want the priest, you can't have the bell ringer either.'

Smilzo began to shout: 'The *de profundis* has already been sounded by the machine guns of your associates!'[51]

'I have no associates.'

'By refusing to ring the bells, you are insulting the dead!'

'By burying the dead with a civil funeral, you are insulting God.'

Bigio intervened: 'Reverend, in this way you are siding with the assassins!'

'I am siding with God.'

'You haven't quite realised the particular political situation of the moment,' insisted Bigio. 'Think again. The dead man's teammates are difficult to handle and we don't know if we'll be able to stop them from coming to ring your bells.'

'Don't worry,' Don Camillo decided. 'I'll stop them.'

A few minutes later, Don Camillo, having climbed up to the bell tower, pulled up the bell ropes and lowered the trap door, blocking it with a beam: so, when Smilzo, Bigio and Brusco returned to hear if he had changed his mind and saw him up there, looking out of the large window overlooking the piazza, they understood that the bells would not be delivering the dreadful utterance Peppone had in mind for the enemies of his people. So, *he* had to speak instead and it wasn't really a great speech, except for its truly unexpected conclusion:

'Citizens, to defend their sacred rights threatened by clerical arrogance, workers fight battles by staining the piazzas generously with their blood, but we must not forget that, to win a war, great actions are not enough: small and bloodless ones are also needed.

'Citizens, you have all grasped the symbolic meaning of the clock that we have installed on the façade of the town hall. It means that, if the one on the church bell tower marks the hour of "God-follow-me", the one on the Town Hall will mark the hour of "let's-be-done-with-it"! The Town Hall's clock will strike the Hour of Redemption, which is not far away.

---

[51] The 'De Profundis' bell rings 'out of the deep' (Psalm 130) in a slow, solemn tolling to remind the faithful to pray for the deceased and souls in purgatory.

'Today the clergy can raise its voice in every sector because it holds the bell monopoly and bangs at will. Here the barbaric dominion will end and the people will have their voice! For we too will be able to ring a big bell, our bell. To rally the people. To celebrate their victories. To warn them of danger. To pay homage to their glorious fallen. To greet the radiant day of final victory! Citizens, our bell, with its powerful voice, will make the stones of the old mediaeval manors vibrate, flushing out the black clerical owls from their holes and forcing them to face the light of day...'

*

A civic tower went up in a flash because anti-clericals of every hue liked the idea and coughed up the necessaries.

Square, squat and built of exposed brick, it did have something threatening about it. Once up, the clock was transferred from the façade of the Town Hall.

Then, the denouement – the arrival of the big bell.

Don Camillo caught his breath when he saw it. It was enormous, as tall as a man and with a sound bow that was chasmic.

There was to be nothing at all inside the tower other than this bell, which would be lifted in three stages by a colossal hoist. After the first lift, the carpenters would place a supporting beam under the bell. Then, having installed the hoist higher up, the process was to be repeated a second and third time.

'Three stages – like Sputnik was launched with a three-stage rocket!' observed Smilzo, while they were hooking the hoist to the upper brackets of the bell.

'Sputnik!' exclaimed Peppone. 'Sputnik! There's the bell christened!'

When all was ready, he chased everyone out of the tower except the men operating the winch chain.

'I don't want the slightest noise,' he shouted. 'The first one who speaks I will strangle!'

The hoist chain tightened and even the people gathered in front of the tower held their breath, as very slowly, Sputnik was lifted off the ground.

In a minute it reached a height of one metre, in another, two metres. The first stage was supposed to end at five metres altitude, but when it reached three and a half, a scream was heard that made the people's blood run cold: the hook of the hoist had broken and the scream had come from one of the men operating the winch chain.

The poor guy had wanted to say: 'Peppone, get out of there or the big bell will fall on you!', but he only managed to let out a high-pitched, heart-rending wail.

The massive bell fell to the ground, which as yet had no floor, and the great poundage made the houses all around quake.

The bell, planted a hand's breadth into the ground, remained upright. People ran to it and crowded around it, stunned as if petrified into a fossilised form.

Don Camillo arrived, panting.

'Who?' he asked.

'Peppone,' they said as one.

'Where is he?'

'Under the bell.'

Don Camillo's angry shout woke them up and they all set to work furiously. They managed to hook the bell to the hoist chain again and when Sputnik began to rise, the people retreated in horror and closed their eyes.

Don Camillo, however, opened his ever wider, and throwing himself flat on the ground, took up a position. As soon as the mouth of Sputnik was half a metre from the ground, he jumped up, plunging his hands under the rim, grabbing what he found under his fingers and giving a tug that would have uprooted a pillar.

Peppone was curled up on the ground like a porcupine, in a desperate attempt to make himself smaller, all his nerves taut, tense and ready to break.

As he arose from his bronze tomb, he hit his head on the sound bow of Sputnik and the bell vibrated. It was a good head-butt, enough to bring him back to his senses. He looked around in amazement, but he was alive and intact, and the people let out a cheer that threatened never to stop.

*

It was a week later that the bell finally reached the top of the tower, because Peppone had to stay in bed for four days due to delayed-action terror.

It was with a lump the size of a walnut on top of his head, but fever-free, victorious and very proud, that he climbed up the tower and gave the inaugural blow of the clapper to Sputnik…

Unfortunately, it sounded more like he'd given a hammer blow to a sheet metal pot. Down he went to the floor in a fury black as a priest's cassock, and having pushed his way through the crowd in the piazza, he explained:

'The bell, she must have died when she fell.'

'No,' said Don Camillo, who was, by chance, right there. 'In my opinion, Mr Mayor, you made her die with that head-butt you gave her while I was pulling you out.'

Peppone stopped and turned:

'Thank you for your intervention, Reverend. But you didn't have to bother: I would have gotten out just fine even without your help.'

'I don't doubt that. I don't know, however, if you would have gotten out without God's help.'

'I did not ask myself the question,' replied Peppone very firmly.

*

A week later, at three in the morning, a man was struggling along the road that leads to a certain shrine, the destination of great pilgrimages. He had been walking for a while and was dead tired because he had travelled twenty kilometres, and he still had twenty-five to go.

A cyclist emerged from a small side road and passed him, but then stopped abruptly.

'Are you travelling on foot, Mr Mayor?' the cyclist asked.

'Yes.'

'Can I help at all?'

'No.'

The cyclist got off his bike and walked alongside the traveller.

'If you don't mind, I'll keep you company.'

'I feel bad…'

'We are born to suffer, Mr Mayor.'

'I'd say that you priests were born to *make* us suffer, Reverend Father.'

'It just so happens... What a coincidence that we bumped into each other here, at this hour?'

'No: you've been spying on me for a week.'

'I cannot deny it: I was curious to know if you had asked yourself that question yet, and if so what answer you received.'

'Reverend, there is a God for everyone,' Peppone muttered.

'Unfortunately, yes, Mr Mayor.'

Don Camillo said, 'unfortunately', but thought 'fortunately'.

They walked in silence because it is precisely out of silence that the most interesting conversations are crafted.

The Black Sheep (1960)

THE LONG PEACE ended and suddenly the air warmed up.
In the riots that had broken out in the city, five Reds had been struck by police machine guns, and since one of the five belonged to Peppone's 'Flying Squad', it seemed like we had returned to the hard times of the immediate post-war period, to the days of suspicion and fear.

'With the help of God, today went well too,' Don Camillo said every evening to the Crucified Christ. 'But what will happen tomorrow, if you don't prevent the Devil from putting one of his abominable ideas into the skull of some wretch tonight?'

Don Camillo had good reason to be worried: Peppone and his men, swollen to bursting, were just waiting for a pretext to unleash an earthquake.

It went on like this for about a week and, when it seemed that the situation was finally returning to normal, some lunatic painted a large swastika in tar right on the front of the Town Hall.

The street cleaner noticed it early one morning and ran immediately to warn Peppone, who didn't even finish his coffee, and having gathered the general staff, gave the necessary directives, setting an outbreak of popular indignation for eleven thirty.

At the appointed time, the piazza was packed and Peppone, after having thoughtfully admired the swastika, turned to the people and stated:

'Even though they painted it on the town hall and even though our administration is run by communists, it doesn't affect me as Mayor or as a communist. It affects me simply as a citizen. This infamous symbol is an insult and a challenge to all democratic citizens. Fascism, with the complicity of the clerical government, is showing its claws again: we will cut them off!...'

An anti-fascist front was formed *ipso facto* and, towards evening, the members of the committee appeared before Don Camillo.

'I hope,' Peppone said solemnly, 'that faced with the fascist threat the clergy will also make common cause with honest and sensible people.'

Don Camillo looked at the characters in Peppone's entourage one by one, then replied calmly:

'Exactly. I make common cause with honest and sensible people, who I don't see among you, because sensible people wouldn't take a scribble daubed on a wall seriously. Two brush strokes of tar cannot constitute a danger.'

'Behind the hand that drew that symbol,' Peppone shouted, 'there is a whole criminal organisation that must be unmasked and destroyed.'

'For me, there is simply an isolated idiot,' Don Camillo replied.

'Or maybe a priest,' Smilzo insinuated in an aggressive tone.

'The priest is behind this hand which, if you don't get out of the way right now, will slap you across the face,' Don Camillo remarked, taking a step forward and waving a huge hand as big as a shovel under Smilzo's nose.

Falchetto, who was the leader of the Red Flying Squad, chuckled:

'You can scratch my backside with that hand if you want.'

'Let's not beat around the bush!' Peppone shouted, grabbing Falchetto by the collar and pulling him back. 'We've learned all we needed to know.'

Don Camillo had guts, but he also had a good nose. On a different occasion, Falchetto would have left the presbytery with his head full of bumps as big as walnuts. If, instead, he left with the same head as when he entered, it was because Don Camillo felt that the rope was already tight enough to snap.

Once the committee members had left, Don Camillo went to vent his anger with Christ above the High Altar:

'Lord, I am sure of it: there is no organisation behind this. There are only some wretches who enjoy playing with fire. Lord, will you not enlighten their minds?'

'Don Camillo, you are the shepherd of this flock. The good shepherd must know his sheep, each one. It is up to the good shepherd to bring a lost sheep back to the right path. The good shepherd must have eyes that see even in the dark to be able to unmask the wolf that prowls the flock hidden in the sheep's clothing, even to prevent the black sheep taking advantage of its night-coloured fleece, wandering around the sheepfold to sow discord.'

'Lord,' exclaimed Don Camillo, 'if there is a black sheep that goes around at night causing trouble, I know who it might be.'

*

Dario Camoni had had his own set of troubles with the Reds, but he hadn't budged an inch.

They wanted to make him admit his error and, to convince him, they beat him with sticks and even put him up against a wall pretending to execute him, but they didn't get a thing out of him.

'The more you beat me,' said Camoni, 'the more I'm convinced that I was right in judging you a gang of murderers.'

They didn't give him the satisfaction of killing him perhaps partly because tough guys have a secret respect for tough guys.

'Die on your own, you damned bastard,' they told him as they let him go free. 'But don't show up in town again, or we'll put you in the wine press and reduce you to a cake of grape marc.' [52]

Six months later, Camoni had returned already, but since he was busy restoring his large farm, which had been reduced to ruins, and was staying away from the village, the Reds pretended not to notice.

Time was when Dario Camoni had not only seen Peppone off, he had even forced Don Camillo to swallow half a pint of castor oil.[53]

The taste had stuck to Don Camillo's palate and, even after many years, Camoni was as indigestible to him as that oil.

If, during Mass he noticed his presence in the congregation, it would so disturb him that he would turn to the wrong page of the Missal, and on taking the wine at Communion (should God not help him to detach from miserable earthly affairs) his mind would turn to that cursed glass of oil.

Don Camillo found Camoni in a shed and, even before setting eyes on him, his well-tuned nose told him that he had not made a mistake in naming him as the black sheep. For Camoni was brushing tar on a barrel for the leachate[54] and it was the smell of the tar that convinced Don Camillo he was right.

Camoni continued his work without acknowledging the priest's appearance.

---

[52] A grape marc cake is made from the solid residue left after grapes are pressed for juice or wine.

[53] See 'The American Indian' (*Don Camillo and Peppone*, Pilot, 2016). The episode refers to the Fascist signature practice of forcing political enemies to drink castor oil.

[54] Any liquid that leaches from a substance as it passes through it.

'As long as it is used to paint barrels,' said Don Camillo, 'tar is fine. It is not good when it is used to daub filth on walls.'

The subtle communication left Camoni indifferent.

'*Errare humanum est, diabolicum perseverare*,' continued Don Camillo. 'Whoever drew the swastika in front of the Town Hall has committed a foolish act; if he persists in the act, he is openly declaring himself a scoundrel.'

Dario Camoni stood up slowly, wiped his hands with a rag and, enunciating each word, said:

'Whoever bothers Camoni is committing a foolish act. If he then persists, he is seriously imprudent.'

Don Camillo managed to keep calm:

'Camoni, you know what happened in the past few days...'

'I know what those wretches did to me for a few miserable slaps.'

'You know that the Reds suffered some deaths in their ranks...'

'Too few!' Camoni shouted, turning pale. His blood was poisoned and it was impossible to reason with him.

Don Camillo changed his tack.

'Only a madman like you could have painted that swastika on the wall. Be careful what you do, Camoni: the Reds are at the end of their tether.'

'Let them come here and I'll paint the swastika on their belly with a machine gun!'

'If your soul is so possessed by the Devil, what are you doing coming to church?'

'To see you, Reverend,' replied Camoni, 'and to confess myself stupid because, instead of castor oil, I didn't purge you with lubricating oil.'

Don Camillo grabbed a pole that was nearby and Camoni a large iron bar: but God hadn't lost sight of them and that was as far as it went.

*

The next morning, things became more complicated. Under a cloak of darkness and a storm that had broken out in the middle of the night, unknown hands had painted five more swastikas on various walls, plus phrases like 'Long live Fascism!', 'Death to the assassins of the Resistance!'

The anti-fascist front sprang up as one. In the evening there was a grand rally in the piazza, and gathered on a stage were not only Peppone and his men, but a number of representatives of other parties and even citizens without a party.

'The anti-fascist unity that brought us together in the war has been reconstituted,' shouted Peppone. 'Representation by the clergy is conspicuous by its absence because, for clericals, the fascist danger does not exist. And let's be honest, they are damn sorry that it does not exist! After all, a priest's cassock is nothing more than a blackshirt pulled out of his trousers...'

'Jesus,' Don Camillo implored, turning to Christ above the High Altar, 'what good did it do me to have identified the black sheep?'

'Don Camillo, the black sheep is just like all the others when it cannot take advantage of the shadows of the night to go around sowing disorder and discord.'

'Jesus,' Don Camillo panted, 'give me a hundred eyes and a hundred ears.'

'God gave you a brain and that must be enough.'

Don Camillo also had his own Flying Squad; a 'White Volante' troop that did not engage in violent actions. It acted more with its brain than with its hands, and quietly. He mobilised it and gave it precise instructions.

That night, there was not a single corner of the village that was not monitored.

At first, nothing happened, but the following night, around two o'clock, a furious storm broke out. Don Camillo was keeping watch in the presbytery when a report came in: 'Enemy sighted in Zone 8.'

He launched himself like a rocket and took up position behind the fence of a construction site, where the command of Zone 8 was located.

'He's working in Strinati alley now,' it was explained to him in a low voice. 'He should come this way. In any case, the whole area is surrounded. He can't escape.'

They didn't have long to wait: shortly thereafter the black sheep emerged into the semi-dark street.

That little sheep couldn't have been blacker, because the stranger was wearing a black hat and was wrapped up in a black cloak. He stopped almost in front of the fence and began to act with extraordinary speed.

They let him write, '*Viva il Duce...*' and then took the picture. The brilliance of the flashlight disoriented the black sheep who, dropping his brush, turned and a second flash illuminated his very pale face.

Recovering immediately he ran away like a hare: but every escape route was blocked because there were men from 'Volante Bianca' at all the openings.

The doors of all the nearby houses were closed except one, into which the unidentified man slipped, as planned. In every area they had set up a trap-house from which it was not possible to escape, not even across the roofs.

The men of the squad went in after him and closed the door so as not to arouse suspicion in anyone who happened by on the street.

And Don Camillo headed towards the Mayor's house.

*

Peppone looked out of the window with his eyes still full of sleep but, seeing that it was Don Camillo, he awakened immediately.

'What do you want?' he muttered.

'I've had second thoughts,' Don Camillo explained. 'I'm joining the anti-fascist front.'

'At this hour?' Peppone roared.

'The homeland can be saved even after midnight,' Don Camillo replied. 'The fascist danger doesn't limit its existence to office hours!'

It was a formidable argument and Peppone went down to open the door.

'While the anti-fascist front sleeps, the parish priest works,' Don Camillo explained. 'We caught the author of the provocative writings red-handed.'

'Who is he?'

'We don't know: he was running too fast. Anyway, he's trapped now and we want to hand him over to the committee.'

The storm was over. Peppone contacted Smilzo who lived nearby and Smilzo quickly got dressed and called the members of the committee together.

While they waited, Peppone let Don Camillo into the kitchen and uncorked a bottle of dry white wine.

'I confess, Reverend, that this upshot doesn't quite convince me,' he muttered.

'And yet it is clear and straightforward, Mr Mayor. We simply want to show you that when it comes to a just cause even the clergy is ready to collaborate with you. We have discovered the person responsible for these serious provocations.'

Peppone started: 'All right, but when we go to pick him up, he'll always be able to tell us that he has nothing to do with it. If you didn't catch him in the act, how can we prove that it is him?'

'We took two photos of him: one while he was in the act and one while he was turning and showed his face. The camera lens catches what can escape the human eye.'

Four o'clock arrived before all the members of the committee were gathered.

*

Peppone, Don Camillo and all the most capable men of the committee entered the trap-house, which belonged to one of the White Flying Squad. They had no trouble flushing out the black sheep. A loud snore led them to the barn: the wretch, throwing his cloak over himself, had fallen asleep on a pile of corn and there, snoring, events awaited him.

Peppone lifted his cloak and the face of Falchetto was revealed.

'The Mayor was right,' Don Camillo acknowledged. 'Behind the hand that drew that infamous symbol there is a criminal organisation that must be unmasked and destroyed!'

Peppone remained speechless for a long time, then he turned to Don Camillo:

'Reverend,' he said, 'I knew nothing about it. I swear!'

'It was my personal initiative to keep the boys' bite alive,' explained Falchetto who had reopened his eyes.

'Reverend,' Peppone insisted, 'do you think I'm capable of a trick like that?'

'I don't judge. I will simply publish the photos and the people will judge.'

Peppone, whose forehead was covered in sweat, nodded to Don Camillo and went off with him to a corner of the barn:

'Reverend,' he said in a low voice, 'I will buy those two photos at any price. Name your figure.'

Don Camillo hesitated, but business is business and he gave a figure that made Peppone turn pale.

'It's too much,' he panted.

'Take it or leave it, Comrade.'

'We need a discount.'

'I'm not a shopkeeper,' Don Camillo affirmed. 'At most I can make the payment easier for you: half right away, on the nail, and the rest in instalments over two years.'

Peppone went to discuss the matter with the men of the general staff who found themselves, in principle, in agreement with him. Only Falchetto raised a lot of issues, but in the end he had to admit that Don Camillo had the knife by the handle, and he had to bow his head.

'All right, Reverend,' decided Peppone. 'We are ready to pay the first instalment.'

Don Camillo wore shoe size forty-five, with double soles, and when he had painted fifteen kicks on Falchetto's backside, you can imagine how the little Falcon felt.

'We'll talk about the other fifteen later,' concluded Don Camillo.

'Fourteen,' panted the little Falcon, sticking his head out of the pile of corn. 'I counted them: you gave me sixteen.'

'Fifteen,' said Peppone. 'I gave you the sixteenth in the name of the Party.'

The sum added up.

Tschaika 5506cc (1960)

A CONFIDENTIAL COMMUNICATION came from the Federation that made Peppone's ears prick up and prompted him to summon his general staff urgently.

'Comrades,' he said when he had them all around him, 'Western capitalism has lost all restraint and uses the most vile methods for its propaganda. Now, for example, with the complicity of America and the clerical government, a paid scoundrel has managed to obtain a Russian vehicle and is using it to defame Soviet industry, which is now at the forefront of design and manufacture in the atomic, missile and interplanetary fields, and which has no rivals in any field.

'This miscreant travels around Italy in his car, pretending to be a sales representative. Landing in the most important provincial centres, choosing market days or festivals, when the towns are full of people, he parks his car in full view and visits various shops of interest to him. "A Russian car": imagine that! Word gets around and everyone wants to look at the car and touch it.

'When the scoundrel sees that the car is the centre of general interest, he returns. Everyone is upon him asking him how much it costs, how it works, how much fuel it consumes, if it is comfortable, if it goes fast and stuff like that. He replies that it costs little, is reliable as a clock, has better suspension than American cars, goes like hell, consumes little or no fuel. In short, a masterpiece worthy of the glorious Russian industry.

'On top of it all, the damned man always carries a copy of *L'Unità* in his jacket pocket to make people believe that he is one of us and to arouse the distrust of reactionaries. Then, after reciting the first Act of the comedy, he gets in the vehicle, starts the engine and all hell breaks loose. On one occasion it might be the battery, on another the dynamo, the carburettor, or the fuel pump, another time it's the water pump...'

Peppone's face was dripping with sweat: he mopped it with his handkerchief, gulped down a large glass of wine, then pounded his fist on the table:

'Comrades!' he continued. 'You've already figured out what he's up to. That scoundrel isn't a traveller, he's a first-rate mechanic who manipulates the machine on each occasion so that, at the optimum moment, a certain problem occurs and it needs to be towed to the workshop. He's clever and varies the programme: if in one place he puts on a show because the machine won't start, in another he'll put on a show with the machine proceeding in fits and starts or firing cannon shots or blowing out smoke and stinking, or whistling, or puffing steam like a locomotive.

'He also puts on a show on the open road because, as soon as he gets close to a tavern or somewhere where there are people to entertain, the scoundrel comes forward. And if he comes across a "one-way" street he doesn't miss the opportunity to stop the car and block the traffic and make the drivers of the other cars hydrophobic.

Peppone cleared his throat with a second pawful of red:

'He's organised,' he continued: 'he also has a buddy who doesn't travel with him but in a Millecento of his own. They act according to a precise plan and the buddy pops out at the critical moment, when the other one puts on the show. He's mocking: "With so many cars that there are in Italy," he says, for example, "why, go and get into trouble with a Russian car?..." He provokes the other fellow, who's fussing over the engine: "More than a carburettor failure," he says loud enough to be heard all around, "in my opinion it's a failure of the Five-year Plan..."[55]

---

[55] There were thirteen Five-year Plans between 1928 and 1991, developed by the Russian state planning committee for economic development.

'The mechanic pretends to be offended and, so, they argue making the reactionaries present disembowel with laughter, because the man's buddy always has the telling joke. There's no point in continuing. You know that 2,000 different problems can happen to a car: all of them happen to this one and the result is that if, up to now, 30,000 people have seen that Russian car, at least twenty-nine thousand have seen it either stopped because of a breakdown, or jumping in leaps and bounds spitting fire, smoke, stench, steam, oil, petrol, bolts and body parts. Or while they were towing it. The central surveillance agencies are therefore right: we must keep on the lookout and unmask the scoundrel.

'Here is a description of the car with its licence plate. Whoever spots him, raise the alarm. The scoundrel works intermittently in Lombardy, Piedmont and Liguria: it won't take long before he ends up in these parts.'

*

The blackbird ended up in the net less than a month later; the Torricella cell spotted him and immediately called the People's Palace:

'Everything matches: make, model and licence plate. The individual stopped for a moment in the piazza, but since there was almost no one there, he drank a beer and then set off again. We followed him on a motorbike: now he's stopped on the embankment road, fiddling around with the engine.'

When the unsuspecting man arrived in Peppone's manor, the Mayor and his staff were waiting for him on the edge of the piazza, sitting at the table of the Caffè Progresso. There was half a market in sway and a lot of people were hanging around: the car, a black Tschaika 5506cc colossal, with plenty of chrome and a trunk-like front, could not go unnoticed.[56] It stopped at the cafè and a man of about forty, dressed with great propriety, emerged. He consulted a notebook, asked where the Belicchi shop was, the most important fabric store in the village, and, learning that it was just a stone's throw away,

---

[56] The 'Tschaika 5506cc' refers to the GAZ-13 Chaika, a Soviet-era luxury car produced from 1959 to 1981 with a 5.5 L V8 engine.

under the arcades, he headed there. He was carrying an elegant leather bag and from the left pocket of his jacket, a carefully folded copy of *L'Unità* was poking out.

Peppone was thrilled: but there was no need for haste and he waited.

Everything went according to plan: someone mentioned that the big car was Russian and people rushed to look at it and comment. Then the so-called commercial traveller resurfaced and came to sit at a table in the Progresso. He ordered an aperitif and pored over his notebook of errands.

Then along came his buddy: a sporty, expansive, cheerful young man.

He sat down between Peppone's group and the fake commercial traveller, clapped his hands and shouted that he'd like a cold beer, then, glancing towards the piazza and noticing the large crowd around the big car, he got up and went to take a look. He sat back down, sneering and shaking his head:

'Fancy coming across an American car in a town that is just a stone's throw from the Ferrari and Maserati factory! An American carcass!'

The fake commercial traveller took offence: 'She's not a carcass,' he said, raising his head and looking at the young man. 'And she's not an American car, she's a Russian one!'

The young man didn't flinch:

'I beg your pardon,' he said. 'I didn't know that Packard had a Russian grandmother.'[57]

Filotti and a gang of reactionaries were sitting nearby and the joke amused them some.

'Let's not exaggerate!' exclaimed Filotti, who was a fascist. 'Grandmother, no way: let's say old aunt.'

The fake commercial salesman smiled; he was playing the gentleman that would never lose his temper:

'The habit doesn't make the man and the bodywork doesn't make the car,' he said. 'Russians care more about substance than form.'

Filotti chuckled wickedly, and Peppone fell into the trap:

---

[57] Packard was a prominent American luxury automobile manufacturer.

'The body of American rockets is a thousand times more elegant than that of Russian rockets,' Peppone stated, 'and yet, Mr Filotti, while Soviet rockets reach the moon, American rockets end up in the sea!'

The fake sales rep appeared alarmed: 'I'm sorry the conversation took this turn,' he exclaimed, acting hurt. 'I simply wanted to say that the Soviet automobile industry focuses mainly on mechanical parts. I've already done thirty thousand kilometres in that car, and I can say that it runs like a chronometer.'

He paid, stood up and, cutting through the crowd attracted by the discussion, which had gathered under the portico, made for his big car.

He got behind the wheel and turned the ignition key: it seemed as if the car had a warehouse of scrap metal in its belly. The engine rattled for a few moments, then fired two cannon shots and stopped.

'Damn the chronometer!' his young accomplice sneered.

The fake commercial traveller had meanwhile got out and, opening the bonnet, had begun rummaging through the various parts of the engine. Climbing back behind the wheel, he turned the key and the engine started, but it limped terribly and so he got out again and dived back under the bonnet to adjust the carburettor. The engine roared, running at full speed, but only for a matter of a few seconds: after two cannon shots, a great cloud of smoke rose from the engine. The man jerked out, jumping back as the engine stalled and the people were seized with a fit of laughter: and the poor guy had black hands and face.

'Extraordinary!' his accomplice shouted. 'It's like a Ridolini film![58] Give it another push and you'll see the chassis take off while the body drops to the ground!'

Peppone jumped up, followed by the general staff, and pushed his way to the car:

---

[58] In the silent, slapstick film era, Ridolini was a popular character played by Larry Semon.

'Don't worry,' he said to the fake traveller, who was trying to clean up his face. 'We'll take it to my workshop and I'll fix it for you in two minutes.'

The mammoth Tschaika was pushed to Peppone's shop.

Peppone had organised things neatly and the five best mechanics from the Municipality and neighbouring municipalities were all there, ready to spring into action.

'While we adjust the carburettor,' Peppone explained to the man, 'we'll also give it a general service, so you can travel safely.'

'Really,' stammered the man, 'I am in a hurry.'

'They're all smart guys and they won't spend much time,' Peppone reassured him.

'But,' the fake traveller tried again: 'I need to know about the expense...'

'Don't worry. We make it a matter of honour. We do not want imbeciles laughing at the glorious Soviet industry! Wouldn't you agree?'

The filibuster had a keen nose: he smelled something was up and played along:

'Okay,' he said, taking *l'Unità* out of his pocket and fanning himself.

Peppone approached him:

'Comrade,' he said in a low voice, 'trust us. That's the door to my house. My wife will clean your jacket and give you whatever you want to drink.'

The man smiled, thanked him and got out of his way.

Peppone's plan was simple: investigation, then general overhaul of the car, check every part, tune-up.

Once sure that the car was in order, they would return it. Peppone's motorcycle 'Flying Squad' was on alert and, unnoticed, would follow the scoundrel, who, thinking he is safe, will stop along the road to mess with the car and prepare it for the show in the next town. They'd then jump on him and catch him red-handed, shame him in front of the people and denounce him in public for this dirty manoeuvring.

Then they'd let him go and, at a certain point along the road, they'd stop him and give him a big slap on the wrist.

Their investigation produced the results they had hoped for: one of the two suitcases stored in the rear trunk turned out to be very heavy. It contained a complete workshop and engine parts already 'manipulated' and ready to replace the good ones.

'He must be a godfather, when it comes to engines,' Peppone admitted through gritted teeth. 'As good a mechanic as he is a scoundrel!'

In two hours of feverish work, the car was checked, screw by screw, and fine-tuned.

It was half past ten and the piazza was overflowing with people:

'Comrade,' Peppone said to the fake representative, 'before we let you go, we'll test the car.'

'No need,' the other exclaimed. 'I have complete faith in you.'

'That's not why. I want all the idiots who were sneering a little while ago to see how a Soviet car works.'

Peppone got behind the wheel and the fake traveller sat next to him. They crossed the piazza slowly and the people made way for the big car.

*

'Slow and steady wins the race,' the young boy chuckled as the car passed in front of him.

'With a car like this,' Peppone replied, sticking his head out the window, 'you can go safely even when it goes fast!'

Peppone had pre-arranged what followed and Smilzo and the gang began to clear the road:

'Leave the way clear: the Boss will be back soon and he will be in a hurry!'

The big car sailed calmly and safely on the asphalt of the embankment: all it took was a moment to touch the accelerator and it immediately leapt. Five and a half litres of displacement and 200 horsepower are not medlars!

At Borghetto Peppone reversed and went back.

'It seems to me that it goes like a stopwatch,' observed the fake fabric salesman.

'I'll make them die of rage,' replied Peppone.

The road that descended from the embankment crossed the village, splitting the piazza in two, and Peppone, as soon as he had started down the slope, let out a long howl on his horn and went full blast.

The self-appointed security service had played its part and the street was clear: the people had retreated to the two slices of the piazza and were waiting for the show. By now, everyone understood what Peppone planned to do.

The big car was flying and, so massive and powerful, it gave such an impression of care-free safety that Peppone didn't hesitate. Having reached the centre of the piazza, he let go of the accelerator and pressed his paw on the brake.

He wanted to do what all people, old and young, wise and crazy, expected of him: a lightning-fast braking. One of those brakings that glue the car to the road and ruin a set of tyres. It was a matter of a fraction of a second: the brake on the right front wheel jammed and the big car, after trying to rear up – Khrushchev wouldn't condone it – spun around a couple of times, screeching to the point of breaking your heart.

The furious steel beast grazed past the people, though no one was touched. Peppone and the fake salesman banged their heads everywhere and were pulled out of the car in rags.

*

Peppone recovered first: he found himself lying in his bed with an ice pack on his head and, as soon as he opened his eyes, he muttered:

'And the other guy?'

He was lying on the bed in the next room and Peppone, throwing away the ice pack, joined him.

The fake commercial traveller was pale but the worst had passed for him too.

'I wonder,' Peppone said through gritted teeth, 'whether you're crazy or an idiot.'

The other looked at him in amazement:

'*You're* saying that to *me*?' he stammered.

'If you're the one who's busting our propaganda machine, I'm talking to *you*.'

'I don't understand.'

'We know everything. We found the bag with the tools and spare parts. There's no point in continuing the charade.'

The fake traveller was a tough guy and, sitting up on the bed, looked Peppone straight in the eye:

'Everyone serves their ideology as they see fit,' he stated. 'There are those who serve it using a machine gun and those who serve it using a screwdriver. If my systems are different from yours, you have no right to judge me crazy or an idiot.'

Peppone swelled up like a balloon:

'When a man goes so far as to sabotage the brakes of his own car...' he began, but the other interrupted him:

'Only a madman or an idiot could do something stupid like that. You can touch everything: except the brakes and the steering! That was a joke that the car played on us, on its own initiative.'

He chuckled, and Peppone asked him angrily what he found ridiculous in the matter.

'I think that since she is a Russian car, she should have had a certain amount of consideration at least for you, Comrade...'

Peppone, besides the jolt the fear had dealt, had a collection of bumps on his head and replied brusquely that, on certain subjects, he welcomed neither jokes nor tricks.

'I didn't mean to disrespect Russia,' the other man said solemnly.

'To hell with Russia and all its paradoxical pitfalls!' Peppone replied.

Asylum Seekers (1960)

'THIS,' SAID DON CAMILLO, pointing out a small article in the newspaper to Filotti, 'should be boxed in red and pasted on the bulletin board. As a shoutline you could use: "They prefer capitalist hell to Soviet paradise."'

A commission of young Russian technicians visited a large community vineyard run by Reds in the immediate vicinity of the city, and a comrade has disappeared.

'Peppone will die of rage,' Filotti chuckled, putting the newspaper back in his bag. 'Anything else, Reverend?'

'That's all,' Don Camillo replied.

By now it was dark and Don Camillo, left alone, made himself a cup of chamomile tea and made for the bedroom, but halfway up the stairs, he remembered that Filotti had arrived just as he was about to close the church door and so he retraced his steps.

The church was dimly lit. Having bolted the main door, Don Camillo was about pass by the High Altar, when a soft voice sounded behind him:

'*Signore...*'

He turned and, with the help of the flashlight he always carried with him during his nightly inspections, together with a certain twig of acacia about five centimetres in diameter, he picked out the faces of two strangers from the shadows. A young man and a girl of about twenty-five, in long, rather wrinkled, grey overcoats.

'*Dico!*' Don Camillo exclaimed, affronted. 'Is this the way you put the fright up people?'

'I'm sorry,' replied the girl. 'We want to ask, please, if it is possible to stay here.'

She spoke with a strange accent and showed some difficulty in finding her words.

Her companion muttered something, and the girl explained:

'He doesn't speak Italian, only a little French. He said: if it is forbidden to enter, we did not know.'

'Entering is not forbidden,' Don Camillo muttered. 'Anyone can enter the House of God. But, at night, you cannot stay because the House of God is neither a hotel nor a station waiting room.'

The girl spoke to her companion and then turned back to Don Camillo. She seemed very worried, almost scared:

'If not here, outside. A little corner, a stable, a barn. We cannot go to the hotel.'

He felt sorry for them and took his wallet out of his pocket, but the girl shook her head briskly:

'No, sir,' she said quickly, 'we have the money. We are foreigners and we do not have a passport.'

Don Camillo considered them more curiously:

'That's just great! And how did you manage to come to Italy without a passport?'

'We entered on a collective passport,' the girl explained, showing a certain embarrassment. 'We and other companions.'

'And where are your companions now?'

The girl spread her arms. At which point the young man intervened: the two argued for a while in low voices, then the girl seemed to make up her mind and took a card from her purse, which she handed to Don Camillo.

The young man also handed something similar to Don Camillo who, turning on his flashlight, took a close look at the two documents.

Everything was now clear and he was surprised at not having guessed it before. He set off, motioning for the two to follow him and, passing in front of the High Altar, he bowed and whispered:

'Lord, it's them!'[59]

*

They were as hungry as Siberian wolves and devoured everything that Don Camillo managed to find in his cupboard. With the table cleared, the girl took from her purse a 1,000-lire note, a 500-lire note, and a few pennies.

She explained that in Moscow she worked for Intourist, had attended a course to become an interpreter in Italian and French, and had acted as a chaperone for Italian tourists on several occasions: in this way she had managed to get a few lire together. But, despite eating only bread and cheese and drinking water, the nest egg had been reduced to a pittance in a few days. Their idea was to reach Paris where they had friends who would help them get settled. But they had realised that such an undertaking was, in practice, much more difficult than they had imagined.

'Have you changed your mind, then?' Don Camillo asked.

'No,' the girl replied with a firm voice. 'Rather prison than go back!'

'Take it easy, we'll sort everything out,' Don Camillo reassured her. 'For now, we must only think about finding a bed.'

At this point he was seized by justified scruples:

'Are you two married?'

'No,' the girl replied seriously.

'Magnificent!' exclaimed Don Camillo. 'A woman and an unmarried man embark on an adventure together, as if nothing out of the ordinary is happening!'

The girl looked at him in astonishment:

'I don't understand, Signore...'

Don Camillo lost a little of his patience:

'Where we are, we have one Lord, the one nailed to the cross above the High Altar. I am a priest and my call-name is

---

[59] Famously a year later, in 1961, Rudolf Nureyev defected to the West while on tour with the Soviet Union's Kirov Ballet in Paris. An apparently last-minute decision to seek asylum made him, at 23, the best known male ballet dancer in the world. A glittering career ensued.

"Reverend". All this aside, it is at least incredible that an honest woman does not recognise the impropriety of throwing herself into the fray with a man who is not her husband. Couldn't you have found a female friend, instead of a man?'

'Why?' said the girl, shrugging her shoulders. 'Male or female, it's the same thing. Men and women are equal.'

'Equal up to a certain point!' shouted Don Camillo. 'To the extent that men marry women and women marry men.'

The girl couldn't fully grasp the meaning of that and stammered:

'We don't want to get married.'

Her friend asked for an explanation and when the girl had given it he shook his head vigorously and said to Don Camillo in a language that sounded like French:

'J'ai déjà une femme, là bas. Il suffit s'épouser une fois.'

Brought to that level, there was no need to take the discussion any further and Don Camillo cut it short by sending the girl to the bell-ringer's mother's house to sleep and placing the young man in the attic of the presbytery.

*

Don Camillo had trouble sleeping that night owing to a sort of manic excitement at suddenly finding himself with two specimens of new-generation Soviet citizenship who had chosen to embark on a flight to freedom and were just now out of their cage. It was enough to drive not one but 200 communist mayors (and their entire sections) crazy with rage. His imagination conjured a whole project of sensational press conferences, television interviews and flashing photographs.

The next morning he got up very excited and, as soon as he found himself with the two specimens back in the presbytery dining room for coffee with milk, he told them what he intended:

'Now,' he said, 'I will show you around the village and introduce you to my friends.'

The girl went pale:

'No,' she exclaimed with anguish in her voice. 'Not this, please.'

'And why on earth not?' asked Don Camillo.

'We are afeared,' the girl explained.

'Afraid, here?' Don Camillo chuckled. 'We are in a free country, not Russia.'

'It is not possible,' the girl insisted. 'Our position is not regular. We do not have passport. The commissioner who accompanies us will force the authorities to return us to him.'

'And how will he know that you are here?'

The girl smiled sadly: 'Many communists in Italy. In Italy a strong Communist Party. Communists everywhere.'

Yes, right, but Don Camillo was not willing to give up an extraordinary opportunity. He thought about it and unfolded his plan: 'You are not Russians. You are two French people from the Agriculture College in Lyon and you have come here to visit, to study the main agricultural industries in the area. You are my guests because you belong to the French Catholic Centre. Is that okay?'

The girl spoke to her friend for a long time and then said that, yes, set up this way, things could work...

The landowners, tenants and the most important of the sharecroppers in the area belonged to Don Camillo's gang and they saw the Reds as thorns in their side: Don Camillo sent for Filotti and the other loyalists and explained the situation.

'To sum up: notify everyone. Officially they will arrive on the farms as French undergraduates on a study visit and, in front of outsiders, family members, and labourers, they will have to be treated as French. Then, in a separate location, after the anolini and tortelli and a few glasses of wine, the two French will go back to who they are and speak about life in Russia. You can do three farms a day: a sharecropper for breakfast, a tenant for dinner and a landowner for dinner.'

The loyalists set off like a rocket and, early the next morning, the tour began.

*

Loroni was one of those famous sharecroppers who, when the time was right, had bought the owner's farm: the two 'Frenchmen' were amazed to see how the farm was cultivated and what animals were in the stable.

During breakfast – caffelatte, zabaglione with Marsala, cooked shoulder, freshly baked bread, sparkling white wine, black cherry cake, nocino[60] – the girl sincerely acknowledged that, in Russia, it was a completely different thing. They talked about life in the kolkhoz, answered a hundred questions.

At ten o'clock, Bocci, the tenant of Torretta, came to pick them up in a Millecento.

Torretta was a farm three times bigger than Loroni's: it was equipped with every type of machine that God created and at one o'clock in the afternoon, when they sat down to dinner, the two were rather overcome.

Langhirano ham with melon, anolini in broth, boiled beef, veal and capon, roast turkey, fruit, assorted cakes, lambrusco, fortanella, trebbiano, sour cherries in alcohol: the two 'Frenchmen' reconciled themselves with life and, at Don Camillo's request, explained the reason for their dispirited demeanour. As usual, it was the girl who spoke:

'We, even though we fled, love the great Russia that is our homeland and, considering the sacrifices that the Soviet people have endured and continue to endure, it is disheartening to compare the results obtained by you and us in the field of agriculture.'

Here, again, they answered all the questions that were put to them.

At three in the afternoon Bernaschi's Duemilacento arrived to pick them up. Bernaschi was the owner of Calunga, a 200-hectare estate, a big deal down there in la Bassa, where the land is cultivated down to the last centimetre and where there are three harvests. Bernaschi, who ran the estate economically, lived in an old patrician house with a vast park full of centuries-old trees.

At Calunga, the two French had an opportunity to come to terms with the extraordinary results that can be obtained in the industrialised agriculture sector. Orchards that produced apples and pears worthy of an earthly paradise, breathtaking

---

[60] A dark brown liqueur from the la Bassa region, made from unripe green walnuts.

tomato fields, beets as long as an arm, stables, a dairy, pigsties, beef cattle farms, vineyards with grapes worthy of a world exhibition. Every now and then the two 'French' looked at Don Camillo in amazement and much was said in their eyes.

Entering the house they were nervous. When they introduced themselves to Bernaschi's wife and two daughters, the girl looked at their clothes and shoes, spellbound, then apologised:

'I had to abandon my suitcase when we ran away and I'm wearing all that I own. If I could have brought my suitcase with me, my dress would be just as poor but clean.'

'We understand your situation perfectly,' said the lady, smiling. 'If you won't take offence, it will be a real pleasure to help you.'

She nodded to the girls, who, taking the French girl by the arm, carried her away. Bernaschi's son did the same with the boy and, when the two friends returned, they were dressed afresh from head to toe.

Culatello di Zibello, salami from Felino, mushrooms and artichokes in oil, consommé, macaroni pie, new chicken alla diavola, mixed salads, fresh fruit, fruit salad, zuppa inglese, ice cream, fine wines, high-class liqueurs, coffee, recorded music: the two of them poured out their bitterness at the system at home and the young man wanted to have his say more than once, and the girl translated promptly.

Late in the evening they returned to the presbytery with two suitcases full of stuff. And before leaving them, Bernaschi – who personally drove them home in his Duemilacento – put an envelope in the girl's hand, saying:

'Please accept this from a free citizen of the West as an act of solidarity with two citizens of the East, who want to live free.'

The following day, the programme, with a sharecropper for breakfast, a tenant for dinner and a landowner for dinner, was repeated.

After three days, Don Camillo gave up:

'From tomorrow, you will have to fend for yourselves.'

They managed magnificently on their own and, every morning, they left with their old tattered suits, returning dressed again and with suitcases full of stuff.

It went on like this for ten days and the two were living as if in a dream.

But every dream has its awakening.

*

This guy, a young man with a crew cut, large Togliatti-style glasses and the grim, gritty mien of a communist functionary, presented Peppone with credentials that stood him to attention, particularly as he came from Rome headquarters.

He was a man of few words:

'Comrade: twelve days ago, two young people from the Soviet commission that came to visit the cooperatives and social wineries of Emilia ran away and we're looking for them. We need to fish them out and bring them back to Rome before the commission returns to the Soviet Union.'

Peppone spread his arms. The official took two small photographs from his leather bag and showed them to him:

'Do they mean anything to you?'

'Those,' he exclaimed, 'are the two French from the Catholic Centre of Lyon that the parish priest has been taking around the farms for about ten days!'

The young man put the photographs away.

'Take me to the parish priest,' he said, rising.

'But the parish priest...' Peppone tried to object.

'Don't even think about it, Comrade.'

Don Camillo was not very cordial and the young man didn't say anything that would make him more welcoming:

'Reverend,' he explained, showing him the two photographs, 'I come from Rome to pick up these two Soviet citizens.'

Don Camillo jumped to his feet:

'If you have come from Rome, you can go back there,' he roared aggressively. 'The door is still where you found it when you came in.'

The man did not flinch:

'You are harbouring two foreigners without documents and presenting them as French while they are Soviet citizens. A priest, in addition to agreeing with the laws of the Vatican, must also agree with those of the country in which he carries out his activities. It is better for everyone not to stir up controversy and to settle matters *in camera caritatis*.'

The young man had the upper hand and Don Camillo could not tell him what he was thinking:

'I did not steal those two young men from the Soviet Union,' he said. 'They came freely and will leave freely. Even at the risk of causing the biggest scandal of the century, if the two do not intend to leave, no one will remove them from where they have found sanctuary!'

The young man realised that he was dealing with no pushover and proposed a compromise solution:

'Let me speak to them.'

'Yes, but here and in my presence. Tomorrow at half past ten.'

He himself went to fish out the two Frenchies and bring them home, full to the brim and well dressed again from head to toe.

'They have come to take you back,' Don Camillo explained when they were in the presbytery dining room. 'You will listen to what they say to you and decide: if you do not agree to return to Russia, no one will be able to make you return. You will have complete freedom to decide.'

The girl talked animatedly with her companion and, in the end, stated categorically: 'Unless you send us back, we will never return to Russia.'

The official arrived accompanied by Peppone, and as soon as the two young people appeared, he showed them some documents and began to speak in Russian.

'Stop,' Don Camillo stopped him. 'You speak in Italian and the girl will then translate what you say.'

This caused the official visible embarrassment, but Don Camillo was not willing to compromise.

'Your comrades are waiting for you,' the official began. 'They know you and are sure that you will never betray the great Russian homeland.'

'We do not want to betray anything or anyone,' replied the girl. 'We only want to be free to lead our own lives.'

'Your life belongs to your homeland that has given you everything.'

He spoke of the terrible sacrifices of the people, of Stalingrad, of the threat from the West.

'Here we are in the presbytery, and in the presbytery communist rallies are not held,' Don Camillo interrupted him. 'Change register.'

The official thought for a long time, then decided:

'If you have put your comrades from your minds, I hope you have not forgotten your parents. If you did not return it will bring shame on your parents.'

'That is not true!' protested the girl. 'They know me and they know that I will never do anything shameful.'

'It is shameful to betray your country! Your comrade, in addition to his parents, also has a wife and a son: do you know that?'

'Of course I do.'

The girl translated diligently for her companion and, when he had listened to the long speech, he jumped up and said something in Russian to the official.

'Translate!' Don Camillo ordered.

'He says that he takes care of his wife and son and the Party must not take care of them,' explained the girl.

'The Party takes care of everything,' replied the official with a sarcastic chuckle. 'And it cannot look favourably on the father, mother, wife and children of a traitor.'

'Parents and relatives have nothing to do with it,' shouted the girl. 'They cannot be held responsible for what we do!'

The official threw up his arms:

'Sentimentality is a bad bourgeois manifestation and the Party cannot take it into account. Think on that.'

'You are a bunch of scoundrels!' shouted Don Camillo, jumping to his feet and putting his fists under the official's nose.

The two fugitives talked for a long time in low voices, and then the girl turned to the official and said a few words to him in Russian.

'What do you mean?' asked Don Camillo, while the girl lowered her head.

'She said they were going back to Russia,' explained the official, smiling. 'I'll be here tomorrow morning at seven in the car. You'll leave as you arrived. With the same luggage, I mean.'

He gave Don Camillo a short bow and walked out stiffly.

'And so,' Don Camillo said to the girl, 'you have given up!'

The girl raised her head and looked at him with eyes full of tears:

'Reverend!' she whispered in anguish, 'you don't know the Party officials...'

'I do know them,' Don Camillo replied in a harsh voice.

Peppone, who had been standing there with his mouth open, came to his senses.

'Good night, Party official!' Don Camillo said to him in a voice full of contempt.

*

At one in the morning, Don Camillo was still eating his heart out, pacing up and down the living room. He hadn't even bothered to close the door, and so Peppone burst out in front of him like a ghost.

'The car is ready outside,' Peppone said. 'Call those two out.'

'Now?' Don Camillo roared. 'Weren't you supposed to come at seven?'

'That was him. I was supposed to come now. If you have any support in Milan, hurry up and write. I'll take them there.'

'And tomorrow, when he can't find them anymore?'

'He'll find me again and I'll explain to him that, since he let them escape out of pure laziness and lack of sense of responsibility, it would be better if he didn't tell anyone that he found them.'

Don Camillo shook his head:

'I wouldn't have dreamt it,' he muttered. 'You're less of a functionary than I thought.'

*

All three were sitting at a table in a café in Milan, listening to the jukebox.

'I had a great time!' the 'functionary' suddenly exclaimed: 'Twelve days from one place to another, they stuffed us with turkey, culatello and Lambrusco!'

'If you hadn't come to save us,' said one of the comrades who had chosen freedom, 'they would have been the end of us – smothering us with fine linen, clothes and money!'

'Do you remember, Don Camillo explaining to us the existence of God and telling us about the life of Christ? And just think of it, a communist leader, after having saved us by duping the Party, gives us 20,000 lire from his own pocket!'

The 'functionary' and the 'fugitives' chuckled.

'There's nothing to laugh about,' the girl replied. 'When I think of that priest and this big man, I don't know, tears come into my eyes.'

The functionary made an impatient gesture:

'Mariolina, if we start being sentimental, the game is over!'

'Indeed,' the girl replied. 'It *is* over. I am not going to play at it anymore.'

'Me neither,' the other fugitive muttered.

*

'Lord,' Don Camillo was whispering to Christ above the High Altar, 'place your holy hand on the heads of those two poor children.'

Christ didn't answer, but smiled because he had already done so.

The Eye of Stalin (1960)

IN RUSSIA, STALIN had long gone out of fashion, but in la Bassa, the 'moustache' was still very popular, even among the Reds, because over here we like guys to have a precise physiognomy, as that makes it easier to choose whether to love or to hate.

Now, while the Russians had given the thing I'm going to tell you about a name that meant nothing, in la Bassa we christened it 'The Eye of Stalin', because that made it easier to choose how we felt about it.

The thing was one of those satellites that are shot into the sky and then continue to circle the Earth until the Eternal Father throws them onto the cosmic garbage tip. A thing as big as a thirty-story building that everyone could see pass in the sky every so many hours with the naked eye, and which, at night, looked like a shooting star.

The Americans had also put a piece of junk into orbit some time earlier, but it was just a balloon full of gas, while The Eye of Stalin was a real piece from the USSR wandering in space, because it contained radio and television stations and incredibly powerful photographic equipment.

In addition, on board the spaceship, there were no dogs or monkeys, but men and women who, after a year of space wandering, seemed to be doing very well.[61] So much so that one of these spacemen, to celebrate the entry into orbit of the The Eye of Stalin, had married one of the space auxiliaries who were his comrades in adventure: not content, the two wretches had given birth to – if you can say so – a male child.

At the time of our story, the unfortunate little boy was already three months old and, as reported by the daily bulletin issued by the The Eye of Stalin radio station, was in excellent health. This unsuspecting little boy was to allow the Russians to pull off a colossal coup.

In fact, there was a great congress of Soviet science in Moscow, during which the experiences collected and communicated by the crew of The Eye of Stalin were summed up. The meeting's conclusions, later disseminated throughout the world press, were of extraordinary interest, but they would have been even more important if – as the space experts said – they had been allowed to examine and study the child born up there.

'We will be happy to send him to you,' the father and mother of the phenomenon immediately announced by radio. 'Although born in space, he is a son of great Russia.'

The world was left breathless: scientists, politicians, writers, journalists, religious figures, fathers and mothers from every country felt involved and a furious controversy arose. For a whole month this was the main topic discussed by tens of thousands of daily and weekly newspapers and by commentators on the most important radio stations on Earth.

When the uproar had reached an intensity that was difficult to control, the Number One of the Soviet Union intervened and, after explaining that the superior interests of science required that the enterprise be carried out, and that, on the

---

[61] The reference here to dogs and monkeys appertain to two space shots: in 1951, two dogs, Dezik and Tsygan were the first of their kind to be propelled into space by the USSR. Tsygan died on a subsequent flight when the return parachute failed. In 1949, a rhesus macaque monkey, Albert II, aboard a US rocket, was the first mammal to travel to outer space. He too died due to parachute failure.

other hand, the spaceship possessed the appropriate equipment to bring it to a successful conclusion, set the precise date and time of the experiment.

It was a memorable event: that day, people forgot everything else and remained glued to their radios. When it was learned that The Eye of Stalin had communicated that it had sent the rocket containing the child towards Earth, the entire world held its breath.

Don Camillo, as soon as he heard the news, felt his heart gripped by anguish and ran to kneel before the Crucified Christ above the High Altar.

'Lord,' he implored, 'forget that this is a diabolical machination of Bolshevik propaganda and save this innocent child!'

'Don Camillo,' Christ replied with a sorrowful voice, 'why do you forget the respect you owe to your God – so much so as to believe that *in* your God there are miserable resentments unworthy of a man?'

'Lord,' moaned Don Camillo, 'forgive a poor country priest with a head full of confusion.'

'Wretched is he who cannot distinguish the voice of pity from that of fear, because the voice of pity is the voice of his God,' Christ admonished.

And the confusion disappeared from Don Camillo's head because, now, he heard only the sweet and serene voice of Christ.

Don Camillo, having forgotten time and fear, was emptying his heart of all bitterness, when a sudden roar that made the old walls of the church tremble came to tear him violently from meditation and prayer.

Patching up a cracked bell is not like gluing a patch to a bicycle tyre and Don Camillo had deluded himself that it wouldn't matter if it took a matter of months for Sputnik to be repaired.

Peppone had acted at night. The bell had been taken down, delivered back to the foundry, recast and put back in place without Don Camillo knowing a thing about it. Then, when suddenly there arose from the civic tower the booming of Sputnik, the effect was one big shock. The first stroke of the bell exploded like an atomic bomb in the stillness and silence that weighed on the village and the countryside.

Then came Peppone's voice, magnified by loudspeakers:

'The missile launched from the spaceship has touched down at the pre-established location. The child has not suffered in the least from the journey and is in perfect health... The greatest victory of science bears the mark of the Soviet Union!... A new era begins!...'

The piazza was filling up with a screaming crowd: the engines of a thousand motorcycles were crackling. The Reds, leaping on their saddles at the first sound of the bell of the civic tower, were rushing towards the village from all the hamlets of the Municipality.

Don Camillo climbed up the bell tower and, looking out of a large window, he saw, below him, a sea of frenetic people.

He went back down and stopped halfway to spy through a hole that looked onto the piazza: all the Reds were there, but there were also others. Those who until that moment had maintained a cautious position of equidistance between the Reds and the Whites while waiting to throw themselves on the side of whoever was actually the strongest, and join in. Now, they had made their choice.

Don Camillo went down to the ground floor and locked himself in the presbytery, covering his ears with his hands so as not to hear the uproar that the Reds and their new friends were creating in the piazza. But, when he heard the crowd rioting in the street in front of the presbytery and someone knocked violently on the door, he had to show his face from a window on the first floor.

Don Camillo's appearance was greeted by a wild shout, but Peppone stepped forward and, with a gesture, silenced everyone.

'Reverend,' Peppone shouted, 'the unanimous citizenry celebrates the greatest victory of humanity. What of the clergy?'

'For the clergy, as for all Christians, the greatest victory of humanity is not today, but dates back to the day when Our Lord Jesus Christ, son of God, became man to redeem us from sin and to show us the way to Heaven.'

'The merits of your Lord Jesus Christ are not up for discussion,' Peppone replied. 'The fact is that, while your Lord taught you how to go to heaven, he did not teach you how to return to earth. Soviet science, on the other hand, taught us both the outward and return journeys!'

The crowd sneered and Don Camillo shrugged: 'This is not written in the books of the Church.'

'It is written in the book of history!' shouted Peppone. 'And, if your bells ring to announce midday, they can ring to greet the radiant dawn of a new era!'

'We have already had occasion to discuss this matter,' explained Don Camillo. 'I do not receive orders from the Communist Party.'

'Not for much longer!' roared Peppone.

'It depends on what God has decided, not what the Mayor has decided.'

'It depends on what the Soviet Union has decided, which today dominates, unchallenged in heaven, on earth and everywhere!'

'Amen,' said Don Camillo, withdrawing and closing the blinds.

The Reds remained talking for a while longer under the windows of the presbytery, but, even with the all-powerful titular ruler of heaven and earth behind them, a double-barrelled shotgun loaded with buckshot is still a damnable tool that can play nasty tricks and so, after many words, the Reds, instead of taking action, departed.

One of the usual summer storms or, perhaps, the worrying announcement of a devastating cyclone?

*

Suddenly, a real mess: on television they were broadcasting a variety show, when the screen fell into darkness and every voice fell silent.

Shortly afterward, the screen re-lit, but instead of actors, a man appeared and read a short statement in an unsteady voice:

'Soviet troops transported by truck have occupied some localities in the Emilia. Treacherous aggression, conducted with a brigand spirit and style...'

The voice and the light were extinguished. After a few seconds, the screen lit up again; the announcer had changed, his voice confident, read out a kind of proclamation:

'Italians! Responding to the invocations of countries oppressed by American capitalism, the Soviet Union, by the will of the working people, comes to liberate you! The soldiers of the glorious Red Army present themselves to you not as enemies, but as brothers. Help them fraternally in their struggle that will lead to the dismantling of the American bases and the elimination of the criminal clerical-fascist clique subservient to the interests of the United States of America...'

It was ten o'clock at night and no one slept that night: fear ran wild, grinning through the dark and deserted streets. As soon as the broadcast of the proclamation was over, the electricity again went out.

Telephone and telegraph stopped working.

People barricaded themselves in their homes.

Around midnight, a few rifle shots began to crackle here and there.

At the first light of dawn, Don Camillo was still praying, kneeling before the Christ above the High Altar.

Suddenly, the door of the church flew open and a group of people entered.

'Lord,' said Don Camillo without turning around, 'if my last hour has come, give me the strength to die as a worthy servant of God.'

But they were only poor people, loaded with children, bundles and terror. They had arrived on a truck that had broken down a few hundred metres from the village. They brought the first direct news:

'They have arrived in Piacenza...', 'They are destroying all the bridges on the Po...', 'They have very fast tanks...', 'Mongolian troops...', 'Terrible...', 'They are setting fire to everything, smashing everything...'

The arrival of the refugees shook the village from its torpor, and first the church and then the piazza crowded with people.

The refugees were forced to repeat their frightening story a hundred times, but old Doghetti was not impressed:

'They'll do no harm, have no fear. They will be men like everyone and if one doesn't bother them, why should they hurt us? The important thing is that one stays away from wherever they pass.'

The refugees replied that, where the Russian soldiers did not pass, others did. In every city, in every village, communist squads went around killing all the unfortunates who were on their black lists. They wore black jackets, a red armband, and were armed with machine guns and bombs. The Russians gave a general dusting as they passed through, while the others took care of the detail.

A second group of desperate fugitives arrived: 'If those damned people continue at this rate,' they said, 'they'll be here in an hour.'

'But why here?' old Doghetti asked stubbornly. 'Why do you expect them to care about this rag of a country?'

'They care because it is on the right side of the Po and they want to spread out along the embankment and isolate Emilia from the North, while others isolate it to the south of the province, blocking the roads to the Apennines, and still others are stationed from the Po delta all the way down to Rimini and beyond,' someone explained, 'to ensure a safe base for landings from the air.'

'And this "rag of a country", as you call it,' Don Camillo explained to the stubborn old man, 'is on the north side of the triangle of death within which we will remain enclosed if we do not cross the river and take refuge on the north bank.'

The situation was now all too clear and everyone was gripped by the frenzy of crossing the river, even as they were, some of them, in their shirtsleeves.

Then Don Camillo knelt before Christ once more, and said:

'Lord, forgive me, but I must transform myself. From a soldier in the infantry of the Lord I pass into the landed infantry.'

'God's will be done,' Christ replied in a low voice.

The people, overcome by fear, began to shout: 'To the river! To the river!' and headed towards the embankment, but they did not get far because they suddenly found Don Camillo before them with a machine gun in his hand and, to the right and left of Don Camillo, were Filotti's son and Dario Camoni, also with machine guns in their hands.

'If you were not crazy sheep,' Don Camillo shouted, 'you would have listened to what the refugee who explained the tactics of the advance said. In Portovecchio the people threw themselves into boats to cross the Po, but not a single person made it over there alive because the Red squads, stationed along the bank, killed everyone with bursts of machine gun fire. If we cannot defend ourselves from foreign Reds, we must at least defend ourselves from our own Reds. Whoever owns a weapon and is not afraid to use it to save the lives of his children, his parents, his wife and his brothers, let him take it out and gather here.'

*

Don Camillo divided the men into four squads: one marched toward the river, at the head of the column of refugees, and one behind it, while the third and fourth stretched out from the road on the embankment to the river, to cover the flanks of the column.

The Great River flowed calmly and no wind was blowing: everything that could float was put onto the water and the passage began.

After unloading the first block of refugees, the fleet returned to take on board the second and everything worked well, and it went well when it was the third block's turn.

But while the last group of refugees was embarking, Dario Camoni, who was scouting ahead, arrived:

'The Russians are coming!' he shouted.

'Which Russians?' Don Camillo asked. 'Those of Peppone?'

'No, Reverend. The Russian-Russians. Peppone, Brusco, Smilzo and the others are mining the bridge over the Stivone, the Ponte Nuovo, the embankment and the Molinetto road.'

Some 'booms' were heard nearby and Camoni rejoiced:

'They did it.'

Don Camillo was perplexed: 'I don't understand their manoeuvre,' he exclaimed.

'It's simple' explained Camoni. 'They are trying to delay the Russian advance to allow the last ones to cross the river.'

'Leave a squad to protect the embarkation from infiltrations and call all the men together!' Don Camillo shouted, starting to run.

*

Peppone had behaved like a little Napoleon: having blown up the bridges and the Molinetto road and knocked out half a kilometre of embankment, he had started up the pumps that were there for a major canalisation job and, driven by powerful diesels, they discharged a deluge of water onto the ruins of the embankment and the fields all around.

Two tanks which had attempted to make a forced crossing across a ploughed field had become bogged down.

The Russians, blocked by the unexpected resistance, were blasting away, but without developing the firepower that one might expect.

'I thought they were more capable,' observed Don Camillo who had arrived alongside Peppone, crawling.

'You'll see when they get us in the middle!' replied Peppone. 'There are only a few cats left there making a racket to keep us busy while the main body goes around to reach the bank on the other side.'

In the meantime, people were getting on board and, finally, the last raft broke away from the shore.

Smilzo arrived with something to say, concluding: 'Chief, we can cut the rope and escape too.'

'No we can't,' replied Peppone. 'We must resist at all costs, until they have crossed to the north bank.'

'But, if the squads arrive from Torricella,' Don Camillo observed, 'who will stop them from that direction?'

A bang was heard from there and Smilzo chuckled: 'We haven't sat on our hands waiting for Divine Providence, we've undermined the embankment on the Grosto drain and set up a defence in that direction too. The clergy can easily cut loose: they are covered on that side too.'

'The clergy will stay put and, if you don't shut your mouth, the clergy will kick your backside,' Don Camillo replied with beautiful simplicity.

The fleet was sailing slowly towards the left bank, but there was still a long stretch of river to cross. Smilzo, who had dashed off on his motorbike, returned with bad news:

'The defence at Grosto is giving up: a tank managed to get through and, before being blown up, it took out Bigio and his entire team.'

'Stay here with Brusco's men and the Reverend's auxiliaries; tell the others to come with me.'

Peppone arrived at Grosto just in time: the resistance was about to disintegrate. The mined embankment had made a quagmire of the ploughed fields all around: the tanks were blocked, but men could get through and while the Panzers' guns and machine guns were spewing torrents of fire, the Russians had, in fact, begun to advance.

The machine guns of Peppone and his men delayed the action, but the good times didn't last long because ammunition was running out alarmingly and it was prudent to save shots and aim at the man.

'If we hold out for just a quarter of an hour,' Peppone exclaimed, 'they should all get through.'

A metre to his right, a machine gun began to sing and Don Camillo was operating it, while Camoni was crawling over to him with boxes and boxes full of magazines.

'Ah, damn you!' Peppone roared. 'You had the machine gun hidden in the presbytery! And *you* talk of *us*!'

Peppone crawled up to Don Camillo's side after ordering Camoni: 'Everyone go over there, behind the sewer, where there's no defence. The two of us will be enough to keep this clear.'

Don Camillo's machine gun, manned by Peppone, made music that sounded like a Verdi chorus and the enemy's fire was concentrated on it.

A bullet scratched Peppone's cheek: 'Damn, they shoot well!' he exclaimed with admiration.

'There's a lot of them!' Don Camillo replied through gritted teeth. 'Seems like 500 against two!'

'One and a half,' Peppone specified, inserting the last magazine into the machine gun. 'A priest is worth half a man... Damn...'

Peppone, hit by a burst of gunfire in the middle of the stomach, collapsed.

'Wait for me,' Don Camillo shouted. 'I'm coming too.'

'I can't,' Peppone panted. And he still had the strength to whisper: 'God help me!...'

Don Camillo barely had time to say, '*Ego te absolvo*,' before being struck down by a burst of machine gun fire as his machine gun fired its last cartridge.

*

Don Camillo found himself sailing in the sky and, up there was a great silence and a great peace.

Standing on a cloud, Peppone waited, and Don Camillo, passing by him, said brusquely:

'Let's go.'

'I don't need you to show me the way,' Peppone replied.

'Hurry up!' Don Camillo ordered and Peppone came alongside.

'I didn't have time to see if they managed to get across,' Peppone observed.

'I saw: they all arrived safe and sound on the far bank.'

'Thank goodness,' Peppone rejoiced. 'It wasn't a wasted effort. Be careful, Reverend!...'

Don Camillo, who was looking up, barely had time to move away: a damned cantaloupe melon as big as a thirty-story building passed at full speed, two fingers from his shoulder. And it was The Eye of Stalin.

They both fell in line, close up to get a good look at it and followed it for a few dozen thousand kilometres.

'It's not that much,' Don Camillo concluded, getting back on track. 'Little more than a cardboard box.'

'Let the Americans make a better one, if they can,' Peppone replied.

In the upper layers they encountered other, smaller pieces of junk: balls, tubes, rockets.

'Crazy men,' Don Camillo sighed. 'Instead of thinking about cleansing their souls, they waste their time trashing the universe.'

They reached as high as the moon. Don Camillo deviated and, once on the other side, he beamed with satisfaction:

'Here it is, how she looks! I knew it. I knew that the Reds' famous photograph was a trick. Tricks and betrayals: these are your weapons!'

Peppone protested and Don Camillo went on the attack: 'You wretch, have you already forgotten what happened down there? Who killed you, the priests or your Russian comrades?'

'You shouldn't judge by mere details,' Peppone tried to object. 'In any case, we can't know how things really happened...'

The discussion couldn't continue because, suddenly, the two stopped and a great light appeared above.

Peppone lowered his head because that light was blinding him, but Don Camillo, instead, raised his eyes because it was a light that filled his heart with sweetness.

'Lord,' said Don Camillo, falling to his knees, 'here I am before you to pay for my sins.'

The voice of Christ was heard, a voice that spread throughout the universe:

'All sins are forgiven to those who have kept their hearts pure. Get up and come, Don Camillo.'

Don Camillo rose and started to walk, but immediately stopped: 'Lord, what about him?' he asked, pointing to Peppone who remained motionless with his head bowed low.

'He was an instrument of the Devil and this is not his goal,' explained the voice of Christ.

'Lord, he did not do it out of malice,' replied Don Camillo. 'He is a poor idiot, a victim of propaganda.'

'I know, Don Camillo: that is why he was assigned not to Hell but Purgatory.'

'Lord,' implored Don Camillo, 'I cannot leave him alone. Allow me to keep him company in Purgatory. I will help him atone.'

Peppone fell to his knees: 'Lord,' he groaned, 'do not make my punishment worse! With him at my side, Purgatory will become pure Hell for me!'

'This is also true,' replied the voice of Christ. 'With him, Paradise will become a Purgatory for you. Get up and come too: God's mercy is great...'

So, they started to climb again and the light became more and more dazzling and now Peppone could look into it too.

They climbed and very sweet music floated on the air, whereupon Peppone's harsh and sacrilegious voice resounded: 'Instead of promising hypothetical rewards in heaven, the priests would do better to give the working people a little justice on earth!'

'Here too?' Don Camillo shouted indignantly. 'Here too?'

*

Don Camillo found himself in the presbytery dining room, sitting in his old armchair. Peppone was haranguing from the top of the civic tower, loudspeakers amplifying his voice.

Don Camillo jumped up:

'Lord,' he said, 'how could I dream so many stupid things in just one hour of sleep?'

'They weren't all stupid, Don Camillo,' replied the voice of Christ.

The lights in the piazza came on, as the first shadows of the evening arose from the Great River. The Eye of Stalin passed in the sky, sparkling like a travelling star, and everyone looked up.

Don Camillo, too, approached the window, looked up and then implored:

'Lord, why not let it fall on his head?'

'God has more serious and important things to think about,' explained Christ. 'Such as, what is that business of a machine gun hidden in the presbytery, which Peppone spoke to you about?'

'Lord,' exclaimed Don Camillo, 'Do you listen to what that unfortunate man says even in a dream?'

'In every dream there is a splinter of truth.'

'Certainly, there's always some truth to a dream...,' agreed Don Camillo, who had hidden only the machine gun tripod in the presbytery, while the rest was tucked away in the attic.

'But a part is not the whole.'